DISCARDED BY
MT. LEBANON PUBLIC LIBRARY

Mt. Lebanon Public Library
16 Castle Shannon Boulevard
Pittsburgh, PA 15228-2252
412-531-1912
www.mtlebanonlibrary.org

CRIME FACTORY: THE FIRST SHIFT

PRODUCT INFORMATION

Machinery assembled in Roisin Dubh (Brunswick, Melbourne), from parts made in USA, Ireland, South Africa and Australia, and edited in Melbourne, San Diego and Arizona.

CRIME FACTORY:
THE FIRST SHIFT

Edited by Keith Rawson,
Cameron Ashley, and
Jimmy Callaway

A NEW PULP PRESS BOOK
First Printing, August 2011

Copyright © 2011 by Keith Rawson,
Cameron Ashley, and Jimmy Callaway

All rights reserved. No part of this book may be reproduced or transmitted in any form or by any electronic or mechanical means including photocopying, recording or by any information storage and retrieval system, without the written permission of the publisher, except where permitted by law.

This book is a work of fiction. Names, characters, places, and incidents either are the products of the author's imagination or are used fictitiously, and any resemblance to actual events or persons, living or dead, is entirely coincidental.

ISBN-13: 978-0-982843-64-2
ISBN-10: 0-9828436-4-X

Printed in the United States of America

Visit us on the web at www.newpulppress.com

ALSO FROM NEW PULP PRESS

badbadbad, by Jesús Ángel García
The Bastard Hand, by Heath Lowrance
The Science of Paul, by Aaron Philip Clark
21 Tales, by Dave Zeltserman
Flight to Darkness, by Gil Brewer
The Red Scarf, by Gil Brewer
A Choice of Nightmares, by Lynn Kostoff
As I Was Cutting, by L.V. Rautenbaumgrabner
Bad Juju, by Jonathan Woods
Rabid Child, by Pete Risley
The Disassembled Man, by Nate Flexer
While The Devil Waits, by Jackson Meeks
Almost Gone, by Stan Richards
The Butcher's Granddaughter, by Michael Lion

UPCOMING:
In Nine Kinds of Pain, by Leonard Fritz
Hell on Church Street, by Jake Hinkson

THE LINEUP

Foreword, David Honeybone VII
Stinger, Dennis Tafoya 11
Two Men and a Car, Andrew Nette 17
Amateurs, Jedidiah Ayres 26
Half-Jack, Roger Smith 35
Glory B., Josh Converse 42
The Decider, Charlie Stella 50
Microprimus Volatitus, Greg Bardsley 58
Ladykiller, Hilary Davidson 69
In the Stretch of Dare, Kieran Shea 76
Prophet Wells and the River of Swine, Nate Flexer 87
The Prevailing Wind, Cameron Ashley 96
Experience Preferred, Patricia Abbott 104
The Method, Chad Eagleton 112
Bedlam, Ken Bruen 123
Of Course, You Realize This Means War
    Jimmy Callaway 133
The Mind Prison, Dave Zeltserman 147
The Ravine, Steve Weddle 158
Through the Valley of the Shadow of Roosevelt's Nose
    Craig McDonald 166
Laughing at Dead Man, Keith Rawson 173
Shafted, Leigh Redhead 181
2,984,000 Pounds of Pressure, Anonymous-9 195
Hearing Voices, Jonathan Woods 201
Juun Hundred Ounces, Liam Jose 211
Budget Cuts, Dave White 216
Green By, Chris F. Holm 224
Luz Verder, Frank Bill 233
The Ladder, Adrian McKinty 238
Hundred Proof, Scott Wolven 255

FOREWORD
David Honeybone

Melbourne. 2000. I was sitting behind the counter of the crime bookshop I used to work at, trying to dream up a title for a magazine I wanted to launch. It was quiet and I was between customers. At the time, they seemed to be split into two factions: those who knew exactly what they wanted or those who just came in to crack-a-fat* in the true crime section. I had been in my adopted country for two years and I really wanted to DO something. I had a lot of ideas and the first word of a title but I needed another. I scanned the shelves seeking inspiration. And then Crime...
FACTORY!
Yes!
I still can't actually remember whether it was the Derek Raymond books or Eddie Bunker's *Animal Factory* that gave me the idea but *Crime Factory* immediately had the type of intriguing yet sleazy ring I was after. Especially if you said it often enough, which I did just to gauge people's reaction.

Some weeks following this Eureka moment a louche youth with a fever for comics entered the shop and we struck up a conversation. Cameron Ashley is still his name. You may have heard of him.

Crime Factory grew out of a need to do something. Something tangible and finally something I actually might enjoy doing. Hands up those of you doing that right now? It lasted for nine issues over three years, until my wife told me it was no way to live a life. And she was right. Again.

Let's avoid too much sentimentality; suffice to say that from the start it was a blast and I got to meet some great crime writers and crime lovers. One Peter Temple launched the magazine on a blisteringly hot summer's day in Melbourne. Ian Rankin was full of compliments when I handed out the first free issue to a room full of startled people in a pub in St. Kilda in February, 2001. Thanks, Ian. They weren't there to see me! And Ken Bruen gave me his father's watch when he came over for the Sydney Writers'

Festival ("for the time you gave me"). It never failed to amaze me how generous people were with their time or how gracious they were about the magazine. And it's what I will probably take most from those three years in the Factory.

So I was pretty amazed and flattered when Cam Ashley and Keith Rawson wanted to resurrect *Crime Factory*. They almost persuaded me to get back on board. And for about 24 hours, I was there. But deep down and in the cold light of a hangover, I guess I just didn't have the passion anymore. Or the energy. And did they really know what they were getting themselves into? Well, Ashley et al have shown that they do and have packed a lot in to six issues (at time of writing) already. This *Crime Factory* is different but, as an online zine, the mag has really taken on a new dimension. And it's available through Amazon. Who'd have thunk it!

A lot has happened since the first version of *Crime Factory*. That little thing called the Internet was around but has now been harnessed by writers and publishers alike, and online publishing opportunities abound with great zines like *Plots with Guns* and of course *Crime Factory* itself. Add to this an incredibly active crime blogging community, and you have a new generation of crime writers flexing their creative muscles in a self-made environment.

And now the anthology. An ambitious, daunting prospect? Not for these guys.

As I was reading these stories, I was struck by the spread of authors, not just geographically but also in terms of career. Back in 2002, Ken Bruen had just been published in Australia and had a growing following. He was pretty much ploughing a loan furrow for Irish crime writing. And now? Well, he's the toast of America and at least two of his books have been made into films. And how many great Irish crime writers are there now? So I wouldn't be surprised that over the next ten years we see some of these talented young gunsels, whose work populates these pages, with book deals and more besides.

To be honest, this is a curate's egg (hardboiled naturally) of a book. The good, the bad, the ugly and the downright indifferent. Don't worry that will be edited.

First take the established writers: McKinty and Bruen, Leigh

Redhead from Australia, South Africa's Roger Smith (Samuel L. Jackson to play Zondi? I can't wait) and then Americans Dave Zeltserman, Charlie Stella, Dennis Tafoya and Craig McDonald (who contributed some great stuff for the first *Crime Factory*).

And then add to the mix the new contenders: Patricia Abbott does a nice line in grifting ("Experience Preferred"); Hillary Davidson ("Ladykiller") shows how revenge is a dish best served cold (in a cell); Andrew Nette ("Two Men and a Car") and Cameron Ashley ("The Prevailing Wind") show a glimpse of an Australian underbelly that doesn't feature in any tourist publicity; an Old Testament nightmare of a character stayed with me for some time thanks to Nate Flexer ("Prophet Wells and the River of Swine"); Scott Wolven's stark prose left me wanting more ("Hundred Proof") and Dave White's story ("Budget Cuts") takes something relatively mundane but imbues it with enough menace until it boils over.

V.S. Pritchett's definition of a short story is "something glimpsed from the corner of the eye, in passing." In the case of this anthology the eye is blackened and swollen and probably oozing something unpleasant, the result of a fist, gun butt or just plain bad language.

So, in conclusion, don't read this book if:
    you are of a religious, temperate disposition
    you believe in the innate goodness of humanity
    you like crime books where the cat solves the crime
    you expect a happy ending (the cat finishes as road kill)
Do read this book if:
    you like your crime served black and bitter
    you delight in the criminal as protagonist
    you like alcohol
    your one true religion is noir

The crime bookshop where it all began closed some years ago when the then-owner got his visa and promptly sold the name in a heartbeat the better to stay in the Lucky Country, count his money and pursue his taste in Thai boys.

Enjoy.
David Honeybone
Melbourne 2011
*Australian slang for an erection.

STINGER
Dennis Tafoya

They met in Arraignment, and she knew he was the one. Sandra and another woman were in the second row of benches of Courtroom 13B, cuffed and waiting for their hearings. The other woman was broad across the shoulders, her belly pressing against the orange jumpsuit. The woman asked if Sandra had a cigarette, and Sandra had just asked when she was due. The woman put one hand on her belly and opened her mouth to speak when the men came in and they both turned to look and the woman went quiet.

There were four men, all handcuffed, wearing the same orange jumpsuits the women wore. The guard leading them stopped and looked around and then at a clipboard he carried. The man on the bench, who Sandra assumed was the judge, began firing questions at the bailiff looking at his clipboard, and she knew the men weren't supposed to be there. The men and the women weren't supposed to be together, Sandra knew. She'd been in the system enough to know that. The bailiff started arguing with the judge, and another guard, a man with gray hair and tired eyes, led the chained men over to sit in the first row of benches and told them not to bother nobody.

Wade was first in line, and taller, bigger across the shoulders, the fabric of his jumpsuit taut around his biceps. He looked right at her, and when he sat, he turned and kept looking at her over his shoulder like he was waiting for her to say something, as if they knew each other, as if they had planned to meet there in 13B on a Thursday morning at ten-thirty. Like a date.

Before the pregnant woman asked for a cigarette, Sandra had been thinking about her mother, about the things they'd said to each other when they'd gotten home from the hospital. She remembered going to her room, her face hot, her body feeling emptied out, hollow and ringing inside, looking in the mirror at the bruises on her face and arms. She'd gone to the door and looked down the hall at her sister's room, and her sister's doorway was filled with light, almost glowing, and it meant something, not just in the moment but something, something, Sandra's room on the dark side of the house, her sister's on the side that got the sun all day.

"Why you here?" he said, and waited. The man next to him was nodding, his eyelids heavy and the whites of his eyes a frank yellow, like the yellow of an egg. She could smell them, the men, their smell a heavy tang of sweat that left a metallic taste on her tongue. She looked down at her shoes. He said, "You don't look like anyone who ever fucked up before." He closed one eye. "Shoplifting."

The bailiff with the gray hair said, *Shut up, Wade*, so then she knew his name. *Wade, I ain't fooling,* he said, but the big man didn't turn his head or respond. He kept looking at her. "You were at the Galleria with your girlfriends and somebody dared you to put something in your purse." She looked at the pregnant girl, who had a tattoo of a devil's horns on the hand she kept protectively on her belly.

"Okay," he said. "Okay, you got stopped holding a little weed for your boyfriend." He was intent, dipping his head to catch her lowered eyes. One of the other men, a young Latino with a shaved head started talking to the girls, and Sandra caught the word *bolillo*, something the Spanish boys said that meant like a cracker, a dumb white guy, and Wade turned and looked at the boy and the boy stopped talking and dropped his head. When she glanced up, Wade was looking at her again and the pupils of his eyes were black, like painted dots, and she could see his teeth. *He thinks he's smiling*, she thought. *He thinks that's what a smile is.* So then she knew. Knew he was the one she needed.

Now he said, "A DUI," so she shook her head.

"Dirty urine," she said. "Two weeks left on my parole."

He nodded. "So you're up for a Gagnon, right?" She lifted a shoulder, let it drop. "Gagnon One hearing, right? For the violation," he said. He looked up at the bench. "Okay, that's why Macklin's here. Not the judge, just a whatever, a Trial Commissioner. Where's your lawyer?"

She shook her head. "I don't know."

He leaned in, his mouth tucked into his swollen bicep and his voice low. "Macklin's easy. Tell him your mom is waiting for you, you got family looking after you. Point to the back of the room, like they're all just waiting outside the door." He pointed with one discreet hand and nodded toward the back of the room and she wanted to look, to see if maybe they were really there, outside. Her mother, her sister in the wheelchair, maybe a lawyer. "Look all helpless and innocent and he'll put you on the street." She couldn't help herself, she turned her head to see the door swing on the empty hall. Nobody.

He nodded. "Right. That's the look. Just like that."

Three days later they were in Atlantic City. It was night and they sat in a Ford pickup Wade had taken from the lot of a theater in Marlton. Those were the things he knew. Where to take cars, how to unload stolen jewelry. And the system, he knew that. Appeals and prison rules. What they had to give you. Outside, he was hesitant, relied on her to handle money, count change, order their food. Negotiate for crack from a man in Hunting Park. Get the room at the motel on Roosevelt Avenue up in the Northeast.

They'd head back there after this. They were going to take somebody's money, Wade said, as they were watching people come out of the casino into the parking tower. She'd look like she needed help and Wade would put a knife against his side and they'd get him and his car and that would keep them for a few days. Wade knew a guy who would take the car, he said. She didn't listen, just watched the smoke trail from his mouth. The pipe was a death's head.

Sandra nodded and looked out through a gap in the concrete

wall at the city, the yellow glow of the streets. There were insects swarming at the lights on the side of the building, with big, gauzy-looking wings bleached white by the bright floodlights. Banging against the glass, the walls with ominous clicks and taps.

There had been something, she had tried to tell her mother, a distraction, a flash at the edge of her vision that might have been a fly or a bee. *You were drinking*, her mother said, as if that was all there was to know. Yes, but, Sandra said. Yes, but, there was something in the car, a bee, a wasp, I don't know. She was terrified of wasps, their folded legs and obscene, curled bodies dangling. I'm a good driver. *She's your sister,* her mother said with her red, wet eyes staring.

Wade stood over the man, the dead man, his eyes rolling in his head. He offered nothing, no excuses, just pointed with the knife and shook his head.

"There you go," he said. "There you go." Like stabbing the man was an argument settled. They were by the side of a road somewhere out in the Barrens, one of those razor-straight cuts laid through the pine woods north of the Atlantic City Expressway. She had followed Wade and the man driving his car, a long old sedan of a type Sandra didn't recognize. They had made random turns in the dark, heading vaguely north and east, and then the car had stopped and she had pulled in behind them. The man had gotten out, standing near the rear so that he was lit red by the taillights.

Sandra had watched from the pickup, watched Wade take the man from the parking lot. She had stood between two parked cars looking lost, searching the ground with her eyes and fishing in her purse. The first man who came up had a little girl with him, so Sandra waved him off. After a few minutes another man came to talk to her, a small brown man like maybe he was South American or Indian or something, and he had a smile on his face. Wade stepped out from behind a pillar and she turned away and got in the pickup truck to watch.

She watched Wade get the man to open the door and let him in, somehow talk him into driving away from the lights of the casinos. She never saw Wade pull the knife, just saw his mouth moving, his lips forming words with a manic intensity, and she wondered what he was saying. Touching the man's arms, his collar, the sleeves of his jacket. The man rigid, afraid. A small man next to Wade with his wide neck and shoulders, the man's eyes flat and dry while Wade's glittered like black metal.

When the car stopped in the woods, Wade had gotten out and the man had done something. Made a move, taken a nervous step toward the dark, and Wade had been on him. They went down, the big man covering the small one, his elbow pumping, pumping, and then they both lay still. She watched. For a moment she thought they were both dead and she reached up and touched the gear shift, ready to pull away. Then Wade got up slowly, the knife pointed out and dripping so that she thought of something sharp that was part of him, a spur of bone. A horn, something that grew out of him.

She went to stand beside him, the two of them in the headlights, the sounds of the insects a roaring metallic droning in the black trees. Wade siphoned gas from the man's car, choking and spitting, then poured it over the man and in through the open windows. She thought to ask what the plan was, but she knew watching Wade's eyes that there was no plan, had never been any plan but to kill the man and run. He moved in quick jerks, looking over his shoulder. He wanted to go back to jail, she saw. He was frightened of the dark, the insect noise, the immensity of the black night and the swirl of stars. For a moment they clung to each other like children. She watched him splash the gas heedlessly and then fumble for a lighter.

They were arrested two days later at the motel, the pickup parked at the curb, Wade's arm covered in grease where he had burned himself in the woods. She had thought he'd kill her, but she couldn't make it happen. Meeting in the courtroom had made that impossible somehow. He saw her like he saw himself, as a victim of the system. Manipulated and betrayed. She called him stupid and he just laughed and nodded; she slapped his face and he hung his head. So she went finally to the lobby and made a call while he was sleeping off the last of the base.

In court she turned to look at the crowd of reporters, the curious.

The family of the dead man, their faces distorted with rage, the detectives who had asked her why it had to happen. And there was her mother, standing next to her sister's wheelchair. She hadn't been expecting it and her eyes burned to see them there, a physical sensation like something chemical poured into her sockets. Her mother's hair with its streaks of yellow and black, her look of endless, bottomless disappointment. Her sister, head bobbing arrhythmically, eyes unfocused, long fingers tapping the arms of the chair.

Her mother stepped forward to grab the arm of Sandra's lawyer, her mouth moving fast to explain or excuse or damn or curse her daughter. Tell everyone about the car turning over and over and Sandra drunk at the wheel. Sandra didn't know and couldn't hear it. She clapped her hands over her ears and turned to face the judge. The bailiffs moved, the judge lifted his gavel, the courtroom retreated from her and she raced forward in her mind to the end. The gurney, the last silent moments, the straps they wouldn't need as she beckoned to them to bring the needle. Her teeth clenched against the sting, the final sting, the pumping venom and the rush into darkness.

TWO MEN AND A CAR
Andrew Nette

Chance opened his eyes to find the world upside down and Shaw headfirst through the windscreen.

He blinked. It hurt to move his eyelids. It hurt everywhere. He felt like he was floating but there was no water, only a blast of cold wind from the hole in the windscreen.

Shaw had been driving. He'd taken one hand off the steering wheel to reach for the mobile phone ringing in his jeans pocket, feeling around his waist in an attempt to find it. When that didn't work, he unbuckled his seatbelt and took his eyes off the road just as they were about to take a corner. He lost control and their car swerved and shot over the side into a ravine.

Chance released his own seat belt, opened the passenger door, and crawled onto the snow. He lay there, patting himself down in search of serious injuries. Nothing appeared pierced or broken.

He pulled Shaw's body from the overturned vehicle and laid it on the snow, grimacing as he felt for a pulse and found nothing. He stood up and took in the surroundings.

It had been at least half an hour since they passed the last green pre-fab buildings in Marysville, erected to replace those devastated by the bush fire that ripped through the town two years earlier. A blanket of snow covered the slope on either side, blackened tree trunks protruding like gnarled hands trying to claw their way out from underneath.

The terrain, the twisted car, Shaw's body, made Chance think of Afghanistan, the time a roadside bomb had taken out the lead truck in the Australian army convoy he'd been part of in Oruzgan province. But there were no flames, no smell of burning rubber, no whirring of choppers in the sky, only two men and a car, one of the men dead, the other lost. Chance forced his mind back to the present and more practical considerations. It was going to be dark soon. He was dressed in jeans, sneakers and a hoodie. Good clothes for knocking off an ecstasy lab, not for spending a night in freezing weather. The deceptively deep snow had already soaked through his sneakers, causing a slight numbness he knew would eventually lead to hypothermia.

He sized up Shaw's boots. At a guess, size ten, one size smaller than Chance took, but they'd do.

"Sorry, mate, I need these more than you," he said, unthreading the laces. Then he eased the polar fleece jacket from the corpse, wiping it against the snow to remove the worst of the blood. He found a thick roll of money in one of the pockets. Shaw must have swiped it during the robbery when Chance wasn't looking.

He started up the ravine, paused and headed back to the car. He reached into the open passenger door, extracted a clear plastic bag full of tablets that looked like tiny sweets, and tucked it down the front of the polar fleece.

It was almost dark by the time Chance reached the road. He walked down the middle of the two lanes, unsure which direction he was headed, hoping to Christ to see headlights in the distance.

The cold was becoming unbearable. Chance was on the verge of surrendering to the urge to lie down and give up, when out of the corner of his eye he caught a pinprick of light several hundred meters to his left. He ran towards it, almost colliding with an iron gate. It was padlocked. He clambered over it and walked briskly down a track recently cleared of snow.

The house was old, a bushfire survivor. Soft light glowed in the windows, smoke curled from the chimney. Chance crouched next to a woodpile and scoped the area. There was no sign of any dog and the carport to the side of the house was empty. He fingered the 9mm Beretta in his belt, thought better of it. He put the gun inside the bag of drugs, tied the plastic tightly and stashed it under the domed lid of a nearby barbecue half-submerged in snow. Then he stepped onto the porch and knocked.

He was about to knock again, when the door swung open to reveal a woman. She gazed at him impassively, as though strange men whose clothes were covered in blood appeared unannounced on the doorstep every evening.

"Please, I don't mean you any harm," Chance said. "I've been in an accident. I just need something to eat and a place to stay tonight.

"I promise I won't be any trouble and I'll be gone in the morning," he continued in the face of her silence. "I have money." He fumbled for the cash. "I can pay you."

She stepped aside and nodded for him to enter. Chance rushed past her to the far end of the room where a large open fire crackled. He sank to his knees in front of it and stretched his hands towards the flames.

He showered and changed into fresh clothes the woman had placed on the bathroom floor for him, gray tracksuit pants and a faded Harley Davidson T-shirt.

Chance stood in the kitchen doorway, drying his short blond hair with a towel slung around his neck, and watched the woman stir something on the stove, her back to him. She was tall as him with a slim, almost boyish figure under her tight blue jeans and black turtleneck sweater.

"Thanks." Chance kept rubbing his hair with the towel.

"For what?"

"For letting me stay."

She turned, a wooden spoon in one hand and looked him up and down. "My mother always told me to help strangers in need."

"Mine told me never to talk to strangers, let alone allow them in the house. Lucky for me they must do things differently where you're from. Where's that?"

"A long way away."

Chance nodded, not pushing her further. Her accent sounded Eastern European, exactly where Chance couldn't tell and didn't suppose it mattered. Probably somewhere cold, poor and remote, not unlike where she was now.

"Is it possible to wash my clothes?"

"Leave them by bathroom door," she said turning back to the food on the stove. "I'll do them later."

Chance leaned against a bench and looked sideways at her. The woman had a heart-shaped face and large blue eyes framed by dark rings accentuated by the whiteness of her skin. She had a crooked mouth that sat in a slight pout when closed. Her shoulder length jet-black hair was unkempt, the fringe falling over her forehead. There was a small tattoo of a black star on her neck.

"If you're not going to tell me where you're from, at least tell me your name."

"Manya."

"Manya, I'm Gary."

She nodded and said nothing.

"So, Manya, do you live here by yourself?"

"No." Her attention remained focused on a large saucepan of food on the stove. "With my husband, Rocky."

Chance hadn't noticed any sign of a male presence in the bathroom or the rest of the house. Come to think of it, the place was empty of the usual tell-tale signs of co-habitation, photos on the wall, papers, the shit that couples amass in the course of their lives.

It suddenly occurred to him that he'd seen no telephone or computer either.

"Where's your husband?"

"Rocky works during the week in the city, comes home on weekends."

Today was Wednesday. He tried to imagine what this boyish woman with a strange accent did with her days in the middle of the Victorian bush. Perhaps she cleaned. At least that would explain the other noticeable thing about the house: despite being old it was spotless. Along with the absence of personal effects, it made the place feel like a movie set.

"You must get lonely during the week," said Chance. "Do you have friends, people who visit?"

She shrugged, her gaze fixed on the pot on the stove. "Rocky doesn't like visitors."

"People you go and see?"

"Rocky doesn't like me leaving the house."

"I see. What else doesn't Rocky like?"

"People who ask too many questions." She inclined her head in his direction and gave him a thin smile to take the edge off her statement. "Now go back and sit in front of the fire. The food will be ready soon."

To one side of the open fire a large flat screen television was on, the sound turned down. It showed an aerial view of a nondescript brick veneer house, flashing lights, people milling about, before throwing to a female reporter speaking earnestly to camera. Behind her, police lifted blue and white checkered crime scene tape to allow a body to be wheeled out on a gurney.

Chance sat on the edge of the couch, looked around for the volume control, then shrugged his shoulders, sat back. It wasn't as though the reporter could tell him anything he didn't already know.

He'd busted Shaw selling speed to a couple of underage girls in the men's toilet of the nightclub he was bouncing in. Chance was about to throw him out when the dealer started going on about a sweet little score he was hatching to knock over an ecstasy lab that was cooking a batch to sell at a major dance party in the city the coming weekend.

Chance had drifted after Afghanistan. There was nothing fucked up or post-traumatic about it, his old life was just a skin he'd shed; when he tried to put it back on after returning it wouldn't fit. He needed the money, a circuit breaker to get him out of Melbourne and started somewhere else. Shaw needed back up.

"It'll be a piece of fucking piss, mate," Shaw had promised. "In and out, like a priest in a knocking shop. Just stand there and look scary, I'll do the rest."

Chance entered through the back while Shaw rang the front door bell. The two cooks made no effort to resist, just looked up from their chemistry equipment and smiled.

"Old man Aydin is going to be mighty pissed at you two," the taller of them said.

Chance recognised the name from stories in the city's tabloid newspaper. *Aydin* was supposed to be Turkish for "enlightened," not a term anyone would have ever used to describe one of Melbourne's most feared drug dealers and his extended family of pit bull sons.

Chance shot Shaw a "what the fuck" look.

"Don't tell me you two brain surgeons don't even know who you're ripping off?" the tall one added with a laugh, at which point Shaw shot him twice in the chest. He would have shot the other man had Chance not restrained him.

After that, there was nothing to do but grab the drugs and drive.

He and Manya ate in silence in front of the television, one of those shows about forensic scientists, well-dressed people combing over a crime scene. The irony wasn't lost on Chance.

After she had cleared the dishes, she led him to a single mattress in an empty room at the back of the house. He fell asleep as soon his head touched the pillow.

Chance was woken by something poking him in the side. The dawn light came through the crack in the cheap floral curtains. Manya stood in the corner in a dressing gown, hugging herself, a look of panic or fear in her face, he couldn't tell. A flat-featured heavy-set woman in a tight blue security guard's uniform was nudging him with her foot.

As Chance clocked the small truncheon she held in one hand, with a fluid movement she raised it brought and it down, sending him crashing into darkness.

He came to face down on cold hard tiles. The bathroom. His head throbbed. He made to get up but one of his ankles was cuffed to the metal pipe connecting the old-fashioned cistern.

The heavy-set woman sat on the edge of the bath, smoking. Manya sat at her feet, a purple bruise on the right side of her face, the dark ring around one of her eyes more pronounced than before.

The woman threw what was left of the cigarette on the floor and ground it under her boot as she looked at Chance. "Did you fuck her?"

"Rocky, nothing happened, I promise," said Manya looking up pleadingly at the woman.

Rocky gave her a hard stare, raised a booted foot and brought it down on Chance's hand.

Manya turned away as he shrieked.

"Hey, you, fuckface, you hard of hearing or something? I asked you a question. Did you have sex with her?"

"I didn't touch her," Chance said cradling his throbbing hand to his chest.

Rocky's eyes remained fixed on Chance as she produced an asthma inhaler and sucked deeply.

"Whatever, I'll get the truth out of her later. For now I got more pressing matters to discuss with you, like where you put the ecstasy."

"What ecstasy?"

"Please, don't bullshit me." Rocky ran a hand across her short brown hair. "I hate people lying to me. Makes me very fucking cranky.

"Manya here tells me you turn up covered in blood, saying something about being in an accident. Meanwhile, I hear on my scanner the cops found a wrecked car several kilometers down the road from here. Said vehicle matches the description of one last seen leaving the scene of a drug heist in the outer eastern suburbs of Melbourne yesterday afternoon. Two people were seen driving away in the car, but the cops only found one body."

"Honestly, I don't know what you're talking about."

"Okay, okay, have it your way." She shook her head, stood up and left the room.

"I thought your mother told you to help strangers?" Chance said looking at the ceiling.

"Rocky came home early in the morning, saying something about having a fight with the people she usually stays with in Melbourne," Manya said moving closer to him.

"How the fuck did you get mixed up with her, anyway?"

"I am illegal in your country. Rocky says she will report me to immigration if I try and escape. I am a prisoner in this house. Now you are too."

"What if I just tell her where the drugs are? She'd have to let me go."

Manya shook her head. "No, she will kill you anyway."

Chance thought for a moment. "My gun. It's with the drugs in a plastic bag underneath the barbecue out the front. You have to go and get it."

"What do you want me to do with it?" she whispered.

Before he could answer, Rocky returned, carrying a heavy gunmetal toolbox, placing it on the floor in front of Chance. Opening the top, she fossicked around for a moment, held up a large pair of wire cutters for him to see. Then, with surprising strength, she grabbed Chance's aching hand, splayed his fingers out and rested the little finger between the cutter's blades.

"This is how it's going to work. I'll ask you nicely once more, and if you don't answer, I'll cut this little finger off. Then I'll start on the others, working all the way down to your dick, comprehendo?"

Manya spoke rapidly, English interspersed with a language Chance couldn't understand. "Rochelle, *dorogay*—darling, please, he never did anything, I swear it."

"Shut up with the mongrel yapping of yours, woman," Rocky responded, still holding Chance's finger in the cutters. "Go and get something to clean the bathroom. This is going to get messy."

"Okay, hot-shot." Rocky looked at Chance, the cutters poised. "Where are the drugs?"

"Rocky, please, come on, mate, there's no need for this. Surely we can negotiate something—"

Chance screamed, nearly passing out as he watched his blood gush from the severed joint of his little finger.

Rocky took a hit on her inhaler.

"I'm afraid the time for negotiating is over, sunshine," she said moving the blades to the next finger.

Manya reappeared behind Rocky, raised the Beretta in both hands and aimed it at the nape of Rocky's neck.

Rocky turned around and said something but the words were drowned out by the gunshot. Manya kept firing, Rocky's body jumping at the impact. The smell of cordite and smoke burned Chance's nostrils.

Glassy-eyed, she swivelled slightly and aimed the gun at Chance.

"Manya, what are you doing?" Chance could hear the panic in his voice.

She squeezed the trigger. Chance raised his arms in a futile gesture to shield his face, but the hammer only clicked on an empty chamber. Chance heard the hollow metallic click several times until Manya slowly lowered the pistol and dropped it on the floor.

She bent down, took a key from Rocky's trouser pocket, and unlocked the handcuff on Chance's ankle.

"There's bandages in the cabinet," said Manya, looking almost absentmindedly around the blood-spattered bathroom. "I have to clean up this mess."

She was dousing the kitchen with petrol from a can when Chance emerged from the bathroom, his hand wrapped in bandages. He'd also swallowed several prescription painkillers he'd found in a bottle.

He slowly changed into his freshly laundered clothes in front of the flat screen. A morning chat show was on, two heavily tanned women talking about how to keep the romance alive in long-term marriages.

Chance went outside. The cold morning air felt good. He went over to the barbecue. The plastic bag lay open on the ground, half melted ecstasy tablets strewn on the snow.

He turned at the sound of a revving engine. Manya sat in the front seat of a large four-wheel drive ute, her eyes straight ahead. Chance climbed in next to her and she took off without a word.

In the rear view mirror he could see the first tongues of fire rising from the house, framed against the clear blue sky.

AMATEURS
Jedidiah Ayres

They were two days into the trip when the train shuddered and the hiss of steam, fighting the brakes applied, caused his bowels to revolt. Through the window, Tip caught a glimpse of a hooded figure standing beside the tracks with a torch. He fought the urge to throw up on his own feet. The Pinkerton across the seat from him chuckled, casually thumbing the cylinder of his Colt and easing back the hammer.

Beside him, Charlie Holland squinted at the night through the glass. "What's going on?" he asked. Tip dreaded hearing the answer.

The Pinkerton winked at them. "Looks like an unscheduled stop."

Tip sat up and pressed his face to the cool window and spied more torches among the trees. Beside him, Charlie said, "Sonsabitches."

The Pinkerton nodded. "Reckon they gonna wanna talk to you two."

The train came to a full stop and Tip heard loud voices saying his and Charlie's names, but not talking to them. He fought the futile urge to try slipping his manacles and duck beneath his chair. Instead he sent up a silent prayer for quickness, if not justice. Charlie attacked his bonds with admirable verve as he levelled a steady stream of curses under his breath. "Motherfuckers. Sonsa-chink-whore-bitches. Cock-suckin-Lincoln-lovin-rot-ass-mongrels."

The Pinkerton stood and showed Tip his palm. *Stay.* As if he could run. The detective meant to see them killed no doubt, only not here and now, which made him their only refuge at the moment. Tip looked over his shoulder at him moving to the front of the car and taking a position beside the door. Tip noticed he'd removed a second pistol, tiny. You could conceal it in an eye patch, he thought.

The approaching mob was announced by murmuring from passengers in the other cars and the fierce vibration of violence in the air growing stronger by the second. Charlie began to pull on his chains and Tip's arms were jerked to his right side. Charlie had slipped one boot between his wrists and was attempting to force the cuffs over his hands. "Shit." He wiggled his thumbs trying to make them touch the far sides of his palms. "Don't just sit there, Tip, c'mon, gimme support."

Tip squeezed his eyes shut instead. He listened for the still, small voice of God his mother had told him of, but it was in the storm this time. There was a dull thud against the door, followed by the sharp crack of splintering wood, and three men in potato sack hoods rushed in. The first one called out to them, "On your feet." Charlie paid no heed and pushed with renewed strength. The irons were moving and taking several layers of skin with them.

"Get up," the second hooded man said. "The devil await ye."

A hand reached out and roughly pulled Tip to his feet and another struck him on the mouth and he fell back into his seat. Charlie lay on his back on the floor, absorbing kicks to his ribs, still pushing with his foot between his hands, up in the air.

From behind, the Pinkerton appeared and put the barrel of his Colt under the chin of the first hood and the lady stinger in the ear of the third man. "The devil gonna have to wait a spell."

The second hooded man stopped reaching for Tip and looked at the Pinkerton. His muffled voice appealed to reason. "We got no strife with you. We only want justice."

"You'll have it. Just gonna have to wait a bit."

"Bullshit," said the voice beneath the first hood. "These boys kilt Bob Manuse plus another posse."

"And they'll hang for it. In Rawlins," said the detective calmly.

"Not good enough. Rawlins awful far from here," said the third man.

"I'm employed by the Union Pacific to bring these men to Rawlins," said the Pinkerton. "That's where they're going. You wanna see them swing, you can buy a ticket like everybody else."

Behind them, a fourth hooded man entered the rail car. "What's the hold up?"

The first man addressed him, "Union Pacific."

The fourth man, clearly the leader said, "Mister, we got no strife with the railroad. Nobody else needs be hurt today." He held up his palms to show that he was unarmed as he approached. "But we will be having justice from they." The Pinkerton dug the barrels of his guns into the flesh beneath the hoods, causing the first and third man to strain their necks for relief. The fourth man moved cautiously around the huddle of men till he was facing the detective. He bent forward to remove his mask.

What he revealed himself to be was middle-aged, about thirty, and balding. He was in need of a shave, but not unkempt. His features looked soft and healthy, but there was granite behind his eyes. "Sir, my name is Felix Vincent Warden, and I am kin to Robert Manuse by marriage." Here he paused and looked directly at Charlie struggling on the floor and then into the returned gaze of Tip. "I intend to see these die men tonight, I'm sure you understand. Ain't no cause for they to be responsible for no other deaths, but if you don't stand down, we will do what we have to."

The detective sighed and said, "Mr. Warden, I will shoot the very first one of you to put a hand on my prisoners and then I'll shoot one more of you for good measure." He nodded his farewell in a gentlemanly manner and added, "Kindly step the fuck off the train."

Charlie groaned with the effort of straining against his cuffs. His wrists were scraped raw and bleeding, but he'd moved the right side almost over the thumb knuckle, which gave with a crack and a cry from Charlie. His hand slipped through, and he leapt to his feet and lunged at the second man in a hood, who calmly took a single step back and shot Charlie in the belly.

Charlie dropped to Tip's feet. Tip winced and dry-heaved between his knees. The detective, cat-quick, shot the second hooded man up in the fatty part of his arm, with the tiny weapon, causing the man to drop his own gun. The little pop from the toy gun hardly seemed real, but the blood that bubbled out of the flesh wound was convincing.

Charlie lay curled on the floor, cursing and gargling blood, while the man who shot him sat in an empty seat and grabbed at the hole in his arm. "Would one of you shoot that son of a bitch!" he said.

The Pinkerton re-cocked the lady stinger, and the hooded men flinched and turned their heads slightly to Felix Warden who had taken on a purplish color. "Now listen here, you fancy son of a bitch—" he said. The Pinkerton fired a shot, from the Colt this time, through the ceiling right beside the first hooded man's ear. The man descended to the floor clutching at his head through the hood and the Pinkerton levelled the Colt into the second man's face.

Below them, the first man had pulled the hood off of his head and was screaming, "Shot my fuckin ear out! Shot my fuckin ear dead! Can't fuckin hear anything!" His eyes were wide and he was looking from hood to hood for recognition that he was indeed saying something. Receiving none, he scrambled to his feet and ran out the door.

From outside the train there was a commotion of voices calling for Warden to tell them what was happening. From the next car more men could be heard approaching the door. The Pinkerton told Felix Warden, "Tell them to stand down or I'll shoot the first one through the door."

Warden commanded in a level voice, "Stay back. Do not come in. Everything's under control."

"That's good, Felix, now—"

Warden continued, his voice raised, "But you boys hear any more guns, you come in shooting!"

Tip knelt beside Charlie on the floor. He tore the hem from his companion's clothing and tried to staunch the flow of blood with Charlie's own shirt. His partner looked up at him with hatred in his eyes. "Why didn't you help me, you fuckin coward?"

Tip gagged on the smells of blood and vomit mixing and filling the car. "Shh, Charlie, don't talk, now."

Charlie tried to spit at him, but only drooled bloody saliva down his chin. "Chickenshit backshooter," he managed. "Never shoulda hooked up with such a yellow-ass-mutt. Fuckin left you to die's what I shoulda done."

The detective looked at Warden, disappointed as if with a child. He started to speak, "Felix, I believe we can work something out." Felix Vincent Warden waited for his offer. The Pinkerton looked first at Tip wiping a string of drool from his chin and Charlie bleeding and bubbling shit all over the car floor. "I'll give you *one* of em."

Supported between two men, Charlie Holland was led off the train into a circle of other hoods and train passengers come out to watch, gathered around a telegraph pole. Two men were struggling with fashioning a noose and Charlie slumped on the ground waiting for them to finish. Felix Warden called out for haste, "Git him up before he bleeds to death."

The Pinkerton poked Tip in the ribs with his Colt. Tip stood from his seat and walked to the front of the car, watching the mob through the windows, feeling a mix of gratitude and shame that Charlie was dying and not himself. His captor and savior led him all the way to the engine where the driver regarded them warily before turning his attention again to the lynching. The Pinkerton spoke, "What are you waiting for, get this heap moving."

The engineer didn't look at him. "Can't. Rail's blocked." The detective put his head out and inspected the track for himself.

"So get your men out there to clear it."

"Pinch it. Let em watch." He turned to look at Tip. "Shoulda let em take both."

"Ain't your concern. Just get us moving along, pronto."

"Case you hadn't noticed, half my passengers are out there to watch. I ain't leaving without them. Why don't you just go back to your seat, you don't wanna see it for yourself?"

The Pinkerton motioned for Tip to step off the train and he did. Tip fell to his knees when he landed, and the detective put a hand under his arm to help him to his feet. "If you don't want to die with your friend tonight, you'd best help me clear this track. Soon as he's stretched, they're gonna want you."

They worked together, clearing away the barricade the mob had hastily placed across the track. They'd lit a fire in front to make it more visible and simultaneously obscure the shoddy obstacle they'd erected. The blaze was reduced to a few smoldering, mostly smoking, patches of timber. It was primarily still-green tree branches and even the trunks of a half dozen saplings lying in a pile.

"Amateurs," said the Pinkerton.

A loud cry rang out when Charlie was lifted to his feet and assisted atop a patiently waiting ass. Charlie began to vocalize his final thoughts. They mostly consisted of objects and animals those gathered round were advised to fornicate with and how he wished he'd killed more of them. He claimed further that Robert Manuse had died like a coward, begging for his life and even sucking on Charlie's cock for mercy before he'd shot him.

It wasn't true. They'd been holed up in a cave for a week, hiding out from a botched train job, when the posse had found them. Tip had been taking a shit across the way when the popping sounds of gunfire had sent him scrambling down the hill, goodbye forever to the gang.

He'd been a road agent before joining up with up with the McKinny-Jan gang that'd failed to stop a train outside Rawlins. He'd been party to bushwhacking and rustling and cheating at cards, but it was an attempted robbery that had brought this end. He and Charlie had busted up the tracks ten miles outside town, but a UP lineman discovered the damaged rails and had the train stopped before it got anywhere near them.

Union Pacific had a posse formed and out before nightfall with an inflated bounty placed on them, and the gang had disappeared up into the mountains. A week after, he'd heard the shooting and began his pilgrimage east without even stopping to wipe his ass. Weeks later, he'd chanced upon Charlie again at a saloon they both knew in Kansas City and heard confirmation from him the tale of the shootout he'd read about in newspapers. A railroad detective and a citizen were killed in the ambush, and Jensen and Collins shot dead from their own company. McKinny and Jan had escaped far as he knew.

Charlie claimed pure dumb luck had saved him that day and that fate had brought them back together that night. He bought Tip a round and a whore and later claimed innocence and bewilderment when they'd found the Pinkerton waiting for them in the bath house.

Upon arrest, the detective had advised quiet if they wanted to survive the trip back to Rawlins, but apparently word had got out they'd been apprehended. Telegraph messages outran any horse, carriage or train. Newspapers were probably printing stories of their capture already. Fuckin Charlie'd testify to that much.

His hands bound behind him and the noose placed around his neck, Charlie was made to sit atop the miserable looking ass who could not then be coaxed to move. Two men pulled on the stubborn animal's reigns and a third pushed from behind while Charlie abused them with words.

Finally the reluctant ass took three steps and then stopped, leaving Charlie, stretched taut, holding onto the animal's hind quarters with his heels and wriggling his head in the rope, until one of the men brushed his feet off. Charlie swung low, his feet missing the ground by inches. He made a wide arc and as he swung back, he kicked his heels in a rhythm that added to his momentum. He was finally able to grab the telegraph pole with his heels and holding himself still, wriggled his head with savage determination until one of the mob knocked his feet loose and Charlie commenced to swinging again. With each swing, the knot slipped a hair. At the zenith of the fourth swing, he fell through the noose and landed on his back. The rope, which had torn both of his ears away from his head, swung empty, garnished with his right extremity and a long strand of hair. The left fell in the dirt. Charlie lay on the ground, heaving wet, broken breaths.

The Pinkerton shook his head. "Amateurs."

They had cleared away the barrier and stood with the engineer who chuckled at the spectacle. Tip couldn't take his eyes off his partner who was left lying in the dust, in shock and too raw and scraped about the neck to cry out, while the mob hurried to fashion a better noose.

Felix Vincent Warden motivated his mob to "make a good one this time." And after a spell, the second version was fitted and cinched tight on Charlie's ragged throat. He slumped, barely upright, atop the mule who'd been cajoled back to the spot beneath the crossbeam of the telegraph pole. Again when the animal was slapped it refused to budge and the same three men set about seducing it away from its spot, but to no avail. Of a sudden, a fourth man stepped forward and shot the dumb animal behind its ear. The mule fell to the earth and Charlie Holland dropped with it, but stopped short of the ground.

Again, he kicked with both his feet and again he managed to get a swing going, but Felix Harden called for a stop to that and two men grabbed his kicking feet and tugged without syncopation until there was a pop. Charlie stopped squirming, went slack and vacated what remained in his bowels.

The gathered crowd became nearly as still as Charlie, whose only motion now was prompted by a dry and dusty wind carrying the smell of him back toward Tip. The Pinkerton urged the engineer to prepare to leave and as the onlookers began filing silently back aboard the train, he and Tip stood up front with the driver watching Charlie tilt and sway.

Tip realized that the detective had been wrong. Charlie's messy exit had left the mob uninterested in his blood and they pulled away without further incident. Several of the hooded men even set about clearing away brush still remaining on the track and others gallantly assisted ladies back to their seats. As he retook his own seat in the otherwise empty car, Tip stared out the window, but the light inside obscured the night and he was left with his own reflection to study.

They were still six hours from Rawlins and maybe six days to execution. The Pinkerton seemed to read his thoughts and offered, "You never know, sometimes a judge gets sick or lost making the trip and another one's gotta be called in. Could take weeks."

Tip considered that as the train pulled away. He glanced back for a final look at Charlie and the detective snorted. "You don't owe that cocksucker nothing. Gave you up five minutes after we caught him in the hills outside Rawlins. Said he knew you had an uncle in Kentucky, figured you'd be headed that way." Tip took the information stoically. It made sense. The Pinkerton watched the subtle changes in Tip's expression and nodded in agreement. "Fuck him. He deserved it."

HALF-JACK
Roger Smith

When the gunmen come at Disaster Zondi, he's lost in one of Erik Satie's intricate piano pieces, the faint, musky tang of the blonde whose bed he's just left still rising from his fingers as they play imaginary scales on the wheel of the idling Beemer.

It is very late—or very early—and he's sitting at a red light in the empty streets of northern Johannesburg, staring up at the floodlit Sandton City Mall and its cordon of office towers, like a shrine to some African god of greed. This is the money-belt of Johannesburg, a city that has fled from itself, rushing northward away from the festering post-apocalyptic downtown, with its high-rise slums, crack whores, Nigerian drug lords and Zairian sex-slavers.

Most people don't stop for lights after dark in the carjack capital of the world, just slow to see there is no oncoming traffic, then accelerate away. A kind of half-curtsey, a bob in the direction of the law. But Zondi's in no hurry to get home to his antiseptic apartment and the insomnia that inevitably awaits him after his nights out on the prowl. These hit-and-run sex sessions scratch some physical itch, temporarily, but they leave him understanding how far he's drifted from human affection. Never mind love.

So Zondi waits at the light, the blue neon from a Mercedes showroom rippling over his dark skin. Satie's complex piano constructions escape out the open car window into the summer night, the odor on Zondi's fingers lost now in the wood-fire fumes that waft in on a warm breeze, drifting over the fortress-like homes of the rich, a reminder of the advancing shack settlements.

Zondi sees a movement, and by the time he turns his head the barrel of a gun rests on his temple, and a skinny black arm has snaked through the open window, releasing the power locks. A second man, fat gut swelling his T-shirt, is already sliding into the passenger seat, his gun on Zondi. He reeks of weed and sweat and stale piss.

The thin man is in behind Zondi. "Drive."

Zondi drives, knowing there is only one way this is going to end.

He started the night drinking at the cocktail bar of the Michelangelo Hotel, a faux-Italianate confection that wouldn't look out of place in Las Vegas. Nouveau rich; Jo'burg's idea of culture. The barman knew Zondi and was already pouring him a neat Stoli before his Cavalli-encased butt settled on the barstool. He nodded to the barman as he lifted the glass, his fingertips chilled by the alcohol, the thick, cold syrup sliding down his throat and cooling the heat in his belly, sending a nice anesthetic buzz to his temples. Zondi closed his eyes in appreciation, and when he opened them he was looking directly into those of the blonde who'd taken the stool beside him.

They were always blondes, the ones who were drawn to his blackness. Natural blondes, with blue veins like tributaries running near the surface of their pale skins. Not something he questioned, this attraction. It was a gift. Or a curse.

She told him her name. Anne? Jane?

When he told her his, she smiled, squinting at him over her mojito. "Disaster? And what's that?" she asked. "Some kind of a struggle name?" Showing him she was cool, this young white woman, knowing that back in the apartheid days, activists had dubbed themselves *Terror* and *Blade* and *AK*.

Zondi shook his head. "No, it's my real name. My parents were illiterate Zulus, and they thought a disaster was something good. Some kind of force of nature." Saying this as he sipped his Stoli, light-years removed from the mud hut he'd been born in.

"And are you?"

"Am I what?"

"A force of nature?" Resting her hand on his knee.

"What you need," he said, signaling the barman, "is another drink."

She smiled at him, in that way, and he knew she would keep her blue eyes open when they fucked, admiring the contrast between his darkness and her light.

The gun barrel prods Zondi at the base of his skull. "Turn here."

Zondi guides the Beemer into a quiet road, luxurious houses lost behind high walls and electric fences. Twenty-five years ago this was open land, the paddocks and stables of Jo'burg's self-made gentry, carved up now by developers.

"Stop."

Zondi stops the car and the small man, barely out of his teens, has Zondi's door open and puts the gun to his neck, ordering him out. Barking at him in that township mix of Zulu and English and Afrikaans.

Zondi obeys. The big man comes round the car, and they shove Zondi back against the side of the Beemer, the skinny guy's hands all over him like spiders, finding his wallet and his cell phone. Then he forces Zondi to knees, the gun at his forehead.

"So," the little bastard says, his sewer-breath hot on Zondi's face, "you want to live like a white man?" Zondi says nothing, looking past the punk's Kangol hat, watching a jet on a flight path to Europe, lights winking in the dark. "Okay, then you can fucken die like one."

The gun rasps as the man cocks it, and Zondi closes his eyes and waits, trying to picture some reassuring afterlife, but all he sees are the feral white teeth of the blonde as she opened her mouth and swallowed him.

But the little runt doesn't pull the trigger, just laughs and playfully prods Zondi's head with the gun barrel. "We not gonna kill you yet, you shit. Not till you give us the numbers of your bank cards."

And they bundle Zondi into the trunk of the Beemer, where

he lies in absolute darkness as the car speeds to Christ-knows-where, but at least he's not floating in some portal between life and afterlife.

Not dead. Not yet.

The trilling Satie has been replaced by the muffled thump of Kwaito, South Africa's homegrown bastard-child of hip-hop and techno. Zondi loathes Kwaito, and it seems unnecessarily perverse that he's going to go to his death with the guttural yearnings of over-blinged township trash in his ears. Because they'll shoot him, for sure, the scum up front, once they reach a cash machine and force him to key in the access code to his credit card.

No way they can let a cop live after he's seen their faces.

And that's what they'll call Zondi when they rifle through his wallet and find the badge that identifies him as a special investigator in the office of the public prosecutor. A cop. Kind of. And that will be his death sentence.

Zondi, with little room to maneuver in the trunk, stretches out his hand and fumbles for the penlight tucked beside the car jack and wheel wrench. He clicks on the beam, and for a moment entertains the idea of looking for a weapon. Dismisses it. What good is a polite German screwdriver going to be against a couple of 9 mils?

Instead he uses the light to find the half-liter of Stoli he wedged into a recess alongside a container of radiator coolant, Zondi too law-abiding to drive with an open bottle of booze inside the car. At least he'll go to his death loaded. He uncaps the small bottle—called a half-jack here in South Africa—and takes a swig, pleased that he liberated it from the blonde's mini-bar.

After a few more drinks in the cocktail lounge, and the carefully coded conversation of the sex-addicted, the blonde had led Zondi up to her room. She was from Cape Town—something in advertising—working on a TV commercial. She kept the lights on and her eyes open, and sobbed three climaxes before his body grudgingly spat out one.

He stayed hard—from desperation more than desire—so they fucked to the point of pain, before he took the vodka and left her sleeping in a tangle of white sheets, looking like an angel fallen from a height.

The car stops and the trunk lid opens, revealing a puke-yellow McDonald's arch straddling a deserted drive-through.

"Hey, he's having a party, this bastard," the fat man says, deep voice thick as mud. He grabs the vodka from Zondi and takes a long pull, splutters, and liquid spills down his chin.

"Out, you fucken cop." The little shit and his gun again, worrying at Zondi's head.

Zondi clambers out of the trunk. The ferret snatches the half-jack from his chunky friend and drinks deeply, his eyes and gun never leaving Zondi. He doesn't cough, just wipes his mouth and urges Zondi forward with the barrel of the automatic toward a cash machine in the empty strip-mall next to the McDonald's.

The scrawny man slides Zondi's MasterCard into the mouth of the auto teller. "Put in your number," he says, taking another swig from the bottle.

Zondi hesitates, and earns himself a smack on the forehead with the gun barrel. He feels warm blood trickling down his cheek, and a drop falls onto the illuminated face of the ATM. Zondi punches in his code, and the asshole grins when he sees Zondi's available balance of ten thousand.

The machine takes a while to produce the cash, its innards whirring and clicking. The 'jackers pass the bottle back and forth, and Zondi stares down the road as a pair of headlamps resolve into a white cop van.

The two men crowd Zondi, guns close.

"Don't fucken move," the small one says.

The van slows to a crawl, the cops looking their way, and Zondi hears the breath of the carjackers, catches the stink of their fear. When the van picks up speed and disappears under a ribbon of orange street lamps, Zondi knows he's missed whatever chance he had.

The skinny guy grabs the money and folds it into his jacket. Still clutching the Stoli, he moves Zondi to the Beemer, opening the rear door and shoving him in, making him crouch on the floor behind the front seats. The runt is in after Zondi, and the big guy gets behind the wheel and they speed away, in the opposite direction from the cops.

As they drive, the small man's breathing turns rough and uneven, and he slumps forward, but keeps the eye of the gun fixed on Zondi.

"This booze," he says, fighting for breath, "it's too fucken strong."

The smooth asphalt gives way to corrugated gravel, and the bottle slips from the shrimp's fingers and lands on Zondi's chest, the dregs wetting his shirt.

"Ay, brother, I'm going to puke," the little guy says, his voice strangled.

"Not in the fucken car, man." Fatso is already slowing the Beemer.

The small man fights the door open, and even before the car has stopped Zondi hears him retching, catches the acrid stench of the vomit. Zondi lifts himself, going for the skinny bastard's gun. But before he can reach it, the big guy rips open the rear door and grabs Zondi and hauls him out.

They're on a gravel track carved into open land, early light tearing the dark sky. Zondi can hear the buzz of traffic on some invisible freeway. Fatso is unsteady on his feet, and there's foam on his lips, but he still has enough strength to push Zondi to the sand and put the gun to his head.

And again Zondi kneels and waits to die, watching the rising sun trickle like blood over a distant spine of hills, the fossil-rich Magaliesberg—the so-called Cradle of Humankind—where early man lifted himself off his knuckles and took his first lurching steps into an uncertain future.

Then the gun droops from Zondi's head, and the beefy guy folds in on himself and hits the ground with a slap of meat. Zondi reaches across and feels a very faint, erratic pulse in the gorilla's thick neck. He kicks away the fat man's gun and crosses to the Beemer where the little guy is slumped half out the car. Zondi grabs him by the jacket and dumps him onto the dirt. He's dead. Zondi frisks him and finds his money, wallet and cell phone.

Half-Jack 41

Zondi stands, surveying what he has wrought. It crosses his mind, for a moment, to call this in, but he thinks, *Fuck it*. The regular police hate Zondi because of the zeal with which he takes down corrupt cops, and he knows they'll kick his ass into a jail cell until his boss pulls strings to bail him out.

Too much grief.

So he draws a white handkerchief from his suit pocket, lifts the skinny man's gun by the barrel and throws it into the stagnant stream that crawls its way through the veld, the water thick with human shit and garbage from a nearby squatter camp. He does the same with the fat guy's weapon.

Then he takes the empty half-jack from the floor of the Beemer and wipes the glass free of his fingerprints, before tossing it into the stream. He pops the trunk and finds the plastic container of antifreeze that he poured into the vodka—after he emptied half the booze into the spare wheel housing—the flashlight clenched between his teeth, battling not to spill the radiator coolant as the Beemer sped through the night. He wipes the container clean, frisbees it into the black water, and closes the trunk.

Zondi nudges the big guy with the toe of his leather loafer. The man's head lolls. He's joined his buddy on the road to wherever.

Zondi starts the Beemer, does a U-turn, negotiates his way past the bodies, and drives back toward the city. He clicks on the Satie, but now the atonal piano seems too cerebral, too northern. He kills the CD and the radio blares out Kwaito. Zondi reaches out a hand to mute it, but withdraws his fingers. It is the right soundtrack, somehow, for this landscape: a fungus of shacks advancing on the low-rent condos crouching behind their blank walls, the saw-toothed skyline of Sandton rising through a blanket of smog in the distance. He pumps up the volume and feels the primitive throb of the music deep in his balls.

Zondi drives home.

GLORY B.
Josh Converse

The Cobra II fought Quinn over every crack in the asphalt. Every twitch and turn sent her into a lurching fit. The clutch was stiff and ornery. The brakes were grabby, the wheel, touch-sensitive. One run, the car would come out of the turn too sharp. The next, she'd barely come out of it at all.

Across the empty lot, through pungent, drifting vapors of exhaust and melted rubber, Glory Bea fumbled a Marlboro into her mouth. She produced a Zippo from the sling that covered her left arm, lit up and took a drag. Her cough rattled across the lot, trailing the observation:

"That ain't likely to cut it, kiddo."

Quinn flipped her off.

Glory Bea slid off the top bar of the shopping cart corral and limped over. She swatted a bee off of her ass. As she approached, secondhand smoke wafted into the car. She held the smoke between her lips, thumbed a belt loop with her good hand.

"Now, you might think that ain't so big a dif'ernce, but you try and gun it outta the position you just left yourself, y' run down two nuns and a mailman just tryin' to get back to the position you shoulda been in right to start with. N' let's do it again, only this time I want you to really snap that back end around. Bootlegger's turn is one of the easiest maneuvers you can pull—" She nodded down at the sling, "—so long's you got two good hands."

"I know, Glory Bea, goddammit. It's like everything in this car is working against me. You know I've done this thing a hundred damn times in a hundred different cars."

Glory Bea nodded. "I know it." She snorted, then spit on the ground. "But not on clean asphalt, y'ain't. Blind person could tell it. We ain't shopliftin' liquor outta some dusty Stop N' Rob out a half-tank past middle nowhere. We right downtown on this deal, now. Tight spaces. Passersby. Now bring that cranky bitch around again, only this time you make sure you get all one hundred and eighty degrees outta 'er. I want that front end tradin' places with that back end, just like this." Glory Bea spun around on her heel, stopping with her back to Quinn.

He frowned. "I should have a smaller car. A little CRX or something."

"You should keep your mouth shut's what you oughta do. Marshall's this close to callin' his guy in from Tampa as it is," Glory Bea said, looking over at Marshall's conversion van, parked a hundred yards off.

"That supposed to make me nervous?"

Glory Bea cuffed him in the back of the head. The lines in her face deepened. "Marshall don't hand out no pink slips, shithead. If he thinks you gonna fuck this up, then all you gonna be to him is a material witness. You get it? No severance packages. Now go again, and this time, get it damn well right."

Quinn went again. This time, as he was about to go into the spin, Glory Bea kicked a shopping cart out in front of the car. Quinn read it and made the adjustment. He let off the gas a little, carved the turn around the cart, but came up short of the full turnaround. The Cobra II stalled out.

Quinn punched the galloping horse in the middle of the wheel.

The door on Marshall's van slid open. Out stepped the mastermind himself.

Marshall crossed the lot. Glory Bea met him halfway. Marshall towered over her. They spoke, looked in Quinn's direction once, twice. Quinn fidgeted with the shifter knob. It was loose. He tightened it down. When he looked up, Marshall's chrome .45 was pressing the corner of his left eye.

The first words Marshall ever directly spoke to Quinn: "So,

Quinn, is it? It's your big shot, Quinn. The big try-out. Right? Final cutdown day. Real simple. I'm gonna stand right over here on this yellow line. That represents the curb, right? And you're gonna go again, one, two, three times, and each time I'm gonna get in the shotgun seat, just like on game day. Got it? Now, if this car doesn't come out of that turn parallel to my shoulders three out of those three, I'm gonna get in and shoot you in the face. And if this car don't come out of that turn where I only need a half step to open that door three out of those three, I'm gonna get in and shoot you in the face. Get it?

"Basically, any scenario that doesn't involve you getting this perfect involves me sitting down in that seat and shooting you in the face, and then calling my guy in Tampa while Glory here Ziebarts your frontal lobe off the upholstery. Grab ya? Good. Batter up."

Marshall handed the .45 to Glory Bea. "All right, Glorious. Enough shopping carts. Battle stations."

Glory Bea took the back seat, driver side.

"Well, now y'all have met."

ATTEMPT 1

Marshall stood a hundred yards away.

The Cobra II idled. Quinn kept touch pressure on the clutch.

Glory Bea lined the .45 up over Quinn's right shoulder, took aim down the center of the hood.

Marshall picked up the bag and put the strap on one shoulder.

Quinn crawled out of first. He went easy on the approach. Gradual, uniform acceleration. The Cobra II responded with an ascending purr. Quinn shifted into second.

Marshall toed the yellow line and pulled a sawed-off shotgun from the bag.

Quinn grabbed the right side of the wheel with his left hand. At twenty yards, he twitched her a tick to the right, then hard full to the left. He clutched and gave the handbrake one firm tug. The back end skidded round. Quinn released the brake, turned into the skid. The Cobra II swung into position.

Marshall reached out and grabbed the door handle. Didn't even need the half step. He tossed the duffel bag into the back, hitting Glory Bea square in the chest.

The bag, weighted with phone books, pinned Glory's gun hand against her body.

Quinn gassed it the instant Marshall's ass touched the seat.

Marshall covered the front end with the sawed-off.

Quinn clutched. Second gear. Third. The Cobra II screamed.

Marshall put his hand up. "A'right. Stop here." He looked in the back seat.

The hockey bag was still resting in Glory Bea's lap as she now struggled to get her gun hand free. Quinn watched in the rearview. Glory Bea was sweating.

Marshall laughed. "Glory's in a fight for her life back here."

"Goddamn sling," Glory Bea hissed. Finally, she was able to push the bag aside. She pointed the .45 out the back window.

"And...bang-bang." Marshall nodded. "Not quite clockwork, Glorious." He turned to Quinn. "That's a lot more like it, kid. Just like that. We move as one. Easy in, hard out. Right? Now let's do it again and we'll see if you're just a lucky fuck."

ATTEMPT 2

Having pulled it off once, Quinn breathed easy. He had the feel of the turn.

Glory Bea took aim over his shoulder again.

Quinn revved the engine, waited for Marshall to lift the bag, and then gunned it. The tires barked going into second. He went into the turn sooner than on the last run. Faster. He brought the wheel sharp left and yanked the brake. The Cobra II sailed through the turn, and with the added momentum, snapped around and rocked to an easy halt.

Money.

Marshall reached for the door. He pushed the bag into the back seat. Glory Bea fielded it clean.

As Quinn clutched for first, the car rolled backwards a hair. Quinn mashed the footbrake and gassed it at once, got the rear wheels spinning. Marshall almost went down with the shift in momentum, but managed to find the seat. When Quinn released the brake, Marshall's head snapped back into the headrest.

Quinn only got it up to about fifty before Marshall signaled him to slow down.

When the car stopped, Marshall took a deep breath. He rolled down the window. Then he jabbed the barrel of the shotgun hard into Quinn's ribcage. Quinn doubled over. Marshall spun the shotgun around and caught him in the mouth with the butt.

Quinn felt the blood run down his chin and neck.

"You cocksucker," Marshall spat. "The approach, fine. The speed, whatever. The position was perfect. None of it matters if you back over me with the door when I'm tryin' to get in. Right? I'm not watching the car, I'm watching the goddamned streets and the sidewalk. I gotta worry about what the fuck I'm doin', you see? You don't have to shoot at nobody, you don't have to grab nothin'. All you got to do in the world is execute a turn and not run me over. Right?"

Quinn nodded and pulled his hands away from his mouth. He checked his teeth. "I got it," he said.

"He's got it, Marshall. Just he's used to drivin' them little Jap numbers, is all."

Marshall shook his head. "We're not turnin' circles around pylons for pussy on this thing, kid. And we're gonna need more than sixty-five miles an hour if anything fucks up. This is a job. Got it? Nobody ever made a getaway in a fuckin' Honda unless they were being chased by a tow truck or a fuckin' truant officer. That's faggot shit. If I wanted any of that 'Tokyo Drift' horseshit, I'd have my fuckin' paperboy drive. Right? This is a fuckin' job."

Quinn nodded and wiped blood from his mouth.

ATTEMPT 3

Glory Bea stared across the lot as Marshall walked back to his mark. She checked the .45 and pulled the brim of her straw hat down.

Quinn heard her sigh. "You'll do fine," he said.

"If I was sittin' up there I'd be doin' better. I'm no damn sharpshooter, Quinn. Leastways not with a damn .45."

"You shoot fine."

"I mean, I can manage. Ain't my especiality, is all. I'm a driver. That's what I always do. Gunnin' is for muscle. I ain't muscle."

"You sure got plenty of muscle in that mouth."

"Lord, he sure is funny," Glory Bea frowned, eyes rolling skyward. Again, she lined up the .45 over Quinn's right shoulder.

Marshall picked up the hockey bag, shouldered it. Quinn eased into first. The shotgun came out of the bag. Fifty yards. Into second, now. Forty.

Wheel.

Clutch.

Handbrake.

Spin.

Quinn had it down automatic.

Marshall shoved the bag through the open window before opening the door, before the Cobra II even came to a stop. Quinn spun the back wheels again. When Marshall's right foot came off the ground, Quinn released the brake and they took off like a shot. Marshall levelled the shotgun on the dash and aimed down the center of the hood.

Quinn kept on line and hauled ass. At seventy, he looked at Marshall. Marshall looked back. Quinn shifted into fourth. Eighty-five.

Then, there was a loud blast. The windshield disintegrated.

Quinn nearly rolled the car. The Cobra II fishtailed wildly, but Quinn calmed her quick. His right eardrum screamed. Smoke rolled from the barrel of Marshall's shotgun.

Marshall got in his face.

"Drive, motherfucker!"

Quinn dropped the hammer. Fifth gear.

The edge of the lot loomed.

Marshall held up his fist, and Quinn slowed again.

"You gotta be ready for that shit, kid. This thing turns into a firefight, I can't have you plowing my car into a fuckin' bus stop. Right?"

Quinn nodded as he parked the Cobra II.

Marshall turned to Glory Bea. She was leaned all the way forward, digging around the floorboards.

"The hell you doing, Glorious?"

"Nothin'."

Marshall nudged Quinn. "She dropped the gun. Didn't ya? I dunno, Glory Bea."

"I got it."

"All the sudden it's not the kid I'm worried about so much, you know?"

Glory Bea narrowed her gaze at Marshall. "Well, try not to throw that fuckin' duffel bag in here like yer workin' the tarmac at Dulles, you blockheaded sumbitch."

He turned to Quinn. "You're a natural, kid. What it looks to me, anyhow."

Glory Bea beamed. "What'd I tell ya? I better watch my ass." She grabbed Marshall's shoulder and gave it a squeeze. "Go on and give him ten more chances. I say he nails ever' one of 'em."

"Nah, I think we got our driver, here. You feel ready, Quinn?"

"Yeah, I'm good."

"Tight in the stomach?"

"A little."

"That's good. That's where you're supposed to be. A lot of these guys, they tell me they don't rattle. Right? I got no use for 'em. Even if he's isn't just tryin' to bullshit me, how alert is a man who's totally at ease? Right? What good is that to me?"

Quinn only shrugged.

"Whatever. Good. All right, I want you back here tomorrow morning, five a.m. Got that? Tonight you get over, see Mikey at the garage. He'll swap out the windshield, and then tell him I want fresh tires in the back. Overinflated. Right, Glory?"

"That's how we do it."

"Damn straight. Then you get over to the do-it-yourself wash and hose this bitch down, inside and out. Got it?"

"Hose down the interior? What about the leather?" Quinn asked.

"What're you, a collector? I want her spotless. Do what the fuck I say."

Glory Bea laughed and leaned forward, rested her chin on her forearm, between the front seats. "Ain't you bein' maybe a bit on the anal retentive side, sugar?"

Marshall snorted. He gave Quinn a wink, then caved Glory

Glory B.

Bea's mouth in with the butt of the sawed-off. Then, in a blur, he turned the barrel on her.

The roar of the shotgun filled the Cobra II.

Quinn opened his eyes. Glory Bea's head was gone.

The back seat was lacquered in blood. Chunks of bone and brain slid down the windows and upholstery. Quinn's breath left him.

Marshall kicked the door open and got out. "Spotless, ya hear?"

Quinn swallowed hard.

"Ya hear, kid?"

THE DECIDER
Charlie Stella

"You remember Hulk Hogan?" Amanda said. "That thing he used to do to get the crowd going, when he wound his hand behind his ear and then pointed. Like this."

She was speaking to the two remaining operators on the third shift. They had been working through the night and would be leaving as soon as the day shift operators arrived. Both were smiling as Amanda stood in front of her desk and leaned back while winding her right hand behind her right ear.

"Then he did this," she said and she pointed straight ahead and up. "He'd pivot and do it to all four sides of the ring. Remember that?"

"The wrestler?" Jim Dixon said. "That guy?"

"Yeah, Hulkamania," Amanda said. "That's the guy. You know him, Sally?"

Sally Piazza nodded. "Sure, I know who he is. My kid brother used to bounce off the walls after watching one of those wrestling shows."

Jim said, "I swear half those guys are gay."

"Maybe," Amanda said. "Anyway, Durr was right in the middle of another of her absurd speeches about how clean the center looked now that Linda is gone. Before that her highness and Carol spent two hours discussing where to place the in and the out boxes. Imagine? Two hours and the entire time they're making fun of Linda, how sloppy she was and so on."

Sally said, "As if that's what's important in a word processing center."

"That bitch gets on my last gay nerve," Jim said. "I like what Steve used to call her, Her Hitler. That play on Herr Hitler. I love it."

"Well, anyway, that's when he did it," Amanda said. "Steve, I mean. Durr was in the middle of her happy speech about the center being clean and Steve stood up, wound his hand, put it up behind his ear and cut the longest, loudest fart you ever heard."

Shocked at what Amanda said, Sally and Jim sat there dumbfounded, their smiles frozen and their eyes opened wide.

"No way?" Jim finally said.

"Way," Amanda said. "I nearly hit the floor. Max from litigation was in here and so was Nelly, Miller's secretary. Max is only a first year so he covered his mouth not to laugh, but there was this great big pause and then everybody let go. Nobody could hold it anymore."

Sally chuckled. "And then what?"

Amanda shrugged. "Her highness fired Steve on the spot, told him to get his things together and get out of the building before she called Security."

"And?" Jim said.

"Steve did it," Amanda said. "He put his IPod in his bag, looked back at Simone, she was here too, and then he cut the cheese one more time before leaving. I don't even think he logged off."

"What her highness do after he was gone?" Jim said.

"Threw a fit," Amanda said. "She told us she didn't think any of what just happened was funny and that it was the most rude display of behavior she'd ever witnessed and if Steve thinks he's collecting unemployment he's out of his mind."

"Steve was diagnosed with cancer last year," Sally said. "He probably doesn't want to spend eight hours a day the last year of his life in this place."

"He looks terrible," Jim said. "Seriously."

"He's been here ten years," Amanda said. "You'd think they'd be more compassionate."

"Durr's wanted him out forever," Sally said. "He refused to

show her fear. That bitch had half this place shaking in their boots, but Steve could care less. She actually said, once he was gone, she can't wait to see him living on the street."

"She said that in front of people?" Jim said.

"She apologized immediately after, but yeah, she said it."

"Too bad it wasn't recorded," Jim said.

Amanda sat on the edge of her desk. "Well, I'm doing this a long time and I don't remember ever seeing something that funny in my life, what Steve did. It was priceless. Between that ditz they brought in from Newark to get things in order...." She stopped to mimic someone speaking. "'Hi, I'm Carol, the perky no-life company girl from Newark who sleeps with her blackberry on her night table so I can be reached while I'm sleeping and dreaming about the firm and I'm here to get things in order.' Every time someone walked in here, she ran up, shook their hands and introduced herself like she was running for mayor."

Jim said, "Tell me she doesn't really say that about sleeping with her blackberry on her night table."

"She does indeed," Amanda said. "And you know her highness loves that level of company girl. Carol the perky becomes one more level of distance between Durr and any form of responsibility. You hear what Durr told Simone about her raise?"

"Something about it being her fault she didn't complain about Linda?" Sally said. "Something like that. Linda mentioned it."

"Yeah," Amanda said. "'We all make decisions,' Durr told Simone. 'You chose not to speak up. That was your decision.'"

"Yeah, right," Sally said. "She gave me shit a few times for forgetting to card in and out. She can see that, but she couldn't see all the times Linda carded in an hour early and was working to get things out before the morning rush without expecting overtime. I heard she gave Linda shit for that, too."

Amanda said, "Durr claimed she didn't know Linda was here so early. I'm telling you, she must believe her own bullshit."

"What she think Linda was doing here at that time, stretching exercises?" Jim said. "All she had to do was ask IT what Linda was doing on the system. That would take, what, five minutes? Ten?"

"Durr takes no responsibility for anything," Amanda said.

"She's the office manager and claims she's clueless about everything going on around her. She depends on her rats, the ones she protects from having to work."

"Like that chunker, Taylor," Sally said. "Those two, Durr and Taylor, don't kid yourself, they're friends."

"Maybe lovers," Jim said.

Amanda clutched her stomach. "Please, don't make me sick."

"Not to mention how when they fired Linda they lost a workhorse," Sally said. "I don't think they have a clue as to how much production that woman was responsible for."

"Except Linda could be a nasty bitch, too," Jim said.

"Whatever," Amanda said. "I didn't get along with her either, but there's no denying how much work she put out. She's the most productive operator I've worked with and I'm doing this twenty-five years. Now they're down Linda and Steve, and guess what? Carol is gonna have her hands more than full before she knows what all. She's so busy putting in her procedures, which some are good, don't get me wrong, but she hasn't taken into account for a minute how much she's losing without Linda. She'll find out soon enough, though, make no mistake about that."

"Durr still wearing those ridiculous outfits?" Sally asked.

Amanda rolled her eyes. "The woman is a virtual stick figure. No hips, no ass, no tits, two pounds of makeup and she wears everything she has two sizes too tight."

"And those shoes, God," Sally said. "She probably spends half her salary on Jimmy Choo shoes that make her look like a witch. Doesn't she realize how ridiculous she looks?"

"All I can see is that beak on her," Jim said. "Reminds me of *Rodan*, the old monster movie. The one that flies."

"That's a good name for her," Amanda said. "Her highness, Rodan."

"The witch," Jim said.

"So, what happens now?" Sally said. "I remember Steve was really pissed off one night after he came back from treatments and he had a run-in with that little piss ant down the hall, what's his face."

"Ress?"

"Yeah. Ress said something to piss Steve off, and he said he was putting Ress at the top of the list of people he'd like to take with him when he died. He was kidding, I think, but what if he wasn't?"

"That was just talk," Jim said. "He'd just gone through chemo. He was probably ready to kill himself."

"I know, but Steve has that dark side to him. That sense of humor of his."

"Oh, come on, he was hilarious. I love the things that came out that man's mouth. And he was quick with it, too."

"And a thorn in her highness's side until yesterday," Amanda said.

"Well, I wish him well," Sally said. "I hope he goes in peace. I know he was a nice guy and all, but he scared me that night."

"You tweaking, girl," Jim said. "Steve was a loner is all. He was just blowing off steam that night."

"Well, I'm with Sally on that," Amanda said. "I liked him enough too, but I don't want to be here if he does come back looking for revenge. On the other hand, I'd pay a hundred bucks to see him do that Hulk Hogan fart again. God, that was funny."

They laughed again.

A week to the day Steve Grogan was terminated for inappropriate behavior in the word processing center of Dash Paris LLP, he gained access to the building through the loading dock on the south side of the street. It was early in the morning. The loading dock security guard was about to go home and mostly ignored the well-dressed man who'd flashed the Dash Paris identification.

"I'm going to have a few boxes to take down in about an hour or so," Grogan said. "Do I bring them here or upstairs in the lobby?"

"Either," the guard said. "But you'll need a pass on your company's stationary."

"No problem," Grogan said. "Freight elevator back there?"

The guard pointed behind him as he reached for his jacket hanging off the back of a chair. "Straight back, through the doors and to the right."

"Thanks."

Grogan went through what was the sub-basement hallway,

through a set of swinging doors and found the freight elevator. He pressed the button and glanced at his watch: seven-fifteen. The kitchen crew in the cafeteria would be working full tilt. Floors eight through thirteen would have a small number of early birds but would be mostly quiet. Grogan had no love for a few of the attorneys but felt they were miserable enough not to kill; killing would be less of a punishment than knowing they'd have to live out their wretched lives. The lawyers he did like would think differently of him once it was done, but that wouldn't change how he felt about them. Grogan believed that good people didn't become bad without getting there on their own.

Earlier he'd slipped his wife the double dose of Benadryl to make sure she'd sleep through the morning. By the time she awoke, it would be long over. He loved her dearly and wouldn't have thought about leaving her early except the combination of illnesses, her debilitating fibromyalgia and his cancer, would cost them everything they had over time. She had lost her insurance two years ago when she was forced to retire. Remortgaging the house was no longer an option and soon he would be dead. It was a cruel ending to a mostly fulfilling life, but Grogan wasn't about to go out without ridding the world of the woman he called Her Hitler. He came up with the name from the afternoon she walked into the word processing center to brag about firing a woman who'd spent twenty-three years of her life working as a secretary for Dash Paris.

"That bag of bones is finally gone," Ms. Frieda Durr had said. "So much for that inconvenience."

Grogan had looked her surname up and smirked when he saw it meant *dry, thin, drought*.

He figured he'd be known as the word processing murderer afterwards, but he figured that title had more honor in it than Her Hitler.

Grogan had worked for Dash Paris LLP ten years and two months. He'd seen it grow from a mid-sized law firm to the brink of what was considered a big firm. Frieda Durr had come four years ago and was universally disliked. A sarcastic woman without substance, she served the company faithfully as the New York office henchwoman. Most workers feared her wrath. Grogan refused to give her the satisfaction of seeing his dislike of her. Even the day he farted to upstage her inane discussion about how much cleaner the office looked now that the latest person to be fired was no longer working there, Grogan refused to show Durr any emotion. He simply passed some gas, was fired for it, then did it again before leaving. He took pleasure in the giggles he heard behind him on his way out.

He could never understand people like Durr, how they talked about people they'd fired as if there was something funny about someone losing their job. He didn't know what she was like outside the job but couldn't imagine how someone who took so much pleasure in other people's misfortune could be someone others would want to be around.

He'd thought about breaking Durr's legs with a baseball bat or maybe her jaw or arms but decided the press and the firm would only make her a martyr. No, it was definitely better to kill her and have done with it. The press and firm would still do their thing, but people who knew her would know the truth and that was all that really mattered.

That and she'd be dead.

The problem was the other twit who'd come to bring order to the New York office, Carol from Newark. Except for the fact she was now the one to begin the process of having people fired, she was mostly harmless. The firm had become her life. She actually bragged about sleeping with her blackberry. Grogan and most other people felt her loyalty to the firm was more pathetic than something to admire.

The freight elevator operator took him to the thirteenth floor. Grogan did a good job of making believe he'd forgotten his key. He greased the guy with a ten dollar bill to unlock the door and then made his way stealthily down the hall to the broom closet around the corner from the word processing center. He'd be safe there unless there was a spill of some kind or one of the toilets in the bathrooms on the floor overflowed.

Durr almost always poked her big nose in the word processing center promptly at nine to greet the morning shift and say goodbye

The Decider

to the night shift, but it was really to make sure nobody left early or showed up late. Durr was a creature of habit and Grogan was counting on her to be on time today.

He started to hear footsteps outside the closet around eight-thirty. A few more closer to nine. He assumed it was the early workers using the bathroom at the other end of the hall.

Then it was nine o'clock, and he removed the Beretta 9000S from the ankle holster he'd worn. He pushed open the door, and there she was walking in the opposite direction, headed toward the word processing center. Grogan felt an adrenaline rush like he'd never felt before. He was behind her in just a few steps and raised the Beretta.

Amanda was standing closest to the door and was going over the work turnover with Carol when she heard the pop, pop, pop. She yelled for everyone to get down and then dove under the desk. Carol had been facing Amanda. She looked from Sally to Jim and then backed up against the wall facing the door paralyzed with fear. Sally's eyes had opened wide at the sound of the second shot, then she gasped and never heard the third. Jim had been standing at the printer furthest from the door but reacted quickly and ran to the glass door and shoved a desk in front of it.

"Oh, God," Jim said when he saw Steve Grogan approaching the door. He saw the gun and that Grogan was waving at him to get out of the way, but Jim didn't move. He could hear Amanda on her cell phone. Sally started to scream and Jim turned to her when there was another shot. He flinched and then dropped to the floor, but he hadn't been hit.

Later the police found a note in one of Steve Grogan's pants pockets. It read: *I had two decisions to make and was able to make one; that was Durr. I'm not sure about the other one and hope for guidance. Sorry for any inconvenience.*

MICROPRIMUS VOLATITUS
Greg Bardsley

"What's he doing?"

"Oh, he always does that."

"Yeah, but what is it?"

"He just loves my hair, especially when I pin it up like this."

"So he plays in your hair, while you sit there and flip through a *Rolling Stone*?"

"You know, or watch TV or something. It's our ritual."

"He's biting into your bun there."

She nods, like she doesn't care.

"Trippy little guy."

"Trippy?" She scrunches her face. "Try cute."

Helmut is the tiniest primate I've ever seen. He's as tall as a canary and couldn't weigh more than a few grams. With his bald head, big nose and giant ears, *cute* is not how I would describe him.

"Just because he's got narrow-set eyes, Helmut can't be cute?"

I nod to her hair. "He could get lost in there."

She stops, looks at me. "Oh, really?"

Helmut continues to clamp onto her hair and shake.

"I'm just saying, you have big head of hair."

Still staring at me. "Really?"

"Doesn't mean I don't dig it. I love your hair."

She returns to her reading, flips a finger toward her head. "Join the club."

Microprimus Volatitus

I watch Helmut gyrate, shake and quiver.

"He looks like a little bald man." I cross my legs, shift my weight and study him. "Like a tiny Kojak?"

She grins, like she's been thinking the same. "Did I tell you he loves to watch cage fighting?"

"A real man's man."

She nods. "And *Jersey Shore*."

"Those guidos?" I take a pull off my Red Hook. "You might as well inject him with testosterone, make him a little wife-beater tank top."

"Randy, he's a dude. You think he wants to watch *Steel Magnolias*?"

"Man, he really likes your hair. You sure that's okay?"

"Dude..." She waves me off. "He's been doing this for four years."

"Every night?"

She nods, adopts a baby voice. "My little Helmut likes Mommy's hair, doesn't he?"

Helmut makes a weird noise, raises his head out of her hair, like a miniature prairie dog. Our eyes meet, and he squints at me.

It's like a staredown.

For whatever reason, I refuse to look away.

He lowers his head and shows me his teeth.

Hell if I don't I curl a lip back, show him mine.

"I just worry." Razelle flips a page. "I mean, I wonder if he gets enough attention."

Helmut glares at me.

"I think Helmut's doing just fine."

"Helmut has some issues, Randy. He's not fine. Just look into those eyes."

The staredown continues

"Now tell me they're not the windows to a wounded soul."

And I'm thinking, *I know his type.*

"They're eyes that hurt."

Hurt? I know what happens behind those eyes. Hell, I'm a guy, too. I know what it's like to stand there sweet and innocent-like—maybe at work, maybe at the grocery store—and participate fully in a conversation, all of it appropriate and respectful, even as another part of your brain multi-processes a continuous loop of thoughts and images so base and carnal they'd make Dr. Ruth blush. Just last week I sat in a conference room with a very professional woman from Procurement, and even though we spent the hour dissecting the J22 Incubation Strategy, never did I stop imagining my cock in her mouth.

For sixty minutes.

The whole time, my eyes sweet and earnest.

Oh yeah, I know what goes on behind those eyes.

Helmut disappears back into her hair, and it shakes.

"Never would've thought something so human-like, so tiny, could exist?"

She nods. "He's like a cartoon."

"I guess he'll never need a shot of espresso."

She looks at me. "Don't even joke about that. He'd die."

I get up, cross the room, plop next to her, shoulders rubbing.

Tonight's the night, baby.

She glances at me and smiles, and my whole chest expands in warmth. I dig Razelle. Seriously dig her. Shit, I like everything about her—the fact everything seems to amuse her, the fact she walks through town barefoot, the fact she calls other women by their last names. The fact I think she's going to fuck me. Maybe tonight.

From inside her hair, a squeak.

I peer into her hair. "What do you call these guys?"

"Little Baldies." She flips another page. "The clinical term I like better—*microprimus volatitus*."

"Volatitus?" I squint, get closer. "You mean, like, volatile? That doesn't sound good."

She shrugs.

"He's quivering." I move a few strands of her hair, get a better look. Helmut has sunken all fours into her bun, clamping hard. "You say he does this all the time?"

"Dude." She laughs. "Chill."

After a long while, I say, "Don't take this the wrong way, but I think he's humping your hair."

She stops, glances at me. "What?"

"His hips are like a blur."

She thinks about it. "No."

"He's really pumping."

She sits up, pokes into her hair. "Helmut, what are you doing?"

I inch forward, lift my chin, and get a better look. "His boner's out."

"What?" She fingers through her hair. "Helmut, stop it."

Helmut's not listening.

Helmut's in another world.

I reach over. "Here, let me try."

"Helmut," she snaps. "You little creep."

Helmut lids his eyes.

"You got him or not?"

"Hold on," I say, and pull harder.

He pants.

She closes her eyes, covers them with a hand. "Pull him off," she whispers.

I finger him at the torso, pull harder. Finally, he releases the bun and snarls at me as I lower him to the coffee table, a pink erection pointed straight up. After a long, pissed-off stare, he darts around the room like the Tasmanian Devil, and all I see are the disrupted items he whizzes past—spinning bottles, knocked-over cups, airborne pencils. I turn to my left, and his black eyes are inches from my face.

I yell out.

In a puff, he's gone.

We're sitting there, trying to let it sink in, when it hits me. I say, "You know what this means, right?"

She sits there, hand still over her eyes.

"It means he's been fucking your head." I rub her back. "Every night…"

Slowly, she nods.

"… for four years?"

At which point, Helmut lands on my forehead and plunges a pencil into the side of my nose.

I don't spend the night in Razelle's bed.

I spend it in E.R., getting three stitches.

The next four days, Razelle won't even take my calls. I guess she figures I should've been *bigger* about the whole thing. Okay, sure, maybe I shouldn't have chased after that little bastard for the next five minutes, slamming into her things, spraying blood over her walls, sofa and armchair, even as she begged me to stop.

The fifth day, I get a text: *Maybe I overreacted.*

I tap back, *Maybe we can start over???*

Maybe tonight.

Maybe I can bring Chinese.

Maybe just Cuervo.

We're so drunk, the bed spins.

Even so, I try to take it all in—her back arching this way, her short meaty legs going that way, her big hips going around and around and around, her rough skin charging my mine in a rhythmic massage that makes me dizzy.

Hell yeah.

"Harder," she slurs, the Cuervo heavy on her breath.

I obey.

Something on the nightstand moves. It's Helmut, sitting there, watching—his eyes huge and eager, his body crouching, his long tail slapping the surface, over and over.

Hold on, Randy.

"Faster," she pants.

I screw my eyes shut and obey.

Oh, God. I'm gonna lose it.

She moans.

I open my eyes, and there's Helmut, fucking her ear, all fours wrapped around her cartilage as his hips quiver over her ear hole.

"Fuck," I snap, but keep pumping.

Razelle has no idea. She looks like she's about to pass out, says, "I'm not feeling too hot."

Helmut sinks his teeth into the top curl of her cartilage and pounds harder, lids his eyes.

"Dude," I whisper, reach over, and try to brush him off.

Helmut glances at me and curls back a lip, showing more teeth.

Microprimus Volatitus

Razelle frowns, slurs, "What's that?"

He keeps pounding.

So do I.

"Here," I say, and try to pull him off.

Helmut hisses through his teeth, keeps pumping.

So do I.

"What—what are you doing to my ear?"

I'm softening.

FUCK.

"Randy, what's wrong?"

Helmut quickens.

"Hey," she says, batting the side of her head. "What the fuck?"

He pounds harder, growls.

"What the fuck are you guys doing to me?"

Helmut keeps pounding.

I fall out, and she squirms away, sits up. "What the fuck is this, a gang bang?"

Helmut keeps pounding.

She pulls at him, yells, "Dude, stop."

I'm going limp, fast.

Goddamn it.

I crawl over, try to help.

He releases a chirp.

"Helmut," she slurs.

His eyes bulge and cross in delight, his body stiffening before it begins to deflate. In a second, he seems sleepy, content.

I sit there, blown away. This little fucker gets to blow his wad into her, and I'm sitting there blue-balled, my shriveled dick drying fast?

Now it's easy to pull him off. Razelle tosses him across the room, onto a stack of pillows. She jumps off the bed, stomps into the bathroom, the tequila suddenly out of her system.

"Razelle, wait."

She slams the door, locks it.

"Razelle."

The shower starts.

And I glare at Helmut over there in the pillows, where he seems perfectly content to lounge, eyelids lower than ever, staring right back at me.

I wake up on her couch with a major hangover, every part of me aching.
    Way too much Cuervo.
    Razelle is standing over me. "We need to talk."
    I sit up, rub my eyes. "Okay."
    "C'mon," she says, motioning me to follow. "I want you both to hear this."
    In the kitchen, Helmut is perched atop the backrest of a chair. He looks content and rested.
    Razelle turns and faces us. "What happened last night was unacceptable."
    I look down, mumble, "I know."
    She raises her voice. "You saw what he was doing…"
    We glance at Helmut. He cocks his head and enlarges his eyes.
    "…and you didn't even stop."
    I cover my face. "I know."
    "You let him do that to me."
    Silence.
    "And you kept going, figuring I was too drunk to know any better."
    "Well, I just—"
    "That's a gang bang, my friend."
    "Wait, I just—"
    "What am I to you guys? Just a couple of holes to fuck?"
    "C'mon, Razelle."
    "It was like you didn't even care."
    "Razelle, listen to yourself. That's crazy."
    She glares at me. "I want you out of my house."
    I bow my head, mumble, "Okay."
    "And take that little creep with you."

Helmut is playing in my kitchen drawers, making a racket.
    "Just us guys now," I say, lifting my shot glass to him.

The racket halts. Helmut pops his head out of the drawer, looks at me.

"Us dudes." I down the shot and grimace, the fire rolling down my throat, warming my gut. I reach for the Cuervo bottle, glance at Helmut, and pour myself a sixth shot.

"Just the two of us."

Still staring, curious.

"At least until..."

He cocks his head, thins his eyes.

"...something bad happens to you."

Helmut dives back into the drawer, tosses a potato peeler onto my counter, then a set of measuring spoons, then an ice cream scooper, then a pizza roller, then my stainless-steel corn holders, all eight of them.

I force a happy voice and motion to the mess he's created. "*Mi casa es su casa*, Helmut."

He tosses more items onto the counter.

The truth is I had to take him home. If I'd refused, Razelle would've told her girlfriends about the gangbang, and that would be it for me and women in this town.

Helmut had seemed devastated. When she put him in his cage and walked us out the door, he whimpered. When I drove away with him, cussing her under my breath, he released a series of suffering chirps, his face sagging, his big ears drooping, his lower lip out. Looked like a very sad little Telly Savalas.

Like I gave a shit. Said, "Never ever gonna see your mommy again, dude."

He sagged even more, produced a series of squeaky moans.

But now, here in my kitchen, he's so industrious.

I reach into my front pocket and pull out the bottle of Maximum Strength NoDoz. Stumbling to the counter, I can't hide my little grin, and I realize I'm drunker than I'd thought. "Your mommy says you like lettuce, grapes and..." I bend toward him, widen my eyes. "...big juicy strawberries."

He stops, studies me.

"Is that right, little guy?"

Cocks his head, chirps.

I pop the lid, my grin turning to a giant, toothy smile, and pour five NoDoz pills onto the counter. I glance at Helmut, pull my garlic press from the drawer and begin to load the pills into the crush chamber.

Helmut watches.

From the shelf above, I retrieve my tiny, stainless steel mixing bowl. I stop, look at him and scratch the stitches on my nose. "What if Uncle Randy cut open a big juicy strawberry?"

Helmut watches as the white substance oozes through the garlic press and drops into the bowl.

"What if he mixed this up with some warm sugar water?"

Helmut shifts his weight, looks up at me.

"And what if sweet ol' Uncle Randy dipped those juicy strawberries into our..." I hunch over, widen my eyes and whisper in mock secrecy, "...secret death sauce?"

Helmut recedes a bit, studies me. He watches as I run the faucet hot and retrieve the strawberries from the fridge—big, fat, juicy suckers. He creeps closer as I slice a few open, halving them, realizing they're like soft and moist vulvas, their sweet meat exposed, glistening. Dripping.

Those lovely openings in the middle.

Ready to be had.

Steam rises from the sink basin.

I think of Razelle's "strawberry."

I think of Helmut stealing it.

Little bastard. Horning in on my action.

I feel my jaw tighten.

Helmut eases his head out, creeps closer.

I pass the bowl under the water for a split second and head for the sugar bowl. I smile at him as I spoon the sugar in, mix it up. "Does this look good?" I soothe.

He chirps, inches forward.

I take a strawberry wedge, dip it into the NoDoz syrup, roll it around in the warm sauce, let it soak into the meat. "Mmmm-mmm," I say, making a big deal about it, talking like a sweet little preschool teacher. "Helmut's gonna go to sleep, for ever and ever."

He looks up at me with that little Kojak face.

"And afterward, Uncle Randy's gonna Ziploc Helmut, pop him in the freezer."

We stare at each other, our faces pleasant.

"And you'll freeze solid, never-ever to see your mommy."

His face twitches, and he steps back.

"C'mon." I ease the dripping strawberry to him, grinning.

He inches closer, examining the strawberry, his nose twitching.

"C'mon," I coo. "Time to die, you little asshole."

Helmut recoils, squints at me and disappears.

Damn, he's fast.

And like that, he lands in my hair, plunges something into my scalp.

"Yeeeeeee-ow."

He's gone.

I feel around my head, pull out a corn holder.

I stumble and slur. "You little fucker."

A corn holder plunges into my temple.

"Okay," I snap, and pull it out.

Another corn holder, behind my ear.

"Hey," I say, feeling dizzy, and snatch it out.

WHAM.

Corn holder into my left ear.

I can hear ringing as I stumble backward, crash into the chairs.

"Dude, stop—"

Corn holder to my nose.

I stare at it, cross-eyed.

"Dude, let's talk about this."

WHAM.

Corn holder in my left eye.

This time, I scream. I bounce off the walls, trying the gain balance, the tequila hitting me harder than ever. Finally, I steady myself, lean against the kitchen door, look around with my good eye.

The kitchen is blurry.

I slide to the floor, roll over on my back. "Dude," I slur.

In my head, I can hear Razelle. "*Randy, he's a dude.*"

Helmut lands on my collar bone, the potato peeler in both hands.

"Dude."

He plunges the peeler into my neck.

Blood spurts everywhere.

I gasp for air.

My vision narrows.

All I see is Helmut, his eyes large and moist as he watches the life drain out of me.

I grasp for him, but I'm way too slow. Helmut recoils, shows me his teeth and hisses. I try to reach for him again, realize I can't even move my arms now.

Oh yeah, I'm a goner.

Helmut creeps up my head, toward my face, a giant sneer on his Kojak face.

I part my lips, but nothing comes out.

Oh, man.

And he's looking at me like he's saying, *You're my bitch.*

His face is right over my good eye. I feel him enter my right nostril, a snug fit, as he bites into my brow. He begins to pump against my nostril.

"You think he wants to watch Steel Magnolias*?"*

My vision darkens. I can hardly see anything. But the pounding, the brutal pounding on my nose—I can feel that.

Take it, bitch.

I feel so hopeless, powerless.

I can hear the low guttural growl as he pounds faster and deeper, and bites harder. And I realize he's fucking my dying corpse. Like some prison badass. He's fucking my freaking corpse.

He pounds so hard, it makes my head jerk back and forth.

Never should've messed with this guy's woman.

It's a distant sensation—an echo, really. The pounding getting harder, the bite sinking deeper, the growling getting louder. All of it, as I fade to black.

LADYKILLER
Hilary Davidson

"You sure you're up for this?"

Tessa glanced at the cop. "You're going to be outside the door the entire time?"

"I'll be right here. He can't hurt you."

She could feel the weight of his gaze, sizing her up, wondering whether she'd be able to go through with it. *She's a big girl,* he had to be thinking. *Bet she can handle herself. He's not going to be able to do to her what he did to that little redhead.*

"Okay," Tessa said. "I'm ready."

The cop opened the door, stepped inside, and gestured for her to follow. Peter sat at a metal table, head in hands. His thinning hair seemed to have gone gray overnight, but maybe that was just the dim light. It wasn't the sort of interrogation cell Tessa had seen on television. There was no mirrored window for the cops to watch through. Instead, there were brown walls, a small window in the door, fluorescent lighting, and an aroma of industrial disinfectant.

Peter was wearing his white monogrammed bathrobe, but it was streaked with rusty stains. *That's the redhead's blood,* Tessa thought, feeling as if she would vomit. He looked up and got to his feet. "Tessa!"

"Sit down!" barked the cop. "You already murdered one woman tonight, Peter Buckley. You're not getting a chance at a second."

"Kiss my ass," Peter shot back. "My lawyer is going to have

me out of here at nine a.m. Then I'm suing your asses for brutality and wrongful arrest."

"Let me talk to him," Tessa said.

"I'm right outside." The cop leaned toward Peter. "Don't try anything, Ladykiller." He retreated and shut the door.

"You bring bail money?" Peter asked.

"But...they haven't set your bail yet."

"The pricks will probably make it five million to set an example. You'll need ten percent of that to get me out of here."

Tessa was stunned by his coolness. There he sat, in a bloody bathrobe, and he was calculating bail. She'd known he was selfish, but this made him seem like a sociopath. "Where am I going to get five hundred thousand dollars?"

"Call my mother."

Peter was a mama's boy, a spoiled rich brat who'd cruised through life on a trust fund and family connections. He'd been handsome once, but that was seventy pounds ago, before his drinking had bloated his features. He was thirty-five, but he looked a decade older.

"She's at her house in Florida right now," Peter added. "But don't tell her exactly what's going on, okay? I don't need her flipping out right now."

"She's going to read about it or see it on TV. She's going to know."

He waved his hand dismissively. "I need her to hear my side of the story first. Then she'll understand."

Tessa let her body sag into a chair. The cold metal against the back of her knees made her shiver. Peter stared at her, his eyes never leaving her face.

"What did you tell the cops about me?" he demanded.

"I said you're my fiancé. I don't know if that's true or not. We've been engaged for two years, but now I find out you're not only sleeping with another woman, you murdered her."

Peter's eyes narrowed, and she realized he was calculating exactly how much truth to tell. "I didn't kill that girl."

"The police said you choked her before you shot her...."

"Bullshit. I didn't lay a hand on her."

"The police were asking me if you like to play...*games.*" Tessa blushed. She'd always gone along with what Peter wanted, but the handcuffs and restraints and whips were entirely his idea.

"Games?"

"They found a bunch of your...*toys*...in your bedroom." It was hard to get the words out. "They asked if you've ever choked me."

"What did *you* say?"

"I told them you'd never hurt me in bed," Tessa lied. The bruises on her throat had healed up during her week out of town. Normally she wore turtlenecks or scarves to hide them.

"Good. Don't answer any more of their questions."

"They only let me in here because I answered their questions. They think if you see me, you're going to..."

"Going to what?"

"Confess," Tessa whispered.

"Are you fucking kidding me?" Peter's expression was pure disbelief. "You think I killed that bitch?"

"The police found a naked woman strangled and shot in your house. What else does it look like?"

"This is a set-up. Someone's trying to destroy me." His expression, and his tone, was completely certain.

"Destroy you?"

"There was someone else in my house tonight. He's the one who killed that girl, not me."

"What the hell was that girl doing in your house?"

Peter's eyes narrowed. "I know what you're thinking, but I didn't sleep with her. She's just this girl from my office. Natalia. They brought her in from Brazil a few weeks ago. She's an analyst. *Was* an analyst."

"Why was she at your house?"

"She had an extensive background in gold mining. I needed analysis of data about a series of mines in South America, and she was the perfect person to do it." It was an explanation that he thought offered enough detail to seem credible.

You lying bastard, Tessa thought, looking down so that her expression wouldn't betray her. An image of Peter and the redhead was seared in her brain. They were tearing off each other's clothing in a hallway with a frantic desire that Peter had never shown for her. Tessa shoved it out of her brain and tried to focus.

"Do you realize how crazy this sounds? It's paranoid. If someone was in the house and killed her, why didn't they kill you, too?"

"Whoever it was wanted to frame me. That's why Natalia is dead." He leaned forward. "You've got to listen to me. Someone else was in the house. When I went upstairs, the light was on in my walk-in closet."

Little hairs rose up on the back of Tessa's neck, but she said, "That's your proof? You probably left it on all day."

"Oh, yeah? Well, what was my mail doing on the kitchen counter?"

Tessa felt her heart skip a beat. "Mail?"

"I noticed it when the cops were going through my house. Mail. On the counter. Someone had brought it inside and put it where I always do."

She opened her mouth, but no sound came out. The mail? Unbelievable.

"I know this sounds crazy," Peter admitted, "but it's the truth."

"What's crazy is why you took a shower while that woman was in the house."

Peter blinked rapidly. "I was really beat, and I had an early morning coming up, so I left her working in the den. I told her to let herself out when she was ready."

"Peter, I've known you for five years. The only time you take a shower before bed is after you have sex. You've got some germ phobia and you go shower for an hour afterwards."

For the first time, his face registered guilt. He'd been caught, and he knew it.

"You're lying to me about not having sex with that woman. You know what, Peter? I'm going to tell that to the police. I'll tell them about every time you tied me up and choked me and pretended you were going to kill me." She stood.

"Tessa, I'm sorry. I swear, it was the first time I ever did anything like this."

His eyes were earnest, but he was still lying. He'd always cheated on her, and she'd been so good at pretending not to notice that he believed she was blind. But now there was a dead girl between them.

"I loved you," said Tessa. "I wanted to marry you. I dreamed about having children with you. And instead you screwed around on me. And now..."

"Listen to me, Tessa. I need you to stand by me. My lawyer says it would look awful if you left. This thing is going to court, and I need you by my side."

As always, it was all about what he wanted. She was supposed to trust him, and he'd do whatever he wanted. But she couldn't do that anymore. Peter was a liar and a cheat. She'd put up with his behavior because, deep down, she thought that he would marry her one day. She wanted to live in his big, beautiful house and call herself Mrs. Buckley. It had all seemed so close, too, since Peter's mother had always liked her. *You should marry Tessa*, the old woman had told her son. *She's a good woman. She'd stand by you, unlike those whores you run around with.* Tessa had overheard those very words as she'd listened in on one of their phone calls. But those days of mute fidelity were over.

"I don't want to stay by your side," said Tessa. "You strangled that woman until she was almost dead, and then you shot her in the chest to finish her off, so she couldn't tell anyone what you did."

"If that was true, why didn't I just put her in the freezer in the basement?" Peter grabbed both of her wrists. "Listen to me. I banged her, then went upstairs to shower. I told her she should get dressed and get out. When I came downstairs, she was lying on the floor with blood everywhere and her eyes wide open. I freaked and ran out the door. I thought the killer might still be in my house." He lowered his voice to a whisper. "I was freezing my ass off outside because I was so scared. Don't tell anyone that. They'll think I'm a fucking chicken."

"You were outside when the police came?"

"I was so freaked out, Tessa. I couldn't help it. I ran up and down the street. Then I finally went to Mrs. Chan's door. She's the only person on the block who says hello to me. She called the cops."

"The police think you're pretending to be paranoid," she whispered.

"It was like my real life ended and a horror movie started." Peter's hands tightened on her wrists. "You've got to stand by me. Call my mother, make her understand I need money, okay? You won't have a problem. She really likes you."

"Okay," Tessa whispered. "Is there anything else you want me to do?"

"Believe in me. Can you do that?"

She nodded and he let go. She got up and left the room without another word.

"You okay?" The cop looked at her with jaded eyes, but there was genuine concern lurking underneath. "I saw him grab your hands, but he kept yapping and I didn't want to break that up."

"It's good you didn't. He would've stopped talking."

"You want to sit down?"

She went downstairs with him and sat on a bench.

"He didn't confess," Tessa said. "He kept saying he didn't kill that girl."

"That's what they all say." The officer snorted. "But he said something else. I can see it in your face."

"He was running around outside, he said. Up and down the block. There's a park just two blocks from his house."

"You think he tossed the gun there?"

"I don't know. There could be another explanation. He thinks...he thinks someone else came into the house and killed her."

"You believe that, I got a bridge to sell you," the cop said. "I'll get uniforms on the park immediately." He stood. "I'll drive you home."

She couldn't answer. Tears slid down her cheeks. In her mind, she was still in Peter's house, walking barefoot down the stairs in a pretty negligee she'd just bought on her trip. She'd heard gasping, animal noises, and she'd watched from the landing as Peter screwed that redhead, right there on the hallway rug. Before they finished, she'd stepped away, hiding herself in the den, just twenty feet away from them. *I'm beat,* she'd heard

Peter announce. *You remember where the bathroom is, right? See you tomorrow, babe.*

The cop handed Tessa a tissue. "They're going to lock him up and throw away the key. You know he deserves that, don't you?"

Tessa wiped her face and blew her nose. Funny how she hadn't cried at Peter's, she thought. After he'd disappeared upstairs, Tessa had stepped out of the den. She didn't remember grabbing the power cord from his computer, but it was in her hands, and then against that little redhead's throat. The woman was so stunned, she'd barely squeaked. When she dropped to the floor, Tessa had thought she was dead. Feeling as if she were sleepwalking through a nightmare, Tessa marched upstairs, planning to kill Peter. She knew where he kept a gun, knew how to fire it, too. But first she dressed in the spare room where she'd left her clothes. He didn't deserve to see her in the negligee now. She'd reviewed all the ways he'd humiliated her. Death was too good for him, she'd decided. She got the gun from its case in his walk-in closet and went downstairs. She'd planned to put a bullet in a dead woman to seal Peter's link to the death, but there was the redhead, twitching and gasping for breath. Tessa put a hole through her heart. Then she'd pulled up the hood of her coat and went outside, down the block to the park. She'd been careful, wearing gloves when she touched the gun. It wouldn't matter that they'd find her prints all over the massive house. She was there so often. It frustrated her that she'd brought the mail inside when she'd let herself in to surprise Peter. But it would be an inconsequential footnote to the police.

"He wants me to arrange bail for him," Tessa told the officer. "I have to call his mother."

"He won't get bail." The officer patted her arm. "You're such a nice girl. What are you doing with a creep like that?"

IN THE STRETCH OF DARE
Kieran Shea

Sometime before two a.m., the Dickey brothers slipped on board from a fifteen-foot runabout that had seen better days.

I'd been awake thinking about Carla and heard their boat's four stoke Mercury engine cut its putter a minute or so before. The Dickeys coasted an approach on momentum in a lame stab at late night maritime stealth. The starboard side of my Pearson sailboat tilted a bit as they tied off and the hull angled a little bit more as the Dickey brothers hoisted their weight aboard one by one. Hardly graceful. As much as they chased waves all year long, those boys couldn't leave the cheap beer and fast food alone.

Down below, braced against the quarter berth, I waited, my Benelli shotgun raised high and leveled back. I knew Faron would be first down the hatch because he had the guts. Timbo would follow because he always hesitated, even on the little things. They'd both be armed, but that was to be expected.

The cramped quarters of my boat's central cabin were dimly lit by a single strip of lights above a small ledge that served as my navigation table, tiny red and white indicators for the batteries, lights, and VHF. In the light's soft-wattage glow, I took in the greasy, creeping spectre of Faron Dickey as he slinked his descent down the ladder. Gun out and leveled, Faron was still looking up toward his brother in the cockpit when I snapped the Benelli out and crushed his ear.

Faron grunted and staggered sideways against the galley sink. He started to raise his weapon, but I'd already flipped the stock and pressed the safety.

"Easy, Faron. You know I can't miss this close."

From above, "Faron!? What the—! Faron!?"

"Tell Timbo to chill or this will be it, man, I swear to God. Tell him now."

Even in the murky darkness, I could see Faron's sweat-streaked face twist with bitterness. Faron had always fancied himself a hard man, the kind of brash idiot who blew car payment money on getting ridiculous neck tats of stars and cutlasses to enhance his poor self-image. He didn't release his gun. Maybe Faron expected his brother to open up through the fiberglass deck. Maybe he thought he was faster than me and could dodge a spread of scorched lead yielding. Maybe Faron believed it was like when we were in grammar school back up in Kill Devil Hills and he felt he deserved a playground do-over.

Twenty-six thousand dollars in cash. Not much room for do-overs.

"Tell me something, Roy...."

"Mmm."

"Why do you do it?"

"Do what?"

"Sell with my brothers."

I pinched the space between my eyebrows. "Carla...."

"Why? You're smarter than them. They're dumber than shit. They're going to get caught and you know it. When those two do, they're going to take you down with them, and it will be awful. It's only a matter of time."

"Everything's a matter of time."

Carla slipped from the sheets and padded over to the motel efficiency's dresser. As a pajama top, she wore my khaki first mate's shirt and it barely covered her stark white tan line that outlined her cheeks. Carla turned and planted her hands behind her on the dresser, crossing her legs. She seemed so small, like a child pretending to be a grownup from moves gleaned from a thousand days of television. Her sun-bleached hair was pulled tight in a ponytail.

Through the blinds, thin bands of North Carolina sunlight scored across the motel room and one of the bands cut across her right eye, the one that roamed a smidge. The room's box air conditioner turned over then, shuddering like a crated animal.

"Then why, Roy?"

"Because I need the money, baby."

"Smart ass," Carla snapped. "Don't you mean *we* need the money?"

Truth was I didn't mean that at all.

Faron's gun clunked on the cabin floor with a dull thud and rattle. It was a stout Smith & Wesson .38 with a lacquered wooden grip. He showed me the .38 once when we were drinking, getting high, and jabbing our way through an epic session of Play Station 3's *World of Outlaws*. Stubbing my toe, I kicked the butt of the .38 halfway toward the bow's v-berth with a spin.

"Tell him to chill, Faron."

Faron drawled, "Be cool, Timbo. Sailor boy here's got a shotgun."

Not wavering my bead on Faron's face, I called up, "Timbo? You hear your brother? Be cool. Just throw your gun over the side."

Timbo whined. "Aw, man. In the water?"

"Yeah."

"No way, Roy. Not a chance. Let Faron go first."

"I'm not fooling around, Timbo."

"Come on, you guys, this has gone too far."

Faron's flinty eyes flicked up toward his brother then back at me. "Just do what he says, Timbo," Faron said.

Timbo protested, "But this is my best gun, dude. I paid a lot of money for this gun. I really like it."

I stabbed the barrel of the Benelli closer to Faron's face, and Faron flinched away. I noticed his smashed ear leaked a dark dribble of blood.

"Tell your brother to throw his precious gun in the water."

Faron frowned. "You're not going to shoot me, Roy. No way. Not out here. Not on your little candy-ass sailboat."

"You so sure?"

"Yeah, I reckon I am."

"Mister Confident then?"

"Yeah. I know you, Roy. I've known you almost all of my life. You don't have the nerve. Never have, never will."

I licked my lips and huffed. "You two tools sneaking on my boat with guns in the middle of the night as a social call? Trust me on this, Faron. Right now I have nerve to spare."

Carla and I lazed on the bed, and like a painter mixing his wares, she trolled a crinkle-cut French fry in a splotch of ketchup. I'd stepped out and crossed down the narrow hot stretch of Highway 12 in my flip-flops and bought a carryout sack of burgers, fruit salad, and some sweet teas from a local bar that had a heavy-handed Edward Teach pirate theme. Blackbeard's infamous legend seemed all the rage for tourists on the Outer Banks the past few years. The trip there and back took a good forty minutes.

It was late August, and the heat was so brutal I came back to the efficiency with my T-shirt soaked through like a damp rag. Even with a five knot westerly coming in across the shallows of Pamlico Sound and the twilight rising, Hatteras held the day's steam like a grudge.

Carla and I talked about my plan.

"God, Roy. Faron will be ticked."

"I imagine so."

"He'll kill you."

"No, he won't."

"You've seen him angry."

"Yeah, but Faron ain't a killer. He'll be angry at me, true, and if he gets me alone he might try to beat me into the emergency room, but trust me. He's not drastic."

"He's been different since he was in jail."

"Six months. Jeez, Carla. Dare County don't count."

"What about Timbo?"

"Timbo is slow."

Carla popped off the bed and gathered her things. I watched her dress. She looped on her yellow bikini top and stepped into a pair of frayed low-rise cut-offs with a stitched Hibiscus patch on the left hip. Carla hardly ever wore any panties, which I kind of always liked.

"What about me?" she said. "You just want me to forget about them like that? That's asking a lot you know. They may be total dipshits, but they're my brothers."

"I guess holidays will be difficult."

"That's not funny."

I sucked some sweet tea through a straw and rattled the melting ice in my Styrofoam cup. "What about you then, huh? What you want? You want to spend the rest of your days on this sandbar wage-slaving it for Yankees and cleaning beach houses? We can start over if we get out of here. And Florida's massive. A year or two goes by, and Faron and Timbo will both either be in jail like you said or onto other things. You know they still talk about doing B&Es and stealing flatscreens from people's vacation homes, and the sheriffs are all over that now.

"Once we get set up we can take some of the money and get you enrolled in some classes. That nursing assistant thing you're always talking about. I'm sure there's good schools down there."

"Nursing assistant...."

"Have you any idea how big health care is down in Florida? Place is like a waiting room for the great beyond. With your personality, I'd bet you'd get a job like that. A good job. Something with benefits. Something with a future."

"What about you?"

"I can always get boat work."

"Boat work, huh? You make it all sound so easy."

"There's other things."

"Like what?"

"I don't know. Construction."

"You'd make a fine Mickey Mouse."

"I would, would I?"

"Be a famous rodent."

I patted the bed. "Sit down. Let me go over it with you one more time."

After a heavy plunk and splash, I told Faron to go up top and move toward the boat's stern—slow hands, out and up where I could see them. After a moment I followed up the ladder.

Once up top, I saw Timbo aft. He backed behind the boat's wheel, ropey arms loose at his sides and antsy as ever. Unlike Faron, Timbo kept his sandy hair shorn short because he always hated going to the barber. Timbo's mouth was slack and he was taking everything in like an unsteady child. The stars were still bright, but the night's thick air was changing. To the northwest, a cold front was shouldering in as forecasted.

I prodded the tip of the shotgun in Faron's back and told him to move on back with his brother. There was some shifting and cursing of me as the two squeezed together like bookends behind the boat's wheel.

In spite of my mouthy show, there was a real tremble and sputter in my gut. If they decided to charge me and I was forced to let fly, neither of them would have a chance. I prayed against the worst.

Faron grumbled, "You're such an idiot, Roy, you know that? Such a total, four flushing jerkoff. You think you can just steal our dope money and sail away with it? You're dreaming, man. Fuckin' dreaming."

"It's not entirely your money, you know."

"Says you. Me and Timbo, we took you on when your Pop up and died and the bank took his charter boat. We made a deal, dude. We didn't have to do that, but we did. We thought, hey, Roy knows people. He can move stuff around on the docks. All those partying fishing charter a-holes down from Virginia and Jersey and all."

"I'm grateful."

"Grateful, my ass. You took advantage. You betrayed me and Timbo. Dude, I'm so going to get you for this. You know I know people. People I know? Guys from jail? Those guys will make you wish you were dead."

"And yet…"

"Yet what?"

"Here we are."

I could feel the bumps of Carla's spine under my calloused fingertips. The bones felt like tiny, hard shells slipped neat in pure, taut silk. I traced a small bubblegum-colored scar on her shoulder she had since she was nine and fell off a slide. After much hemming and hawing over the details, Carla finally agreed to my plan.

I told her I loved her and she cried.

"I get seasick," she whimpered.

I smoothed her hair. "Chewable Dramamine and fresh ginger. You'll be fine. Besides, we'll be on the inland waterway most of the way down. It's just like sailing on the sound and you've been okay with that so far."

"That's different."

"Carla, I need to know you're with me on this. You know I'm set. There's no backing out now, and no room for second thoughts. This could finally be the start of something good for the both of us."

"I'm so scared, Roy."

"Don't be."

She looked into my eyes for yet another shot of assurance and kissed me hard. I kissed her back and slipped my tongue in her mouth.

"I love you," she said, breaking away and breathing into my neck.

I turned and took my duffle from the room's only table and hoisted it over my shoulder. The duffle held pretty much everything I owned except for what I had on the boat. Carla kissed me one more time at the door and I thumbed away the last of her tears. Sniffles and the latch.

We headed out to her car.

I didn't expect Timbo to have any brains.

I don't know why I underestimated him, but I did. A quick glance away from them two behind the wheel because something didn't feel right. It was like the feeling you get when a big school of fish is jumpy and loose and changing instinct. I don't know, maybe it was my dead Pop looking out for me. The big Pearson was his legacy and all I had left of him after the bank took the charter boat. Maybe his ghost was still knocking around the boat's rigging.

Installed on the port side of the Pearson's cockpit, just beyond a gear well stuffed with extra line about shin-high, was a scuffed plastic holster. The holster usually housed a heavy L-shaped detachable winch handle with an ash grip that was used for ratcheting in the jib on reach. I saw that the winch handle was missing. Then I remembered the splash when Timbo supposedly threw his gun in the drink. My heart raced and the butterflies in my stomach locked cold. Timbo's easing hand divulged the rest.

"Timbo," I said. "Let me explain something to you. Before this shot has a chance to spread, both you and your brother die. End of story."

Timbo's hand froze halfway. Faron glanced at his brother.

"You're not a murderer, Timbo," I continued. "You can't clear that gun before I fire. Be smart here, both of you. It's only money. You both can still have a life."

"You tied up our sister," Timbo barked.

"I'm sorry about that."

"And you hit her!"

"Only once, Timbo. Hell, I had to. She struggled."

"You're a thief and a coward."

"Shut up, Timbo. Hey, by the by... how'd you two geniuses find me?"

Faron looked up the changing night sky and then said, "We knew you'd check the weather. Be harbored down here, waiting for the storm to blow itself out. Carla said you two lovebirds anchored down here all the time."

I thought my one mistake over and remembered the scene back at the Dickey's house, how I knocked Carla down and tied her up with heavy weight fishing line, how she called me every name she could think of until I gagged her and shoved her in a dark closet. "That figures," I said. "Look, dudes. I'm real sorry about Carla. I like her. She's smart and she's sweet and all, but like you two, she was a means to an end. She knew when you two would be out of the house, and she knew where you kept the money. You know she planned to go along with me, right?"

Thunder rumbled.

Faron spat. "You set her up. We'll deal with her later."

Timbo stammered, "Y-you know what I think?"

"What's that?"

"I think Faron here's right. You won't shoot us, Roy. Not in a million years. Besides, man, we just want the money back, that's all. We only came out here to get it and scare you some."

I nodded. "Turn around."

Both. "What?"

"You heard. Turn around. You two boys are going to get wet."

Faron sneered, "Fuck you. Make us."

I waited a beat, and I guess Faron saw the uneasiness in my eyes. He lurched a step, and I jumped up starboard as Faron groped for his brother's back belted gun.

Quickly I swung my shotgun and fired a blast down at their skiff's red plastic gas tank and caught the tank clean. The plump ball of flame surprised us all.

Faron fell left with the explosion and both brothers toppled on top of each other. I teetered on the rail for a second, thinking I might fall overboard, my shirt littered with small oily specks of fire, but I got my footing and the wicks of light quickly burned themselves out. I fired my remaining shells out into the sound, stepped, and whipped the gun at Faron's skull like a club as he pushed himself off Timbo. Instead of knocking him cold, I split a gash in Faron's cheek. He gasped and wavered. I swung once more and nailed him square on the side of his skull and he deflated. Then I heard two quick, loud cracks as Timbo's wild aim scorched past my ear.

Lightning split the sky then, and a thunder clap exploded so loud and so close I actually feared Timbo had squeezed off another round and killed me. When I realized he hadn't, I sprang low for his waist. Timbo's gun flew and finally found the water as the squall cut loose on us with all its fury.

Timbo was powerful, and the adrenaline rushing through his muscles made everything worse. We tussled and slipped on the rain hammered deck. He chopped his right fist over and over into the side of my neck until I dipped my head, bit hard, and tore off a chunk of skin near his collarbone.

With a wild, bucking scream, Timbo released me and I crumpled back against the open hatch. I got control of my Benelli from the floor of the cockpit and I sighted him from my waist.

"STOP!"

Like I said, Timbo was always slow on the uptake. If he'd done the math he'd have realized my shotgun was dry. Timbo's hands flew out, pleading. The rain fell so hard and heavy I couldn't hear his cries for mercy.

I got to my feet and prompted Timbo to grab his unconscious brother by the waist and heave him off of the stern. Timbo griped that Faron would drown in the water, and I told him he better make sure he didn't.

With his meaty arms scooped around his brother's chest, Timbo cursed me and fell backward into the black rain-brailed sound. Bobbing in the darkness, he went on and on about bull sharks and hammerheads and Faron's bleeding ear and his own blood from where I bit him. I could have cared less. I started the Pearson's engine.

As they drifted away, I made my way forward, pulled up the anchor line. Covered in fresh mud from the waist down, I staggered back to the cockpit and took the wheel.

Piloting toward the winking red and green marks, I untied the smoldering skiff and set it free before the deeper channel. The storm cranked bad and the boat rocked hard in the gusts but at least the wind was with me and the tide high. The beacons off Ocracoke Inlet wavered in the stinging rain like a mismatched pair of demon eyes.

Unlike my dead Pop, I'd never sailed blue water solo. But I knew if I could ride out the storm, get a few miles offshore, and raise the Pearson's mainsail I could be off the horizon by the time it cleared and the sun came up. Faron was right. Like a good waterman I'd checked the weather. Once the storm exhausted itself, prevailing winds were westerly and in my favor.

A quarter mile off shore I locked the autopilot and scrambled down below. In all the fuss I'd forgotten the running lights and switched them on. I grabbed a cold Coke from the cooler, cracked the tab, and took a long searing drink. Then I quickly checked the charts and my heading.

Hamilton, Bermuda—32° 20"N, 64° 45"W—five hundred sixty-two miles, due east.

Give or take, give or take.

PROPHET WELLS AND THE RIVER OF SWINE
Nate Flexer

For ten years, the man known as Prophet Wells had driven back and forth across the country in an old Lincoln Continental, listening to Red Sovine and The Louvin Brothers, stopping only when the Good Lord told him to stop. Then he'd get out of his car, stretch his long body, and wander through the streets and bars and whorehouses, gathering up sinners, and the words of the Lord flowed from his mouth with the speed and articulation of an auctioneer, words soaked in kerosene and blood. And sometimes passersby would ignore him, and sometimes they'd stop and snicker, and sometimes they'd stare mesmerized. He could have been mistaken for a game show host or a carny, but make no mistake: Prophet Wells was a true believer. He dressed in a frock coat, black trousers, white shirt, and a black string tie. The requisite wide-brimmed hat balanced on his head, shielding a grotesque face beneath. A face burned beyond the recognition of a human face, a face that appeared to have been molded by the devil himself.

El Hornillo, Texas. With a tattered suitcase in one hand and a Bible in the other, Wells stood on the top of Black Oil Hill and stared down at the backwater town below. Derricks and grain elevators and brick buildings and poor man shacks. Drunks and whores. A town full of sinners. He shook his head and spat on the ground.

And then, whispering to the skies, "Earth is his, but not forever." He stayed on that hill for some time, just thinking and praying and crying. Then he made his way to town.

Main Street was dying. An abandoned convenience store, abandoned gas station, abandoned motel. Rusted signs and boarded-up windows. The preacher wandered around for awhile, the wind kicking up dirt, until he came to a little worn-out brick building that said, "Hank's Hotel." He walked up the crumbling steps and kicked open the door. Inside, everything smelled like rotted wood and formaldehyde. An elk's head hung from the far wall. In the corner of the room stood a baby grand, unplayable. Behind the counter was a dwarf of a woman wearing a floral dress and sporting a blue bouffant. She had pasty white skin, cherub cheeks, and a turkey wattle. She put away the flask she'd been sipping from and stuck it beneath the counter. Then she looked at the burnt face and shivered. "How can I help you?" she said.

"Well, what do you think?" Wells said.

"You want a room? Or do you need something else?" She said this with no playfulness.

"I'm looking for a woman. Name of Mary Falkum. She one of yours?"

"Now what do you mean by that?"

Wells scowled, making his face look even more devilish. "I don't have time for this, ma'am. Is she one of yours or ain't she?"

The woman laughed. "She might be. What you want with her?"

"I aim to convert her," he said. "I aim to convert all of you."

The woman laughed, slapping her thighs and looking upward to the heavens. "Well, as long as you pay...."

"I'll pay," Wells said. "What time? What time can I see her?"

"She's a busy one. Don't have an opening until midnight. Can you wait that long, preacher?"

"Yeah, I can wait. Give me a room in the meantime."

She grinned and nodded her head. Then she reached behind the counter and grabbed a key. In the back of the lobby, there was a narrow staircase that Wells hadn't noticed. He followed her up the flight of stairs, a light bulb dangling perilously from the ceiling, creating strange shadows.

The second floor was in bad shape. The lights were flickering, paint was peeling from the ceiling, curling up on itself, and the walls were covered with red graffiti. Against one wall there was a wooden bench, and sitting on the bench was a young woman wearing red boots and a red skirt and a red wig. A cigarette dangled from a lipstick-smeared mouth. She winked at Wells, a despicable act.

The blue-haired woman pushed opened a room door and handed Wells the key. "You watch out, preacher," she said, "or you bound to be flooded by sin."

"I'll take my chances," he said. "Jesus's blood never failed me yet."

The room was as bad as the rest of the ramshackle hotel. Grime scrubbed walls. An unmade bed. A 1950's style refrigerator. And against the wall, a curtainless window overlooking what remained of this living ghost town.

Wells sat down on the bed and removed his jacket and hat. He unzipped the suitcase and pulled out his Bible, a worn leather King James, the pages starting to yellow. *And Gideon said unto him, Oh my Lord, if the LORD be with us, why then is all this befallen us? And where be all his miracles which our fathers told us of, saying, Did not the LORD bring us up from Egypt? but now the LORD hath forsaken us, and delivered us into the hands of the Midianites.*

The power of the passage moved him, and he collapsed onto the bed. Wells was beginning to think that there wasn't a single righteous person in the world. He was beginning to think that everybody had secrets, terrible secrets. He turned over and lay on his stomach, gnashing his teeth and weeping into the pillow.

Wells left his room at a half past twelve, and for the rest of the day he preached outside the local bar. "Let this face be a warning to you!" he shouted. "This is a face of heartache! This is a face of sin! You stay on your present path, and this is what your soul will look like. A raisin in the sun. Jesus saved me, yes, he did. He dragged me from the river of swine and gave me life that I didn't deserve. And in return, I made a promise to him. I promised that I would go from town to town and tell the truth to every last one of you. A life without Jesus ain't no life at all. A life without Jesus is a life with the Devil. A life without Jesus means eternal damnation. And Hell is hotter than a blast furnace!"

And a few people stopped and listened, and a few people laughed or shouted obscenities. But Prophet Wells kept right on preaching, just like he'd done every day for the last ten years. By his count he saved four, had them say the Lord's Prayer, poured a bottle of holy water on their heads. One young man with a wispy mustache tried giving him money, and Wells became incensed, shouting, "I ain't no televangelist! I ain't no b-grade grifter! I'm a prophet for almighty Jesus, and my payment will come in the afterworld!" And the young man picked up that one-dollar bill and stuffed it into his overall pocket, hurrying away with an anxious smile on his face.

That evening was a long one. Prophet Wells sat inside his dingy room, reading his Bible and jotting down notes for a possible sermon, while he snorted apricot snuff and swallowed plum brandy. Well, only Jesus was truly sin free....

Wells had fallen asleep when he heard a sloppy knocking on the door. He rose from the bed, straightened out his black string tie, and pulled back his mud-colored hair. He caught a glimpse of his reflection in the window and shivered. The hardwood floor creaked under the pressure of his footsteps.

Mary Falkum looked like hell. Her skin was wrinkled and leathery, her eyes badly bloodshot. She wore a healthy helping of rouge, lipstick, and mascara, but all the queen's makeup couldn't have hidden the ravaged appearance of her face.

"So you're the preacher I been hearing about," she said. "What about your face? What happened to your face?"

Prophet Wells's eyes narrowed and his expression hardened. "I done it to myself," he said softly.

"Done it to yourself?"

"That's right. Ten years ago. Drenched my face with kerosene and took a match to it."

Mary shook her head. "It don't make no sense," he said. "Why would you go and do that?"

"I was a sinner of the worst kind," he said. "Drinking, whoring, fighting. A marionette with the Devil as my puppeteer. I burned my face," and now he spoke very slowly, "so I wouldn't have to burn my soul."

She looked him over for a long moment and then smiled. "You really think you saved yourself?" she said. "Just by burning your face, you think you saved yourself?"

"I didn't have nothing to do with it. It was the Lord who saved me, made me his prophet."

Mary snorted and shook her head. "Anyway, you gonna invite me in?"

"Yes, ma'am, I didn't mean to be rude. Come on in. Make yourself at home."

She stepped inside and shut the door behind her. She removed a Little Red Riding Hood sweater, revealing a first-row view of her blue-veined cleavage. "You got something to drink, Prophet?"

"I happen to have some plum brandy," he said. "No glasses, though."

"That's all right," she said. "Hand it over."

Wells gave her the flask and watched in detached bemusement as she sucked it all down, a pair of purple streaks dribbling down her chin. She dropped the flask on the floor, smiled a spiteful smile, and struggled out of her hand-me-down dress. "Okay, Prophet," she said. "I ain't got all night. Forty straight in, sixty in the mouth, a hundred up the ass."

Wells frowned and clenched his fists. "I'll pay you," he said. "But I don't want to fuck you."

Mary laughed. "Yeah? What kind of weird shit do you want me to do? Cause I don't do weird shit. Not unless the price is right."

"It ain't weird. And the price is your own salvation."

"I'd rather fuck you. I've never fucked a real live prophet before."

Wells paced across the tiny hotel room, staring at the woman with contempt from the corner of his eyes. "The first thing you've gotta do is stop talking so crudely. A woman of God would never—"

"A woman of God? You can't be serious."

"What you don't understand," Wells began, his voice barely above a whisper, "is that you can't live without Jesus. Not really. I came here...God sent me to...."

"He sent you here? He sent you to me?"

"Yes. Yes, that's right. You're the one. You're the one I need to save."

Mary snorted. "I'll let you save me just as soon as I'd let you fuck me. If the price is right."

"It doesn't work that way. You can't whore yourself to God. God is no pimp."

She laughed at that. "He's worse than a pimp. A pimp beats you for money. God beats you for adulation."

The prophet slapped Mary Falkum hard, driving her to her knees, leaving a welt on her cheek. "That there's blasphemy," Wells said. "I don't care if this *is* a whorehouse."

On the ground, Mary reached into her purse and came out with a spring loaded pearl handle revolver. She pointed it straight between the prophet's eyes. Her hands weren't shaking even a little bit.

"Nobody hits me," she said.

A smile spread slowly across Wells's burnt face, and he nodded his head. "I do apologize, ma'am," he said. "That was wrong of me. But what you said was wrong, too. The Lord wants to save you. He wants that more than anything in the world. That's why he sacrificed his only son."

"I don't need no saving," she said. "Saving's for the self-righteous and ignorant."

Hurriedly she put on her dress, managing to keep the gun pointed at him all the while. "I guess I'll be going," she said. "I've got a date with the Devil."

It was the following evening as the sun set beneath the water tower, when Wells next saw Mary Falkum. She was staggering down the sidewalk—one of her high-heel shoes was broken. She was wearing the same tattered and torn red bridesmaid dress she'd worn the night before. She was gripping a bottle of six-dollar tequila. Walking next to her was a young boy who looked even more disheveled than her. He wore no shoes, no shirt, and his face was hidden by long, filthy hair. His torso was covered with pus-filled welts. He was puffing a thick cigar....

Downstairs, the blue-haired madam was standing behind the counter as before. She smiled when she saw the preacher. "Well, hello there, Prophet. How you liking your girl?"

"She's the devil's mistress, that's what she is," he said. "Who's the boy?"

"Say again?"

"The scraggly-looking kid I seen with her. Who is he?"

"Oh, him. Why, that's her son. He's a real hell raiser, yes he is."

"What's his name?"

She smiled for a moment too long before answering. "His name is Sin. Ain't that a funny name she gave him?"

Wells nodded slowly. "Yeah," he said. "That's real funny."

Mary and Sin Falkum hadn't gotten far when Prophet Wells stepped outside. Both were having difficulty walking—Mary because of her broken shoe, Sin because polio had shriveled up his right leg.

Wells followed at a safe distance as they made their way from Main Street into a dingy neighborhood along the railroad tracks and finally to a little pink house with garbage and tires and car parts strewn on the dirt yard.

Mary and the boy entered the house. Wells stopped across the street, leaning against a light post. He flipped through his Bible until he found a comforting psalm, rocking back and forth as he read it. Then he got down on his scabby knees, and prayed like he'd never prayed before.

He stayed out there for twenty minutes, maybe more. The sky had darkened, and the moon was the color of jaundiced skin. He stuck his Bible into his trouser pocket and walked slowly toward the house.

Wells didn't bother knocking. He opened the door and stepped inside. The living area was a disaster. Clothes, empty bottles, dirty dishes everywhere. The smell of rotting fish. Mary was sitting on the couch watching a game show on TV, sucking down her tequila. The boy, Sin, was sitting in the corner, a beer can at his side, a cigar in his mouth, his elephant cock in his hand, eyes closed and moaning. When Mary saw the Prophet, she jumped to her feet. "What are you doing here?" she shouted. "Get out, you fucking pervert!" She began reaching for her crocodile skin purse, but Wells was too quick. He kicked her hand away and grabbed it himself. He reached inside, pulled out the gun, and pointed it vaguely at Mary. She slunk back to the couch, trembling.

The boy stopped jerking-off and stared at the Prophet, eyes open wide. Wells nodded at the boy. "How old is he?" he said in a voice all full of pebbles. Mary didn't answer. Wells cocked the gun. "How old is he?" he said again.

"Ten," she said. "He's ten years old."

He nodded his head slowly. "That's about right," he said. "Seems longer, somehow. What I should tell you is this: I'm sorry for what I done to you. I came back to make things right. God is showing me the way."

Mary's face contorted into a terrible vision. "I knew it!" she hissed. "I knew you were the one! You goddamn bastard. Burning your face didn't do nothing. Don't you know, you can't undo the things you done?"

Wells strode over to where the boy was sitting. "We'll see about that."

The boy didn't struggle as Wells grabbed him from beneath the arms and started dragging him toward the bathroom. Mary made a half-hearted move to stop him, but Wells pointed the gun at her. She stood in the doorway as Wells dropped the boy into the bathtub and turned on the bath water. When the tub was full, Wells nodded at the boy. "It's time you got baptized, son. Ain't no sin that can't be cleansed by the Lord."

Wells placed the gun on the commode. He grabbed the boy by the hair and shoved his head under water. Mary Falkum watched paralyzed. "In the Name of the Lord Jesus Christ, I baptize you into the Name of the Father, the Son, and the Holy Spirit."

Initially, the boy struggled, kicking his legs and flapping his arms. But after a minute or more underwater, his body relaxed. A few bubbles arose to the surface, and then there was quiet. Wells released his grip and looked at Mary. Her face was like an ancient mask, colorless, unmoving.

"You killed him," she whispered.

"I baptized him," he said. "It was the only way."

Mary slid down the doorframe and sat on the floor. She chewed on her lower lip until it started bleeding. Prophet Wells grabbed the pearl-handle revolver and placed it in Mary's hand. She held it limp-wristed. Wells stepped over her and walked slowly out of the bathroom toward the front door. With a sudden burst of energy, Mary rose to her feet raised and pointed the gun at the back of the Prophet's head. He stopped for a moment, his shoulders stooped. She cocked the gun but couldn't fire. He continued walking. The gun clattered to the floor. Wells pushed open the door and stepped out into the hot Texas night, the words of the Lord echoing in his skull.

THE PREVAILING WIND
Cameron Ashley

(For Yvo)

Chang Lap Fu's old-man fedora dampens in the fine but constant rain. The boy beside him, puffed up in a thick parka, worries for the state of his hair in the drizzle. The boy looks between Chang Lap Fu and the large Maori bouncer blocking their entry into the bar. The bouncer's 'fro is safe from the wet—he stands under an awning in front of a staircase leading up to the second story bar. Tribal tattoos spiral down his huge, bare arms, sitting crossed against his massive chest.

Chang Lap Fu takes a step back to let some young, mini-skirted things teeter past on heels they don't know how to walk in. Afro Bouncer says to the girls

"What's up."

and lets them through.

Chang Lap Fu stares up at the large bay windows of the bar. He looks back at the boy, says

-Tell him we need to get in.

The boy pulls smokes from his pocket, shakes one loose from the pack. He fires it up with a Zippo. Chang Lap Fu swipes it from the boy's lips, sucks his teeth in disgust and smokes it himself.

The boy says

-He's not letting us in. Seriously. We're not getting in.

-Ask him.

Chang Lap Fu nudges the boy forward. The boy says,

"Hi. Um. Look, can we come up, please? We can pay the cover charge?"

Afro Bouncer grins.

"Are you a midget?"

"What?"

"Are you a midget."

"Um. No."

"If you're not a midget, bro, then you're underage. Is Gramps over there, is he like that guy in that fucken movie? That fucken movie where that guy de-ages? Is he going to, like, become an age-appropriate Bruce Lee or something in the next five minutes?"

The boy sighs.

Afro Bouncer hooks a thumb at the street.

"Then both of you fuck off."

Chang Lap Fu sucks his teeth, steps forward and barks out more Cantonese.

The boy translates.

"Look, my cousin is up there. His mother had an accident tonight. She's in the hospital. My cousin left his mobile at home and my grandpa found out he's here. Please, just let my grandpa get him."

Afro Bouncer sizes up Chang Lap Fu. Chang Lap Fu doesn't back down from the eyeballing. He opens his palms, says

"Please."

Kevin Loong found employment cleaning up after the sixty-seven residents at the home. He engaged them in conversation, helped them however he could, accepted their gifts and generally ingratiated himself into the tiny community of retired Chinese. Never once did he let slip that he was a criminal, convicted of trafficking over a hundred kilos of marijuana. He never said a word about it. Until Keng Wah Wong moved in.

Keng Wah Wong, fresh from Shanghai, complained constantly to Kevin Loong about his continual defeats in the home's mahjong tournaments. Drugs and mahjong make a hell of a pairing and back in China, Keng Wah Wong was a man unbeatable at the game when drugged off his nut. In the circles Keng Wah Wong formerly moved in, you didn't play mahjong without a taste of something. Coke, ketamine or any type of amphetamine were not only standard performance enhancers, they were encouraged, practically required to make it through the frequent all-night games.

So Keng Wah Wong, jonesing, made an off-hand, jokey quip to Kevin Loong

-Don't suppose you could get me some cocaine.

Kevin Loong thought

Fuck it.

He made some phone calls.

Keng Wah Wong, coked off his gourd, winning continuously, felt the spirit of competition bite him. He dropped the secret of his mahjong mastery.

Kevin Loong's order quadrupled within a fortnight, quadrupled again a fortnight later, and a fortnight after that, the old mahjong-playing freaks began to experiment. Pensions, Chinese New Year cash, loose notes squirreled away—it all found its way to Kevin Loong.

Packages brought in by a guy named Alex Au got bigger. Nurses commented on what a good grandson he was, bringing his grandfather all these presents.

Kevin Loong got busted smoking a tiny grayhound of a joint in Keng Wah Wong's bathroom.

No more work release for Kevin, back to the slammer full time.

The largest order yet—purchased in bulk by residents wising up and pooling their cash—went ahead without him.

At the bar, Chang Lap Fu queues and buys a beer from a slightly perplexed barmaid. He looks around for Alex Au. Young white Melburnians size each other up for either a fuck or a fight. He chugs back his pint and goes for a wander, grimacing at the shitty music. He follows the arse of some young Chinese girl he spotted from the corner of his eye through this crowd of Caucasians. The girl, painted into something garish and completely unsuitable for the season, leads him up and out to a rooftop beer garden of sorts. It's encased in a clear plastic sheeting shielding it from the cold and wet. Gas heaters burn. Gym-fit boys, with no subtlety or skill whatsoever, attempt to woo young women through drunken bluster alone.

The Prevailing Wind

Chang Lap Fu feels a stirring and wonders if the Chinese girl with the arse will let him fuck her for cash. In the old days, if she refused, he'd have taken her anyway.

They woke him from a nap filled with dreams of the old days, of endless nights of gambling and whores, of drugs and booze. Of long cruel mornings, difficult staggering walks to the Guangzhou wet markets. Chang Lap Fu, a heroic drinker, was well known to market stall owners, who sold their exotic remedies for everything from fever to impotence. As he aged and grew in stature, so did the tales of his alcohol-fuelled adventures.

Members of his gang nicknamed him Barking Deer, as he consumed it daily to ease his brutal hangovers. It was a name that stuck until his retirement, where the legend of his furious violent urges to kung-fu fuckers was at odds with the cuddly grandfather he had become. Uncle Barking Deer was now the voice of reason, and with this change, mellowed by age and family, he uprooted.

They woke him and told him what happened and begged him to help. The grandfather in him tried to refuse, but the gangster in him, snatched from the dream into the real, had already said
-Yes.
His only questions
-Which one of you bastards can get me a gun? And which one of you bastards will lend me a grandson? I'm not bringing mine into your mess.

He dressed in his favorite suit. He attached his cufflinks, made from two matching American-style mahjong tiles—"Big Joker" written on them. By the time he dug out his favorite hat, the boy who would be his translator was knocking on his door.

As expected, no-one had the means to procure him a firearm. He sucked his teeth. In his day, hardcore gamblers knew as much about guns as they did about mahjong. This collective of gambling grandparents, all they had to give Uncle Barking Deer was their best wishes and a pocket full of coins.

He said to the boy
-You ever visited a prison before?

• • •

Chang Lap Fu stands in the corner watching Alex Au.

Alex, tall and lean, in baggy jeans and a T-shirt with some sort of hip-hop nonsense written on it. The girl Chang Lap Fu followed sits on his lap. There are five others with them, a mix of wannabe hard men and their molls. Pathetic. Designer gangster, all surface, all logo. No balls.

Alex Au drinks beer after beer. Chang Lap Fu goes to the men's room and waits. It doesn't take long. Alex stumbles up to one end of the piss trough. Chang Lap Fu's at the other end, head down, pretending to piss. The guy between them, one of Alex's mates, finishes up, does a double-take at the short old man next to him, and heads back upstairs.

Chang Lap Fu says
-You're Alex Au?

Alex turns slowly, tilts his head at Chang Lap Fu. Silence is punctuated by the drumming of piss against tin.

-Do I know you?
-You delivered packages to my friends.

Pissing stops.

-The–? Don't know what you're on about...

Chang Lap Fu steps forward, cracks Alex Au's head against the cistern three times. As Alex crumples to the tiles, a couple of guys walk in. Chang's knees pop like derringer shots as he drops. He cradles Alex and lets loose a string of alarmed Cantonese. Feigning tears, he switches to English

"Help please. My grandson. My car parked outside. You help."

Somerton.

A shithole.

Filled with industry and business parks, it's cursed with an equally ugly undergut—zombie-men fucked up from chroming or worse, their physiques matching the skinny, cheap cigarettes they smoke. Worn-down, pram-pushing women praying for a lotto win, another man, a new TV, or a good, cheap score.

Chang Lap Fu stares into the house, between a crack in the living room curtains. The boy, with superior night vision, searches the overgrown front yard for a brick or a rock, something, anything solid enough to split skin and break bones.

Alex Au sits in the back of the old Subaru Chang Lap Fu boosted from around the corner of the retirement home before he and the boy hit the city.

Terrified and tape-bound, Alex spilled easily. A slapping and a few spiralling brands from the car's cigarette lighter was all it took.

No balls. No heart.

As the boy cracked the window to let the cooked-meat smell out, Alex not only gave up a name. He also offered GPS-worthy directions in both Cantonese and English.

The boy stands beside Chang Lap Fu, a heavy sliver of ceramic roof tile in his extended hand. Chang Lap Fu takes it, turns it over and over in his old, spotted hands, slides it into a suit jacket pocket.

-When I tell you to look away, boy, you look away.

Chang Lap Fu rings the doorbell. It makes a tinny Big Ben chime.

A big white guy with a crew cut, a beer gut and bloodshot eyes, opens the door.

Chang Lap Fu wears a warm, grandfatherly smile. He holds the boy's hand. The boy says

"Hi. Are you Joshua Hepburn?"

"Nah, man."

Crew Cut turns his head.

"Josh, hey, Josh. There's a—uhh—kid here…"

Crew Cut sniffs, looks the little old Chinese man over dismissively. Chang Lap Fu still smiles. The boy nervously hops from foot to foot. Canned sitcom laughter from the TV inside soundtracks the moment.

Another whitey appears. He's baby-faced, with long unwashed hair. He sees his visitors.

"Yeah? Whoa…"

He looks at Crew Cut but points at Chang Lap Fu.

"Are the mushies kicking in already?"

Laughter from the TV, chuckles from Crew Cut.

Chang Lap Fu steps forward.

-There's nothing funny about robbing old people blind.

Josh scratches his head.

"Huh?"

-You had Alex Au deliver a package full of baking powder and vitamin pills to my home. I know this because Alex told me himself.

"English, mate. Speak some fucken English."

-I know Alex because I used to see him drop off his parcels. I visited Kevin Loong in prison. I threatened to tell the prison guards about the drug deals if he didn't help me. Kevin is a pussy. He told me where Alex likes to spend his Friday nights. Alex is also a pussy. He told me where you live.

"I dunno what you're on about, but you can just fuck off, okay?"

-You need to associate with manlier men.

"You've got the wrong house. No chinks here."

Crew Cut's concerned. He says to Joshua

"He asked for you by name, mate."

Chang Lap Fu looks at the boy. The boy begins to translate, but he's scared and can't remember right. He says

"You owe him twelve grand. He doesn't want to hurt you."

Sitcom over, narration for a show about Tasmanian Devil cancer instead.

Joshua goes

"What?"

-Look away, boy.

Chang Lap Fu palm-strikes Crew Cut in the throat. Crew Cut staggers back into the wall, but he's a big boy and doesn't go down. Still, Chang Lap Fu has surprise on his side and he works it, slipping the tile from his pocket and sticking Crew Cut with its sharp end. Over and over and over between the ribs.

The boy backpeddles into the yard, but can't help watch the violence. He sees Crew Cut hit the lino, his white shirt turning red. He sees Chang Lap Fu, blood coating his hand, dripping from his weapon, advancing toward a retreating Joshua Hepburn.

Chang Lap Fu stops, looks out at the boy, scowls and closes the front door.

He emerges fifteen minutes later. He carries a bulging

pillowcase and drags an old, tan suitcase. He sucks his teeth, says
 -You weren't raised to help an old man with his luggage?

He dreams of filthy Guangzhou back-alleys. A man flailing in the muck, one hand clutching the other, four finger-stumps spurting red.
 He holds the knife. Tells the man to never come back, to never gamble again.
 Yee Xiu Ling gently wakes him. She holds a plate of dumplings. She tells him about her daughter, the Australian husband who beats her.
 Uncle Barking Deer wipes some sleep from his eyes, some drool from his mouth. He stands, pops a dumpling in his mouth, reaches for his cufflinks and holds out his hand for the address.

EXPERIENCE PREFERRED
Patricia Abbott

"I can get you a job as a personal housekeeper. Be a hell of a lot easier. This job's for wetbacks or ex-Commies." Bud was lying on a guest bed, watching Iris clean her final room of the day. "*No habla ingles*," he said, affecting a Spanish accent. "Look, you already dusted that phone, honey. Don't you have a routine—a procedure—so you don't clean things twice?" He crossed his legs and put the remote down on the bedside table, having settled on the Classic Baseball station. "Is that Ernie Banks?" he muttered.

"I have a routine, but you're distracting me. Anyway—this thing's grimy." She sprayed it, watching as the cleanser made its way into the phone's interior. "I said to pick me up at four, Bud, and it's not even three-thirty. You shouldn't be in here…." She looked around uneasily, wondering if the room was bugged. Examples of her inadequacies as a chambermaid kept cropping up at staff meetings. Was a video device somewhere on her cart? It'd be like Mr. Duggan to install expensive surveillance equipment while claiming poverty last month when she asked for a dollar-an-hour raise. Inside the TV? Ernie Banks was still at the plate.

Bud glanced at his watch. "So I'm a few minutes early. Let up a little—the room's clean." He struggled to sit up, putting another pillow behind him. His pony tail, a hair style she didn't care for, stuck up like the comb on a rooster. Seeing her gaze, he yanked it tighter. "Look, here's the thing I came early to tell you—it just occurred to me this morning. I run into old guys who need help all the time at my practice. They're completely lost after their wives die. I can introduce you to one. Probably pay you more than you earn here just to listen to his life story. You got mucho experience as a housekeeper now, right?"

"Sounds swell. Being one guy's slave instead of a dozen's."

"That's what I do mostly—listen." Bud closed his eyes. "Tell you one thing. This is the worst fuckin' mattress I've ever seen. Maybe I can make a deal with the hotel. Set up a massage kiosk in the lobby or something. People gotta get out of bed feelin' like cripples."

"This room's scheduled for refurbishing. Whole floor is. They bring in those pillow-top things, a couple of down items, slap up some discounted wallpaper and then bump up the rates to pay for it. Same rooms on floors one through five are fifty dollars more a night now." Bud was still wincing. "Leaning over that massage table all day long must be murder," she said with sympathy.

She bent over beds half the day herself, lifting the mattresses with the same broken-down shoulder—all of it the consequences of a quick divorce. One minute she was cutting triangular peanut-butter sandwiches for her kids in her primo kitchen in the burbs, next she was unloading suitcases at her mother's place and looking at the want ads. It was enough to bring on whiplash. "Don't you have a deal with one of your pals? Trading massages?"

"Like I'd ever let a man touch me."

"See, that's what I always thought. Must be a hell of lot easier for a woman masseuse."

"I do a hell of a lot more than give massages. You know that."

Bud was an acupuncturist, running a practice that also touted the benefits of vitamin therapy, acupuncture, relaxation tapes, massage—all the stuff flooding the market since circa 1980. It'd only grown bigger since the smash last year. Lots of stressed-out people turned up at Bud's when they'd exhausted everything else, or when their medical plan wouldn't cough up the dough for a real orthopedist. Bud didn't have a degree in anything requiring state licensing, but that didn't stop him from hanging a sign above his office.

Iris had seen through his snake oil pitch immediately. But most of the men she knew—had ever known—were pretty much like Bud. Some sort of scam or dicey deal lurking nearby. The bed creaked as Bud settled in deeper. "So like I was saying…"

"Gonna smooth that out before you go?" she asked, emptying the wastepaper basket while shooting him a black look. "The bedspread, I mean. And watch out for your shoes, Buddy," she added, modifying her shrill tone. "Hell to get scuff marks off that fabric." She picked up a stray tube of lip balm from the floor and tossed it. "Hotel world's still bonkers for polyester—even after thirty years. You should see how nasty cigarette burns look on that sheen. Bet the place goes down in flames eventually."

He laughed lightly, his pony tail shaking. "You sound like a regular little *hausfrau*, Iris. That's why this idea I have—"

"Nobody's offered me a job on any runway. And if you knew what I knew, you'd think twice before rolling around on that spread. They never launder them, you know."

Bud jumped up, giving the spread a swipe. "See, no wrinkles. It's magic." Holding his palms out, he sang the words like the old Sinatra song. Bud was a big Sinatra geek. Most guys she knew were—even, what?—a decade after his death. She preferred John Mayer. Bud walked over and rubbed her neck. "Jeez, you're wrapped tighter than a mummy."

"Makes me tense having you here. Like it or not—which I don't—I need this damned job. That doofus, Duggan, shows up here and finds you, I'm gone."

He sniggered. "Duggan's probably nailing one of the Latinas in a room down the hall."

"The only thing that could raise his flag is a room resemblin' a surgical site. Anyway, wife's got him on a short leash."

"You'd be surprised how much wiggle room six inches gives you. Come on, old girl. Room was clean ten minutes ago." He raised and lowered his shoulders impatiently. "I'm startin' to get the idea you're avoidin' me." He paused. "Thing is these guys—the ones that come into the office—they're so ready to turn their lives over to someone. And not just the household chores. They're used to a woman paying the bills. Givin' them advice on everything. What else did that generation have to do? Watch soaps? See where I'm going, baby? Get it? In the palm of your hands in days."

Iris wiped the wastepaper basket off, placing it under the desk. If it were up to her, they'd put plastic bags inside. There was always a coating of dust or grime or sticky stuff from the crap people pitched. God, she was beginning to think like her mother. Spend too much time on wifely duties and shit happens.

"Looks tacky," Mr. Duggan told her when she mentioned her idea about bag inserts. "Plus an added cost. Just wipe them down." He had demonstrated the proper method on one already pristine, his eyes narrowing with attention to the task. "Hotel's already paying you, right? Why'd we want to pay for a bag, too?"

Duggan had trained Iris himself, going through the room with undisguised pleasure, showing her the common mistakes. He dusted the light bulbs, for instance, and vacuumed the inside of the closet. " 'Course, you'll have to complete each room in a timely manner. If it's been trashed or if time's short, these niceties can be dispensed with." The room he'd chosen was already clean so he finished in about fifteen minutes. "Not that fifteen minutes should be your benchmark at first," he said, running a hand along the windowsill and wincing as his hand came away coated with grime. "I'd like to nail these damned windows shut. Look at it outside. Why do our guests feel the need to open the window? Cities are filthy places."

She'd like to see Duggan take on the typical trashcan she handled. More days than not, she'd find a used condom inside, although she'd rather find them in the can than in the bed. Sometimes she'd miss one, yank the sheet off, and send it flying through the air. God, she hated this job. Oh, and gum; gum was bad. No one would believe how many people tossed chewed gum, opened cans of soda, half-filled coffee containers, cigarettes still lit, and a variety of paraphernalia into those little, fake brown leather cans.

Amazing the number of guests who assumed she wouldn't rat them out for their drug use. Did they think she took some sort of a secrecy oath? A confidentiality pact? Did they think that a lousy two bucks on the desktop after a long weekend's stay was a fitting reward for fishing needles and assorted drug supplies out of the trash can? For having to flush unflushed toilets? For crawling around on her hands and knees to retrieve things from under the sink because they couldn't be bothered to aim better? And speaking of a better aim...

She'd also suggested wearing gloves to Mr. Duggan, who said gloves implied their guests were riddled with germs. "People see you coming out of a room in gloves and they'll think we have Legionnaires' disease in here. Or swine flu."

Well, the rooms *were* riddled with germs. She could attest to the germ issue by the sheer number of tissues, swabs, and medications displayed openly in the guests rooms, from the bandages, bottles of antiseptic ointments and heating pads, from the odors of decay that hung in the air when she walked in. Most people were a walking medicine chest.

Bud was talking again. "Look, there's this patient—nice fellow—you'd love him—who needs help right now." She'd no idea what he was talking about. "Practically begging me to help him out." His mouth was inches from her ear. "Never know where somethin' like this might go, Iris. We could make out real good."

Was he rubbing his hands? Iris looked at him blankly. "What? Help who out?" Was Bud asking her to service a client? Give someone a blow job perhaps? Bring men up here for sex?

"A housekeeper, Iris! What do you think I mean. This old dude I know needs a housekeeper." Bud shook his head. "Ever listen to what I'm saying? Anyway, his wife died and he's damn near helpless. Took care of everything for him, I guess. He's coming in to see me for neck pain." His fingers absentmindedly massaged the air. It was kind of sensual. Bud had nice fingers, and she wished they were on her right now, gliding up and down her thigh, her stomach, her breasts, her back.

"Keep his accounts? Stuff like that, you mean?" she said, finally shaking the image of Bud's fingers off, shaking off too the idea of her on her knees with some old fart. Getting the gist of what he meant. "Cleaning and cooking? I'm not the greatest cook if that's what he's after."

"Guy's not after anything much. Idea of a housekeeper hasn't even occurred to him. *Yet.* That's where I come in. You can easily take care of this guy. Kowalski'll be so thrilled to have a good-looking woman around, he won't even notice what's on his plate. And who knows what you'll come across in that house. He seems rich to me. Had some fellow drive him in. Like a car service, I guess."

Bud got up, walked across the room, putting his arms around her waist. "One of those rich guys who never spent a dime. Probably has millions sitting in a bank account, making 1% interest." Bud took a good look at Iris—trying to gauge her interest in what he was saying. "Watching you bend over in that shiny, black polyester number gets me going. What're we gonna do about it?"

Iris could tell as much as he pushed up against her. She shrugged him off for the moment and squirted the mirror with glass cleaner. "Pretty much anything gets you going, Bud. Look, I don't feel sexy in a uniform I've been cleaning in all day. Does that count for anything? What I feel?" She lifted her arm and sniffed. "Not pretty, Bud. Does it count that I'd rather *not*—at least not here? That I'd like to be in the mood myself, feel sexy, too?"

She was lying, but it didn't do to show him he'd won her over. They'd done it before in hotel rooms here, but she'd lose her job if someone walked in on them. Or if there was a recording device somewhere...

"So take a shower first," he suggested, his eyes lighting up. "We can both take a shower. Those little hotel soaps are sexy as hell. Slipping down over your breasts, your thighs. They fit inside the tightest places."

She whirled around, her uniform crinkling. "You'd like that, wouldn't you? Then I'd have to scrub the tub again."

She *was* beginning to really feel like doing it now. Using those little soaps, maybe just not in the shower. Women were programmed to be turned on by erections, by images of strong fingers even. Where'd she read that? *Cosmo*? She couldn't help it. Bud's fingers aroused her. His profession made them strong, agile, useful.

"*I like your attitude.*" He was making shiver-inducing contact without removing a garment. She pretended to shake him off, not wanting to make things too easy. He'd be up here all the time if it was a sure thing. Being his own boss, he could schedule it in. She'd soon be his two o'clock appointment. And a dinner out might not be necessary—movies either.

Iris wasn't supposed to shut the guest room door. It was in the protocol manual in bold writing: *Hotels rooms are not to be used by staff for any form of fraternization. Hotel rooms are to be treated as if they belonged to the guest: the guest's privacy and possessions are inviolate. The guestroom door must remain open when staff is inside the room for any purpose.*

She walked over and kicked the doorstop away; the door had only been open a few inches anyway. It slammed the way hotel doors always did—loud and with a click. No one would be checking in for another two hours—the entire hallway had emptied out after a dentists conference ended earlier that day. Maria, scheduled to clean the other end of the floor, had sneaked out fifteen minutes earlier to meet Stefano for lunch. Wouldn't be back till tomorrow probably.

"Got too hopped up before we started," Bud said, buttoning his shirt fifteen minutes later. "You were thinking about remaking the bed the whole time. Wondering if any hairs had gotten loose. Any fluid. Admit it."

But he didn't offer a hand in remaking the bed. She'd never known a man willing to lift a finger with household tasks. "Have to make it over from scratch," she said, examining the sheets. "Lipstick or blood?" she asked, holding up a corner. He shrugged. She sprayed it with a can from her cart, waiting impatiently for the spot to dry.

"So tell me more about this guy. The one who needs a housekeeper. How needy is he? Not in diapers, is he? Not some randy old goat? Wouldn't have to read to him, or change any dressings."

"You're gonna like Charlie," Bud promised. He pulled her down next to him. "This is the way we're gonna play it."

She spent another week working at The Philadelphia House. Taking advantage of her situation, she came home with several bags of items taken from rooms she never cleaned.

None of the items were worth reporting—the sort of objects a guest wondered about later, wondered whether he'd left the item on the vanity, or on the back of the door, or under the bed in that hotel in Philadelphia. Maybe left it on the airplane. The kind of stuff a person meant to call or write the hotel about but never did. Hotel gift shop stuff. Mementos from the souvenir shop at the Liberty Bell or Independence Hall. No one would want them bad enough to pursue it.

Her new job began on Monday. Bud was teaching her what to look for, how to take advantage of documents she came across. She had to make her way in the world now and she had only Bud for a guide.

THE METHOD
Chad Eagleton

Zoë Bendix sat in her BMW, watching the roadside through cracked glass, waiting for the body to move. It hadn't moved since she straightened out the snake curve about a mile back and it rebounded off the hood, smashed the windshield and soared somewhere out there in the grass, the scrub and the litter.

"Who the fuck does that? Middle of the road? Middle of the night? Middle of goddamn fucking nowhere? Ah fuck!" She repeated it like a club mix hook as her heart *dooorooompt* the bass line, a cocaine drumbeat with a vodka and Red Bull-fueled groove.

She shook her hands out, brought them up to her face and breathed. "'kay, okay," she said. Her face dripped. "Deep breath—ohhh." She wiped her hands on her short, purple dress. Her sweat smelled like cigarettes and alcohol and drugs and fear.

"Okay." She began turning toward the side window. Her heart started... *doooo*... something pale lay in the darkness. She thought it was a shoe.

"Ohhh, God—fuck!" She jerked from the window, trying to scramble for the passenger's side only to crack her bony hip against the steering wheel. "FUCK!" She screamed and kicked the pedals with her platforms.

Her cell phone rang.

It pushed her back from the brink. She gasped and looked at

it. The display glowed. It shimmied on the far edge of the seat. A snot bubble burst from her nostril.

Zoë pulled a tissue from the visor and picked up the phone. She sniffled, looked at the number and didn't recognize it. Wiping the screen cleared nothing but the display. Her thumb hovered above the answer button. She scratched it with a nail and—the phone quieted. The voicemail symbol flashed. It beeped at her once.

Zoë brushed her hair back, shook it away from her neck and rubbed the display again. She sat it on the passenger's seat, both hoping and afraid it would—ring again.

She answered it. "Hello?" She sounded loud. It scared her.

"Ms. Bendix?"

She didn't recognize the voice. "Yeah," she said, softer now—too soft. "Yes."

"My name is Terrence Bledsoe. Do you know who I am?"

She nodded. The line remained silent until realizing, she said, "I do." The oncoming tears didn't show on her face, but sounded in her voice. "You'll help me? I didn't mean to," she said. "I know I shouldn't have been driving, if anybody knows that it's me. I don't wanna make *People* again. But—who the fuck does that? Middle of the road? Middle of the night? Middle of goddamn nowhere?" The words exploded from her mouth quickly like she had just remembered her line. Her heart *doooroooompt* again.

"The first thing, Zoë, I'm going to do is ask you some questions."

She fussed with her dress. The fabric felt moist. She had an ingrown hair just below the short hemline. "'kay," she said and scratched it.

"Have you been drinking?"

"Yes." She nodded.

"How much?"

She fretted her lip then picked at the steering wheel with her thumbnail. "A couple."

"Mixed drinks, beer, or hard liquor?"

"All of 'em—whatever. I don't fucking know."

"How many is a couple?"

She grabbed her cigarettes from the cup-holder. Her thumb couldn't spark the lighter.

"Are you smoking?" he asked.

The lighter fired.

"Are you smoking?" he repeated.

She calmed. A final spastic breath-sob escaped, before she exhaled and coughed. Bledsoe remained silent.

She lowered the window and smoked her answer back, "Yes."

"Don't toss your butt out the window. How many, Zoë?"

"Don't know."

"Two? Four? A dozen?"

"I don't know—three beers, two—three or so mixed drinks...glass—a lot."

"Drugs?"

"No."

"Zoë?"

His voice sounded like her mother's, and for a moment she hated him. Looking away, trying to find something else to focus her anger, she found, instead, only that single, white shoe in her mind, bobbing like a buoy that offered only rocks.

She stared at the wheel until her voice found the desperation mastered during five seasons of children's programming. "Two lines—just two—of coke with Jack Prine. *Sunset Squadron* hit 400 million overseas."

"Did you fuck him?"

"No," she said and caught her face in the rearview. It looked old.

"Who were you with earlier, besides Smiling Jack?"

"I was at a party."

"Who were you with?"

"No one."

"And now?"

She looked around, avoiding the window. The car remained empty. "I'm alone," she said. "But he's out there. I can see his shoe."

"The man you hit?"

"Yes."

"It's a man?"

"I think so," she said. Her I's creaking like old doors. "I didn't see him until I was already hitting him, I think."

"Where are you?"

"Off the highway."

"Which?"

She coughed and tossed the cigarette. She made a face he could hear. "101."

"North or south?"

Zoë opened the door and leaned out of the car. She scooped the cigarette butt up, raking her nails on the pavement. Her middle finger chipped and she dropped her phone.

"What happened?" His voice from below.

Almost falling, she snatched the phone then jerked back inside the car onto the damp seat. She slammed the door and held the up button on the window too long. "Dropped phone."

"You opened the door."

"I dropped my cigarette."

"North or south?" he asked again.

"I don't know directions. I was just driving."

"Up or down on the map?"

"Up."

"Your car have GPS?"

"Yes."

"Do you know how it works?"

"No."

"I'm going to tell you."

Bledsoe walked her through it. His voice remained even and clear, a little commanding without being angry or bossy. She liked that.

"Good," he said, after she read him her position.

"Terry?" she pleaded.

"Terrence. I'm still here Zoë."

"Sorry, got nervous."

"There's nothing nearby?"

"No."

"Anyone driven past?"

"Someone did about ten minutes ago. Flying. Shook my car."

"Did you call anyone else?"

"Just Marcus Crevello," Zoë said.

"Your manager?"

"Yes."

"You sure?"

"Didn't he call you?"

"Ethan Houghton did."

She leaned forward, squeezing her legs together, and feeling very cold. "I'm fucked. They'll recast me. I fucking needed this."

He ignored her. "You call your mother?"

"No," she pouted.

"Bullshit."

"I started to."

"Texts?"

"No," she said and then, "Terry—Terrence—there's lights. In the rear-view. Bright."

"Are they flashing?"

She squinted and sunk down in her seat, sliding easily. "Not like cop lights—like when you signal their turn."

"That's me."

The headlights died. She blinked and wanted to rub her eyes. "I'm hanging up now and getting out of the car," he said.

Zoë righted herself in the seat. She leaned her head against the steering wheel. "'kay," she said to the empty car. "I can do this, I can do this, I can do this."

Outside something flashed.

She looked up.

FLASH.

Bledsoe moved around the car taking pictures.

FLASH.

She felt her head starting to spin. Something rose in her stomach. Already, she could smell the vomit rising, the—

FLASH.

Bledsoe opened the door.

"I'm Terrence Bledsoe," he said.

She stared at him. She was a terrible judge of height and beard, knowing well how they could be manipulated. His thick dark hair, turning gray, was swept back from his broad forehead. His large nose looked like it had been broken before. She didn't like that she couldn't read his eyes.

"Zoë," she said.

Bledsoe picked up her phone and sat it in his lap while slinging a case from his shoulder. He unzipped it and pulled a USB cable from his windbreaker.

"What are you doing? Shouldn't we go?"

Bledsoe's phone beeped. He ignored it and typed quickly. "E-mailing pictures of your car."

"Why?"

"Don't have time for questions." His eyes raced across the screen and then he was repacking.

"You're going to follow me, Zoë," he said. "It's not far."

"I thought you were going to help me."

"I am. You're going to follow me. We're going to meet someone who works for me. A former stuntman. He's going to lead you through staging an accident."

"Why?"

"Hide an accident with an accident."

"How's that gonna help—can't we just—get rid of this body and I'll go home and you can get my car fixed and I can just—go home? I want to go home."

"Not my decision—Houghton's. He's gambling with controversy. Controversy killed *Proof of Life* at the box office, but pushed *Mr. and Mrs. Smith* into record books. Houghton's footing the budget for this."

"Please, I don't wanna—I'll—I can do things. For you or for—"

"Houghton has girls. Ones that cost considerably less than you." He checked the phone. "The police will arrest you."

"I don't want to go to jail—again."

"You'll be released before TMZ gets your mug shot. Your manager will make a heartfelt plea urging you to get help. You'll get Judge Rice. Rehab has been arranged."

"I should have worn panties," she said.

"Probably, but in two weeks, they'll announce you're making

remarkable progress. You'll do talk show spots. When production starts, you'll have a camera following you around for the series."

"A series?"

"A reality show."

"Why?"

"You killed a man with your car. This is the last in a long line of fuck-ups. Houghton has already sunk a lot of cash into *The Exile Letter*. He wants to cover potential losses and—"

"It's advertising."

"Advertising, exactly. The DVD will drop the Tuesday before opening weekend. Saturday they'll air a marathon. Houghton assures me, 'It'll be gloriously mind-numbing.'"

Bledsoe continued paging through the phone and Zoë realized—*That's my phone!* She reached for it. "What are you doing!"

Bledsoe grabbed her fingers and twisted them, pushing her wrist toward her own chest. "Ahhh, fuck!"

He pushed harder. She tried to rise out of the seat. Zoë realized her dress had risen up and Bledsoe looked bored by her pussy.

He released her hand. "There's your call to Crevello. There's a call to your mother. And there's a call to Jack Prine."

"So!"

"You're a fucking liar. I need truth for this to work. Or I walk."

"I fucking hate you."

He shrugged. "That I believe," he said, returning her phone. "Truth or walk."

"Jack Prine wanted to fuck me. That's what I'm doing out here. I got fucking lost! Got lost on the way to fuck Jack Prine!"

"Your mother?"

"I fucking hate her," she sobbed, "but she's still my mommy. It went to voicemail. I didn't leave a message."

Bledsoe opened his door. "Follow me."

She glared at him through raw, red eyes.

"Do you know—"

"My lines?" She wiped her mouth and sniffled. "Yeah, I do. I fucking do."

The dead man wasn't wearing white shoes.

Just to be certain, Bledsoe wiped the sneakers clean of blood and mud.

They still weren't white.

Bledsoe walked around the darkness, looking for something white. He didn't find anything, before returning to the body and rolling out the plastic. He rolled the man over and onto the bag.

He slipped latex gloves on.

The man looked about twenty-five or so. Tight shirt over a thin chest. Tight dark jeans, tighter at the crouch. He couldn't tell anything about the face. It was all pulp and little rocks and something rubbery.

Bledsoe felt for a wallet.

Nothing.

He scanned the distant road once and searched the front pockets. A packet of condoms and six crisp hundred dollar bills.

Bledsoe pocketed the money and zipped the bag.

After he closed it in his trunk, he walked the roadside with a flashlight. He didn't find anything, but that was okay.

He had an idea.

When he heard Houghton coming down the hallway, Bledsoe stuck the contracts back in the Fed Ex envelope and slid them across the steel coffee table.

Houghton smiled and swept into the room, shaking hands and moving to pose by the award crowded mantel. "You hear about *Sunset Squadron*?"

"Four hundred million overseas."

"My man." He smirked.

"What's the final gross?"

"Just shy of a billion. Once we quadruple-dip the DVD market...billion nine easy."

"Prine's salary is rising again."

"He's worth it," Houghton said. "Let me get your check."

"Not yet. I have a question. How long has Zoë Bendix been your whore?"

"What?"

"Is that how we're gonna do this?" Bledsoe unbuttoned his

sport coat. He crossed his legs. The butt of his 9mm jutted like Houghton's lower lip.

The producer looked around and then nodded. He crossed to the table and opened the art deco case. "Smoke? No? Okay. Mind if I do?" He lit it before Bledsoe could speak. "Years. I see that look, Terry. I know that look. I saved her. From that fucking mother of hers. Come on, man. You watched that show. I know you did, at least once. That bullshit with Zoë's little brother. Caring mother, my ass. She's a pimp. They know it. You know it. I know it. And Zoë sure as fuck fucking knows it. Hell, that bitch didn't know Zoë could act. The only reason she took Zoë in to audition was to twirl her panties in the hope some fucking Polanski-type would get a whiff and she could turn her daughter taking it up the bunny nose into fucking blackmail."

He dragged hard on the smoke. Looked around for somewhere to ash. Shrugged and tapped his cigarette into a vase. "She would have been eaten alive, man." He smiled. "Now I control who eats her and she gets the chance for real acting, brother. By acting like she couldn't act. By playing a part through her entire public life. You dig it? Man, you gotta admit that conceptually that's some Christopher Nolan-type shit there, dude. Wrap your brain around it."

Houghton gave him a moment, before continuing. "The best part is—it's so fucking obvious. She's pisses millions away on purpose. She hasn't even had a movie that broke even in, Christ, for fucking ever. But she still lives the way she does. Still gets work. And still gets to act. She's a girl, dude. A fucking girl."

Bledsoe nodded.

"You know. You're with that Dodge woman. What is she—forty-two? And her career's toast. What's she got left...playing what—teachers in Harry Potter movies? Grandmas in shitty kids films? Or some adaptation of some shitty book a bunch of women take their mothers to so they don't feel bad about not fucking calling them the rest of the year?" Houghton shrugged and ground his smoke out on the vase.

"Prine?"

"That little bastard. The news about *Sunset Squadron* comes in, so I call him. Congratulations on a fine performance. Like the director didn't create it in the editing room. I invite him to the party. I mention some other scripts I'd like to send his way. Maybe we can get together next week and talk about the sequel—*Sunrise Squadron: Race to Dawn* or something. You know what that little prick says to me? 'I'll think about it.' I'll fucking thinking about it." Houghton hurled the vase across the room. It shattered behind Bledsoe. Bledsoe didn't flinch.

"'Warner is offering 2 million more and 5 points. What do you got?' What do I got? What do I fucking got? I got your balls, motherfucker."

"Indiana?"

"That's what I thought. Use the incident you already cleaned up. But no—Zoë. Give Prine some coke. Intro the two of them. I knew he'd want to fuck her. But I knew he'd be discreet. See you taught him well."

"I didn't think he'd forget."

"Zoë cruises out with some H & V hooker I picked up. Like Prine's gonna let some skid row homo suck his cock. But anyway." Houghton drove a flabby fist into a fatter palm. "Bam! Bingo, bango, I got Prine's ass on fucking everything: sex, drugs, delinquency of a fucking minor. And who the fuck is going to believe Zoë hit some fag prostitute in the middle of nowhere within spitting distance of Prine's and he wasn't there? Nobody."

"Good-bye, extra million and 5 points."

Houghton nodded. "I call him up—I tell him, I can make this all go away, *but* I can only all do that if you're my boy. Well, now... Smiling Jack Prine is my fucking boy."

Houghton held his arms out, waiting for adulation. When none came, he went for another smoke. "So, no hard feelings, man? Huh? Are we *simpatico*? I won't use you that way again, promise."

"Sure," Bledsoe said. "But I'm gonna need a new check."

"My man." Houghton pointed with his cigarette. "My man."

Bledsoe laughed. "You know how you can tell you're a Hollywood exec?"

Houghton smiled. "How?"

"You take something simple and muck it up with all unnecessary bullshit and then you want your dick sucked when it doesn't blow up."

"Yeah?"

"Probably." Houghton stuck the smoke in his thin lips and sat beside Bledsoe. He wiped the sweat from his upper lip and almost burned himself. "Ah, shit, you're fucking right? How'd you know?"

Bledsoe pointed at the Fed Ex envelope. "You shouldn't leave contracts out where anyone can see them."

"Why aren't you writing for me?" He blew smoke out his nose and wiped the folds of his neck. "What else?"

"The hooker?"

"Yeah."

"The hooker wasn't wearing white shoes."

Houghton stared at his smoke. "So?"

"She kept talking about seeing a white shoe. There wasn't one. She was method acting. Honing in some memory. Maybe a part in a movie, a television show."

"So, she fucked up?"

"No," Bledsoe said. "She played it too well."

BEDLAM
Ken Bruen

I've been out of the hospital, near three weeks.

I know because I precisely counted and oh so………………… delicately counted the days.

I wish I knew how long I was incarcerated.

The heavy medication, the padded room, you lose all sense of nigh everything.

A room designed to drive you………….madder.

It did.

I alas, remember, months gone by, weeks. Years?

Curled up in the fetal position, and cackling to me own self.

They'd just hosed me down, those fucking lethal sprays of water that bounce you off the freaking walls.

A day came, when I managed to feign taking the pills and slowly, oh so fucking slowly, I began to get back to me own self. Now play the game.

I became the model patient.

It mostly worked.

I was released into general population.

One slight hiccup.

One of the orderlies didn't buy my new act.

Kept on my case, pushing me to reveal my real self.

I did.

When she was least expecting it.

I got her on the early hour of the night shift, drowned her in the toilet. Took a time but then I didn't have any place to be, so I drew it out a bit.

Hear the bitch plead.

Then when I got bored, hung her from the socket, put a placard round her neck, in nice neon yellow,

Said

"I can't take it anymore."

Looked at her for a brief moment then put my hand on her hip, pushed her hard to get that swing going, said

"You're a swinger, babe."

The Government cutbacks were in full bite, they were releasing patients all over the fucking place and with my new model patient status

I was freed.

The mad bastards.

Gave me a bucketful of pills to keep me on an even keel.

Good luck with that.

Four of the CURED patients were bundled into a minivan. Due to be dropped at four separate hostels in Galway City.

The driver had the look of an ex-bouncer/boxer.

The drive to Galway was silent, the other three so medicated they were comatose.

I acted similar, had been doing the zonked gig for so long, it was effortless.

He dropped the other three at their designated hostels.

He checked his list

Said

"They have you in a hostel.............lemme see, yeah, in Woodquay."

I said in my meekest tone

"Thank you so very much."

He was surprised, asked

"What were you in for?"

I near whispered

"Alcoholism."

My head, bowed in shame.

He near smiled, in recognition, said
"Yah poor devil, it killed me Mum."
I thought
"Gotcha."
Said
"I'm afraid though."
He gave a look of part sympathy, mostly curiosity
Said
"Ary, it will be ok, what are you most afraid of?"
I hesitated, as if it was too agonizing to say.
He was in control now, urged
"Spit it out, maybe I can help."
Oh, he was helping alright, tentatively, I ventured
"My old apartment is still in my name and I know I'll have to go there sometime but.............."
He was full hooked, I said
"There's six bottles of fifty year old Black Bushmills there"
I could literally see the Euro signs in his bloodshot eyes, a serious amount of cash there.

His drinker's face, the bulbous nose, the rosacea, the broken veins, the mint pills on his breath nearly disguising the effects of last night's bash, he drooled at the mouth, then all chivalrous, offered
"Now that we can fix right now, I'll take them away for you."
I protested, said
"I couldn't ask you to do that."
He put the van in gear, said
"I insist."
I told him my apartment was at the end of Long Walk and he jumped right in with
"I know them, Jesus, I'll have us there in, like, four minutes."
He did.
Parked at the end of Long Walk, facing the ocean.
I pointed at his feet, asked
"Is that twenty Euro?"
He bent down and I plunged the glass shard I'd honed/smoothed to a fine point.

I moved back as the spurt of blood gushed, he muttered
"Sweet Jesus."

I had to stab him a few more times till he bled out. I took his wallet, nice bit of cash there. I looked round, no witnesses I could spot. Found a black watch cap in his glove department. Pulled it right down over my face. Then I jammed his foot on the accelerator, used a piece of wood to hold it in place. I turned the ignition then slipped out as the van rolled towards the water.

I didn't look back, moving fast. Thought I heard the van hit the water, muttered

"Quite a splash you made, fellah."

I made it into the shadows of the large office complex, turned in the direction of Wolfe Tone Bridge and was on Dominic St. in jig time.

A skip and a reel and I was passing The Samaritans office … and a hundred yards later, I was in Nun's Island.

Where I owned a small apartment. Against all the odds, I'd managed to retain it as a bolt hole. No one else knew about it, I never even killed anyone there. The neighbors were a snotty bunch, never spoke or acknowledged my existence.

Perfect.

I don't do…………..cordiality.

Putting the key in the lock was a real rush, I said

"I'm home, dear."

Absolute silence answered.

Bills were paid by direct debit, not in my own name of course. I'd more aliases than Puff Daddy.

I did have a bottle of Jameson. Who can afford Black Bush?

I poured a large one.

Sank into the battered sofa, took a lethal wallop of the Jay, and waited for the burn.

Come it did.

The fire in my gut, a pale echo of the blast from gutting the van driver, I raised my glass, toasted him said

"Don't forget to feed the swans."

Perhaps they'd see him as take away. That amused me hugely. Truth to tell, nobody amuses me like me own self. You could call it…….Killer comedy. I poured another wee dram of Jay then went to brew some coffee. One of my passions is real coffee. Colombian beans, and the aroma alone gets me amped. Took a while as all real art does. When it's brewed just right, with the Jay as outrider, I feel almost human.

Well, at least an Irish one which allows huge flexibility.

Once I'd eased the cricks out of my body, I stood, pushed the sofa.

It didn't move.

Terrific.

I leaned under it, found the click and hit it. The sofa moved as easy as The River Corrib, without the poisonous face. Beneath it the wood floor appeared seamless.

One

Two

Three.

Lifted the third panel with the glass shard. All intact.

Money

Mobile phones

Coke

Taser

Knives.

I took a thousand Euro, the Taser, few grams of coke and my old favorite Japanese blade—a leather band wound tight around the butt, for controlled grip. Tested it, primed and ready to go. Added two mobile phones. Put the rest back in place then positioned the sofa, re-secured it with the lock and heard the click. I laid out a few lines of coke and snorted them fast. The icy trickle down my throat was near instant and I could feel the clear focus building behind my eyes.

My bookshelves are laden with books.

All poetry.

No true crime or serial killer shite.

I knew my game and better, I knew my act.

My early days in the asylum, one of the shrinks interviewing me had read all the relevant books

Me too.

He asked

"As a child, did you ever torture or kill small animals?"

Gimme a fucking break, the most basic question.

I said

"I love animals, why would I hurt them?"

Then the freaking classic

"Did you ever set fires and as a result, receive sexual gratification?"

God almighty.

I said

"But we had central heating."

He'd caught on to my mind fucking and didn't like it.

Not one bit.

Asked in an icy tone

"Does killing give you sexual release?"

I stared at him, said

"You're a wee bit obsessed about sex and violence, have you spoken to anyone about that?"

He lost it, said

"I know what you are."

"Do share, Doc."

He took a deep sigh, said

"You are a narcissistic psychopath and highly dangerous."

I looked at his name tag, now he had my attention, I said

"Dr. Williams, I don't understand those big words."

He smirked; I liked it a lot, thought

"Later, Doc."

He looked at me with mild disdain, said

"Oh you understand only too well. You are little more than a very sleek killing machine. You can mimic most human emotions, except of course, empathy."

I said

"Doc, aren't you like supposed to be ………..am………..helping me? Calling me names is hardly a good bedside manner. But you are wrong about one thing."

He did that fucking irritating thing of making a tent of his fingers, leaned back in his leather armchair, contempt writ large, asked

"Pray tell?"

I said

"Empathy? I do feel it. I feel so desperately sorry for you."

Rattled his cage, he asked

"That is priceless, why would you feel sorry for me?"

"Because I know the date of your death."

He shot forward, EL HOMBRE again, snapped

"Are you threatening me?"

I responded with

"Touch of paranoia there, Doc?"

He stood, jammed on the alarm bell and in ballad time, two bouncers/nurses appeared.

He ordered

"Strait jacket, the padded cell, Thorazine three times daily and no contact with anyone."

I stood up, let my body go limp, no resistance, said

"Overreacting a wee bit there, Doc."

He waved me away and for the next month, maybe two, I endured what he'd ordered.

Then he got transferred to Galway and I was released into General Population.

God bless the recession and the shambles of the Health Service.

I became a model patient, and when they started releasing patients, I'd my file sufficiently altered to be on the supervised freedom list.

A bright March day, four of us taken in a white minivan to Galway. Staying at the four different hostels. Can't put four lunatics together, we might start a political party.

I had some other minor changes to make, change my hair to black, accessorize my soul. Old 501's, a battered sweat shirt that read

……………………………………..Light my fire.

If you really want to filter through un-noticed, nothing like a dull large cheap parka.

One, it completely hides your physique.

Two, God bless the hoodies.

They've achieved a rep way beyond their actions. You don that gig, people automatically turn away.

I've met, eaten with, shot the shit with, some of the most dangerous predators and never saw one of them with a hoodie.

While I waited for the hair dye to settle, I grabbed a book, sat on the sofa with my drink. The volume

Ann Sexton's

………………………………..To bedlam and part way back.

It sings to me

And on so darkly.

I worship at the shrine of the poets of madness.

On the front page, phew-oh, so long ago, I'd written

Thomas Berryman……….from a Caribbean steamer threw himself

Robert Lowell…………Crown Prince of the disturbed.

Yukio Mishima…………..who ritually disembowelled himself.

And of course, Ann Sexton…………..Queen of The Incitation.

Then I rang Directory Inquiries and what a helpful crew, gave me the doctor's phone number and address.

Coffee-ed

Showered

Parka-ed

I went to visit my money.

Three banks, three IDs and a mountain of cash. Us cuckoos may not have feelings but we sure get a rush from cash.

I began my surveillance of Dr. Williams. Took my own sweet time. He was a bachelor. Not that it mattered a lot. If he'd had a family, I'd have slaughtered them. I try not to kill children. Parents do a much better slow methodical job of that. Anyone else is open season.

Years ago, I'd hooked up with Emil. He had his finger in just about every criminal enterprise. And we'd never met. Just used the phone and PO Box drop. When I completed whatever assignment he'd asked, he'd put the money in the PO Box.

I pulled out one of the mobile phones, called him, said

"Hi, Emil."

Sharp intake of breath, then

"You're back."

I smiled, answered
"And on fire."
He said
"Your timing is perfect, I have a job for you."
I said
"Tell."
Deep theatrical sigh, then
"I like to support the Arts. A young writer, I suggested he write a novella, I put up the money to publish it, promote it and who'd have known, it took off, was made into a movie and fuck, it's been nominated for an Oscar."

He was breathing hard, then he spat out the writer's name and I felt something jar in my memory. He continued
"He now blanks me totally. Refuses to acknowledge my part in his success and says he owes me nothing. There was no written contract, people don't fuck with me and I'm not fond of paper trails. I'll up your usual fee if you can get this done within the week."

Then I remembered, asked
"Wasn't he doing quite well till he had some kind of breakdown?"

He admitted
"Your data base never ceases to astonish me. When they slung him out of the madhouse, he had nothing, nowhere to go. He was nothing. But I, MOI, picked up the shattered pieces, gave him a whole new life and career."

I said
"So, he is a poet of madness."
"Whatever, fuck him."
I said
"I don't kill poets."
Stunned silence then
"Are you insane?"
"Actually I'm an accredited sane person. If I recall, he had a very pretty face."
Hesitancy now.
He took great pains to hide his gayness.

I asked

"Did he sleep on the side of your bed with the lovely Japanese lamp?"

Astonished, he asked

"You watched me while I slept?"

"Think of it more as…………..me watching OVER you. I'll call you next week."

Rang off.

Removed the sim card from the phone, put it carefully in a side pocket.

Six more days of watching my doctor. Then it was D-day. I'd been in his house many times by now and could move around without light. His routine was so familiar to me, I knew, Thursday, he retired early. Precisely, at ten.

Ah, those control freaks, anal retentive.

I dressed in black, pulled the watch cap down over my hair.

Let myself into the house by the back.

No lights downstairs.

Bingo.

I moved silently up the stairs. Paused briefly at the slightly open bedroom door. He was sitting up in bed, bare chest and sipping from a large tumbler of red wine. I hesitated, something was off.

But I rarely turn back, a bad habit that got me caught before. I rushed him, hit him with the Taser, the red wine flowing down his chest and the glass hitting the carpet. I straddled him, got the Japanese blade poised and began the intoxicating moments of cutting his head off.

The bathroom door opened and a young woman, clad in a tiny towel emerged.

We were frozen in a tableau of shock, red wine and blood. I pulled off the watch cap and she gasped

"But you're a woman?"

I raised the blade high above my head, began to approach her, said

"I prefer to think of myself as a poet."

OF COURSE, YOU REALIZE THIS MEANS WAR
Jimmy Callaway

I gotta meet Beau tonight, so I jump the trolley out to State and boost a car outta one of the parking garages. It's a Saturday, so there ain't many cars, but ain't much security either. I grab a white Ford Focus with a big Tweety sticker on the rear window and drive back to El Cajon.

One time, this buddy of mine tells me this story, how he helped some chick out. He was at the mall or something, y'know, and he's going back to his car, and there's this chick, her car won't start. He says she was asking people for a jump and they would just ignore her. So here's my buddy, he's got cables, and this chick's kinda cute and clearly all flustered, can't get a helping hand. So he tells her he'll pull around, give her a jump. Oh, thank you, thank you, y'know, she's real grateful.

So he pulls his car around to the other row, y'know, so his front end is facing hers. But there's this, like, planter in between the rows there with some little flowers and stuff, right? Now, he's all the way in his spot, but she's not, so he can't quite get the cables to reach. So he tells her, take the brake off, put the car in neutral, let it roll forward a bit. So she takes the brake off, but she can't work the, whattayacall, y'know, it's an automatic, and she can't get the shifter outta park—whatever. She's too flustered to be of any help. So my buddy goes over, gets in, turns the car on, puts it in drive and lets it roll forward a few inches. He jumps her car, oh thank you, thank you, and off she goes.

Now, my buddy, you may think he's a nice guy. And maybe he is. But that didn't stop him from boosting her wallet outta her purse on the passenger's seat. And she drives off, and he's feeling pretty slick. He closes his hood and takes off, gets on the freeway. But the dope was in such a hurry or was feeling so slick or whatever, he doesn't bother to check that his hood's closed all the way. He's on the freeway a good fifteen, twenty minutes before the goddamn hood comes flying up and crushes his windshield. Scares the living shit out of him.

He was all right, he pulled over fine and got Triple-A to come out. But that new windshield cost him two hundred bucks, man, and all that chick had in her wallet was a stick of gum and fourteen dollars.

"Man," he says to me. "I'll tell ya, no good deed goes unpunished."

Jesus, I about laughed my ass off.

It's almost three, so I go out to the Tweety car. I check that the gun's still there, and then I drive up to that new Jack in the Box on Greenfield and Main. I take surface streets the whole way, taking it easy. This late on a weeknight, the cops aren't out really, but the damn Highway Patrol headquarters are right next door to that Jack there.

I pull into the lot, and Beau's there, waiting, polishing off a Sourdough Jack. "Nice car," he says. "What're you, a fairy?"

"It's my sister's car," I tell him. "Mine's in the shop."

Beau sucks the grease off his fingertips, tosses his wrapper on the ground. "Slide over," he says.

"What? Hey, c'mon. It's my sister's car, man."

"Look," he says. "I know right where we're goin', so it's easier if I drive. Now just slide over, let's go."

"No, I don't think you understand," I say. "I had to beg her just to use it, y'know, she'll kill me if anything happens to it."

Beau leans on the driver's side and looks down at me, giving me his prison stare. "Look, Milligan, I'm doing you a fuckin' favor here. Don't you forget that. Now slide over."

I let out a big sigh and climb over into the passenger's seat. Beau gets in and has to move the seat back to make room for his gut. "Don't worry," he says, all smiles again. "I'll be careful. Your sister's little fairymobile won't get a scratch on it."

"Better not, man," I say. "I've been in enough hot water this week, I could open a goddamn bathhouse."

Beau chuckles and looks over at me. "Where'd you get the shiner?"

I touch my eye. It's still swollen and tender. "Nowhere," I say. "Don't worry about it."

He chuckles some more. "Fightin' Chance Milligan," he says. "He ain't got a fightin' chance." He laughs out loud, gets sourdough spittle on the windshield.

"Yeah, yeah, very funny," I say. "Can we do this please?"

"You got the money?"

"Yeah."

"Let's see it."

"It's right there," I say and point to the book bag in the back seat.

"Let's see it," he says.

I sigh again, bring it up, and unzip it. "Three grand, man," I say. "Cash. Now let's go."

Beau smiles at me. "Relax, will ya? This'll all be over soon. You're lucky you got a friend like me."

"Yeah," I say. "With friends like these, right?"

Beau frowns. "With friends like what?"

See, I don't drink much these days. I got popped for a little shoplifting last year, and the judge let me slide with a few days community service. I spent the next four Saturdays in a stupid orange vest in the hot sun, picking up garbage by the side of the freeway. Nearly everybody else was there for DUIs, and those poor bastards had thirty, sixty days to serve. So I said the hell with all that, I'm not rolling any dice drinking and driving.

But I still like to go out, y'know, hang out. I'll nurse a beer or two and see what I can see. And I've seen a lotta different kinds of drunks. You got your angry drunks, your blackout drunks, your weepy drunks. Y'know, all kinds. They all tend to mix and match, y'know, but can usually be comfortably placed in one category. And the chatty drunks, man. Those guys are my favorite.

One time, another buddy of mine was all loaded and he told me about how he once banged his girlfriend's sister. Good story. Then, a few weeks later, we were hanging out again, and somebody mentioned sisters, and I was like, Dude, is your girlfriend's sister around?

And he got all bug-eyed, and was like, What?

And I was like, Y'know, your girlfriend's sister? You banged her that time.

And he did not even remember telling me that story, no recollection of it whatsoever. And he was like, Dude, don't tell anybody about that.

And I was like, Who am I gonna tell?

And he was like, Dude. Seriously.

And I was like, All right, man. But I was thinking to myself, Don't drink so much then, you can't keep your trap shut. Y'know?

Beau was definitely chatty. Drunk or not, but especially when he was drunk. At first, I used to hang on his every word. Y'know, he's got a few years on me, and I'd heard he'd done real hard time, up at CRC or San Quentin or one'a those. So I figured I should pay attention, y'know, I could learn something.

But all I learned was what a windbag the guy was. He would go on and on, especially about chicks. Oh, lookit that one, Chance, lookit, lookit, and Oh, that one works at Janet's is a sexy broad, and Oh, we gotta find a bar with more pussy in it. I mean, hey, I'm a single guy, I know the story. But, Jesus. Let's talk about something else for a change.

Of course, by then, Beau had me tagged as a good listener, so I could never get rid of him. And what a shit-talker, too. A guy we know walks in, and Beau's all smiles and handshakes one minute, hey, lemme get this guy a shot. And then whoever-it-is goes to the can, and the next minute Beau's all, Aw, fuck that guy, and Aw, he's a pussy no-account, and Aw, I swear I'm gonna beat his ass one'a these days.

Sheesh.

A windbag, I'll tell ya.

Drew called me on Monday, and he's like, Dude, you're pretty well screwed.

And I was like, What?

And he was like, Mr. Bob Romano's been looking around for you.

Well, right away, I knew I hadn't done anything major. Mr. Bob Romano's a big man, y'know, in the big time. Mostly in San Diego proper, but he's got his hand in pies from up in Poway to down in Chula, and yeah, even out here in El Cajon.

But me? A two-bit stick-up guy, maybe deals a little weed here and again to make his rent? What's he got against me?

So I'm like, to Drew, What's he got against me? I've never even met him.

And Drew's like, Dude, you banged his niece.

And I was like, Shit. I knew which chick Drew was talking about, y'know, it's not like I'm knee-deep in it over here. I met this chick at Cheers & Beers a week ago, a real looker, y'know, a cute little pocket rocket. Some college girl, out slumming it up in the East County, drinking like an alcoholic fish and looking for somebody to give her a poke.

And I mean, who am I to have left her hanging? Y'know?

So I'm like, to Drew, Man, I didn't know who she was.

And he's like, Yeah, well, he sure as fuck knows who you are. Somebody must'a seen you leave with her, word got back to him, and, well... I mean, he ain't gonna kill you, I wouldn't think, but... y'know. It's his niece.

And I was like, Shit.

See, Mr. Bob Romano, he's a real family-oriented guy. Back before my time, the story goes, some bikers went in on a deal with Mr. Bob Romano's cousin. But then they cut him out of it by blowing his head off out in the hills somewhere. It was his cousin's deal, so nobody in Mr. Bob Romano's crew knew which bikers they were or anything. So they just started killing anybody on a Harley. Near about caused an all-out war.

Eventually, Mr. Bob Romano and the Dago Mob had a sit-down. Or maybe it was the UMF or the Peckerwoods, I dunno. The Satan's Helpers, for all I know. All them Hells Angels types look the same to me. Anyways, they had a sit-down and arranged a truce and stuff, but nobody ever did find out exactly how Mr. Bob Romano's cousin got killed, and word is the guy can't even watch *The Wild One* or anything like that without flipping out.

The guy's a bit protective of his family, what I'm getting at.

So Drew's like, Anyways, dude, just a heads up.

And I was like, Thanks, man.

But shit. I had no idea what to do.

None.

One good thing about Beau, he did have one really good story. I was at the Old Dutchman one night, about two or three years ago, a Tuesday, and it's late, and it's pretty dead. Beau was really drunk, and we were sitting in a booth, bullshitting. He leans in and he says, "I ever tell you I was in jail?" He's kinda squinty-eyed when he's drunk, breathing through his mouth.

I told him no, but I'd heard that.

"Yeah," he says to me. "Raw fuckin' deal, I'll tell ya."

"Yeah," I say.

"No," he says. "No, no, no, no, no, no. No, yeah, any guy's done time'll say that. But me. I really got a raw fuckin' deal."

So I says to him, "Yeah? How so?"

And so he tells me.

So in "Bully for Bugs," Bugs takes that wrong turn at Albuquerque and ends up in a bullfighting arena. The bull headbutts him in the ass and outta the arena. So now he's got Bugs Bunny to contend with for the rest of the picture: anvils, boulders to the face, the whole nine.

But there's one part where Bugs almost outsmarts himself. He hides a rifle behind his cape there, but when the bull charges,

Of Course, You Realize This Means War 139

he accidentally swallows the rifle. So now when he hits his tail on the ground, bullets shoot out his horns. Uh-oh, right? Now it looks like Bugs is on the ropes, running around the arena, dodging bullets.

But then the bull runs outta ammo. He hits his tail, but his horns just go click. So now he reloads, swallows a buncha ammo, but elephant bullets, the kind with explosive heads. And then he hits his tail, and instead of higher firepower through his horns, he just blows himself up.

And I remember always thinking, like, Man, if you just hadn't gotten so, y'know...overambitious there, Toro, you might'a won that round. But I guess that sorta thing's good to see, y'know, 'cause a guy can only rely on his own wit for so long. Having really dumb enemies helps a lot.

A whole lot.

A couple days after I talked to Drew, Beau called me up. Kinda weird. I don't even remember giving him my number, although it coulda been a while back and I just forgot.

And he's like, What'cha doin'?

And I'm like, Watching cartoons, what're you doin'?

And he's like, Well, I heard you've been having a rough week.

I paused the cartoons. Elmer Fudd held his rifle at Daffy's head. Daffy's looking at me, his eyes half-lidded.

I got up outta my chair, and I'm like, Whaddaya mean?

And he's like, Y'know. That whole Romano thing.

And I went into the kitchen, phone between my shoulder and ear, and started rifling through the junk drawer. And I'm like, Yeah, I'm kinda laying low, y'know, hoping it'll blow over.

And Beau was like, Yeah, that makes sense, but I dunno, y'know?

And I'm like, What.

And he's like, Well, y'know, Mr. Bob Romano's not one to let things blow over.

And I'm like, Yeah, so I hear.

And he's like, I heard not that long ago, some punk up in La Jolla banged the other niece, Vicki? And a couple'a Romano's guys tracked him down, went up and beat the shit outta him in his own apartment.

There was no duct tape in the junk drawer. I started digging around in the cabinet under the sink. And I'm like, Yeah, huh.

And Beau kinda paused and he was like, You don't sound too concerned.

I stopped digging for a second and just sat back on my feet in the middle of the kitchen floor. And I'm like, No, sure I'm concerned, but, y'know. What am I gonna do? He wants my ass kicked, I guess I'll just have to get my ass kicked.

And he's like, Well, what if I told you I had a better idea?

And I'm like, Then I'd say let's hear it.

And so he laid it out for me:

Beau's been trying to sell tweak out in the East County, which is a lot like trying to sell space heaters on the Equator. But if he could get a buy-in with Mr. Bob Romano's people, then he'd have the muscle behind him to really start making some moves. But unless you got at least five grand to bring to the table, you might as well just stay home. And all Beau's been able to get together is two thousand dollars.

And I'm like, I dunno, man.

And he's like, kinda pissy, You didn't even let me finish!

And I'm like, Well, if I'm hearing you right, you want me to come up with the rest of the money to stake you with Romano.

And he, like, paused. Well, yeah, basically, he says.

And I'm like, So that's three grand we're talking, which is pretty much all I got. Sounds a little expensive just to avoid a beating.

And he's like, Hey, gimme some credit here, Milligan. I'm not just looking out for number one with this. We'll be partners, see? You and me, we'll do this together. Buying your way out of an ass-kicking is just a bonus.

And I'm like, I dunno, man.

And then he started getting mad. He's like, C'mon, man, I'm trying to do you a fuckin' favor here, so the least you can do is help me out back! I'll be doing all the fuckin' work, you just gotta sit home and watch Looney Tunes while your money grows. And if you want out after you get your money back, then you walk

Of Course, You Realize This Means War   141

away. You can't lose, you can only win with this. Quit being such a fucking pussy!

And I'm like, All right, all right, calm down.

And he's like, So you're in?

I started looking in the hall closet for the duct tape. I'm like, Yeah, probably, I dunno. Let me think about it and I'll call you back.

And he's like, Tonight?

And I'm like, Tomorrow, let me call you tomorrow.

And he's like, All right, tomorrow. But don't let me down here, Chance. This is our ship coming in here, don't fuck it up.

And I'm like, Yeah, yeah. We hung up and I spent the rest of the afternoon trying to find that damn duct tape. Couldn't find it anywhere.

The receptionist at Romano & Sons was this middle-aged blonde, nice-lookin' lady. Probably a cheerleader in high school, but not, y'know, one'a those really bubbly ones no one can stand. Nice smile on her, too.

"Can I help you, sir?"

"Yeah, I'm here to see Mr. Bob Romano, please."

"And your name?"

"Chance Milligan."

"Do you have an appointment?"

"Uh, no, ma'am. But he wants to see me."

"Oh?"

"Yeah. Seems I, uh, banged his niece last week."

"Oh, okay." And she smiled at me and led me back into the main office. Nice lady.

She went into Romano's office for a minute, signaling for me to stay put. Then she came back out. "Go right in."

Mr. Bob Romano sat behind his giant desk, this little bald guy. But not like the kinda little bald guy who looks like a librarian. Or even like one'a those little bald guys who goes outta his way to not look like a librarian. Y'know, pretty much like he knows you can't fuck with him, so he ain't gotta prove it.

Anyways, he's sitting there, and behind him on the wall is this big mirror. I didn't look as nervous as I felt, so that was good. Standing next to the desk was this big bear of a guy, about my age, I'd say, long hair and a beard. I'd think he's a biker if I didn't know any better. He was wearing a green T-shirt with the Mexican flag on it, even though he's about as Mexican as I am. Neither one of 'em were trying to hide the surprise on their faces, and I'm thinking to myself, y'know, well played, Milligan.

Mr. Bob Romano said, "Hughes."

The big bear stepped forward and socked me in the eye.

All right, so, maybe not so well played.

I fell back into a chair, but not, y'know, into it, like sitting down. I smacked my elbow against it on my way to the floor, and that's what really hurt, my goddamn funny bone, and I let out a yelp.

Hughes went back to standing next to the desk, his arms folded across his chest. Man, that guy is hairy. His bare arms look like he's wearing a sweater. I sat there and rubbed my elbow, and I could feel my eye starting to swell shut.

Mr. Bob Romano leaned forward out of his chair a bit and looked at me. "You want a chair, Milligan? Go ahead, sit."

I got up and took a chair. My fingers started to tingle as the feeling returned to my elbow.

"Now," Mr. Bob Romano said, "was there something you wanted to say?"

I told him what I wanted to say.

It took me a little while, and then he wanted me to say it again. So I did.

Mr. Bob Romano stared at me. "Hughes," he said without taking his eyes off me. "You get all that?"

"Yeah," Hughes said. He packed a lotta disbelief into that one word. But he also sounded like he believed me anyways. Y'know, just crazy enough to be true.

"Go call Manny," Mr. Bob Romano said.

"Manny's in county, boss."

"Well, then fuckin' call somebody!" Romano said. "Don't just stand there with your thumb in your ass!"

Hughes hurried outta the room.

"Now," Romano said to me. "What do you want from me?"

"Well, I was kinda hoping to avoid this, for openers," I said, pointing to my eye. I could see it turning purple in the mirror behind him.

"Well, that's off the table, clearly," Romano said. "What else?"

"Twenty grand."

"Ten."

"Fifteen?"

"Done," he said. "What else?"

"Um, well, I guess a clean gun and a ride home afterwards would be swell."

Hughes walked back in. Mr. Bob Romano leaned back and stared at me as Hughes whispered in his ear. When he was done, Hughes stood with his hands on his hips, looking at me. I couldn't tell through his beard, but it looked like he was grinning a bit.

Romano leaned forward in his chair again and drummed his fingers on his desk blotter. Then he said, "Hughes, go get Milligan here a phone."

As Hughes went out again, Romano said, "You know, Milligan, when Tina told me you were here, I thought you had some real balls."

"I was kinda counting on that, I think."

"But now," he said, "I honestly don't know what to think."

I smiled. Can't help myself sometimes.

Hughes came back in and handed me a cell phone. "There's two numbers in that phone," Romano said. "The first one, listed under Al, will connect you with a gun. The other number, you call that when it's all over, and somebody'll come grab you up. I'll call them both myself and let 'em know to expect you."

"Okay," I said.

"Then, you come back here and see me next week," he said.

"Okay." I got up to leave, and then I snapped my fingers. "Oh, one more thing, do you have any duct tape I can borrow?"

"Duct tape?"

"Yeah, I can't seem to find mine."

Romano looked at me. Then he said, "Hughes, get Milligan here some duct tape."

• • •

So, two or three years ago, Beau's really drunk, and he tells me about this raw deal of his:

Back in the mid-80s, Beau's selling quite a bit of coke in town. Not enough to really be up on anybody's radar, but enough to keep him from having to work for a living. One of his coke buddies is this guy Vin, who's supposedly some half-assed mob guy. Not like Mafia mob, but y'know, his cousin or his second cousin is supposed to be some local big shot.

But Vin was far from being any kinda gangster. I think Beau said the guy was a carpet salesman or something. But he had money to throw around, he liked to party. And the wheels start turning in Beau's head.

He comes to Vin, he says, Look, man, I got a way you and me can make some easy money. There's these bikers, see, been making a little trouble for Beau and his struggling business. Nothing major, y'know, dirty looks mostly. No rough stuff yet, but that's how these things get started.

Now Beau's a big guy, but he can't take on a whole gang of bikers by himself. So, he says to Vin, can't beat 'em, join 'em, right? Let's say Beau asks for a sit-down with the local Dago war chief or whatever-the-hell. Let's say Beau brings along his good pal, Vin, who's got some friends that got some friends. And let's say Beau brings his pal Vin in as a sorta silent partner. Beau will do all the heavy lifting, all Vin's gotta do is sit there and look connected, and he'll make himself a nice chunk'a change every month.

Well, Vin jumps at the idea like he's spring-loaded. Way Beau tells it, the guy was just itching to get into some kinda business other than selling interior flooring. So Beau sets it up, they're gonna go meet with these biker guys out in Harbison Canyon. Beau drives 'em both out there late one night in Vin's car—he knows right where they're going—taking the long way around up the 8 instead of cutting through Crest or Singing Hills. They get to this old abandoned shack Beau knows, out on the ass end of somebody's property, and Beau puts two silenced bullets into Vin's face.

So here's Beau sitting pretty now. Vin's people don't even know who Beau is, all they know is he was gonna meet some bikers. So now the bikers giving Beau trouble got their hands full, and Beau can start making some moves. He takes Vin's buy-in money to his connection down in San Ysidro, ready to get business moving.

Well, it moved, all right, right up shit creek. Beau takes an extra five minutes at his connection's place to take a dump. Next thing he knows, he's got some DEA agent drawing down on him while he's on the can. They raided the joint, hauled everybody off to the pokey. Beau got off light, all things considered, out in two years with good behavior. But all his well-laid plans went right out the window.

"Raw deal, Chance," he said to me. "Raw fuckin' deal."

Man. Was he ever wasted that night.

"So this broad takes me back to her place, and I gotta tell ya, Milligan, she" blah blah blah blah blah blah. Jesus.

We're just past that new Burger King off the Lake Jennings exit, and I'm thinking I can't listen to this blowhard for another second, although it's only been ten minutes or so. Fortunately, right then, the hood finally pops up and smashes into the windshield. It's a little sooner than I expected, but Christ. Not soon enough, you ask me.

"Jesus!" Beau says, and stomps on the brake with both feet. My seatbelt strains against me, but I just breathe through my nose, stay calm. The rear tires on the Focus scream, and the little shoebox of a car starts to fishtail a bit, but Beau's got his massive paws in a death grip on the wheel.

Just as the car's about to stop, I tear the gun from the side of the passenger's seat. The duct tape holding it there makes a big ripping sound, but Beau's got his mind on other things. He's got his head down, trying to peer through the little space between the bottom of the hood and the bottom of the windshield. Little bits of safety glass are all over like confetti, but the windshield is more or less in the same place, with a big sag in the middle.

I put two bullets into Beau's fat head.

As the car comes to a complete stop, I wipe the gun off with my shirt and drop it on the floor. I grab the backpack full of cash and get out. This late at night, especially on a weeknight, there isn't another car around for miles. Still, I waste no time crossing to my right and jumping the fence into that little office park there. I get myself down to Olde Highway 80, again wasting no time, but moving quietly. I can't imagine night-time security is real heavy out here, but why take a chance?

I get to the 80, the main drag through here before they built the freeway back whenever, and start walking back west. Eventually, I'll get the phone Romano gave me outta the backpack and call for my ride, have 'em meet me down at the Burger King there.

But right now, I'm just gonna walk for a bit. Just wanna enjoy the cool night air. I feel all right, y'know, everything's pretty well wrapped up. But I really can't take all the credit.

It helps to have really stupid enemies.

THE MIND PRISON
Dave Zeltserman

I could tell from their faces that they weren't going to be receptive, but it didn't matter. I already had the Governor sold and the Governor's council sold, and more importantly, I had the State Senate President sold. The best these five could do was put up a speed bump.

I introduced myself as Graham Winston and gave them my credentials: PhD in electrical engineering from MIT and top of my class at Harvard Medical. Before I could start the presentation, a heavyset woman, her voice trembling with moral indignation, stopped me.

"Dr. Winston," she asked, "don't you consider what you're doing inhuman?"

"And why would that be?"

"Because," she said, her pitch rising, "what you are proposing is to warehouse human beings. Basically, you want to pen prisoners up as if they were nothing but fatted calves!"

I gave her and her companions a hard look. I already had approval to start the clinical trials and I didn't really need their support. This was a waste of time. I felt a little anxious as I glanced at my watch. It was eleven o'clock and I was supposed to meet Svetlana at twelve-thirty. It had taken me a week to convince her to see me and I couldn't afford to let this meeting mess that up. I politely told the woman that I believed what I was proposing was far more humane than the system that was currently in place. I asked if she could withhold judgment and questions until I was done with my presentation. I could tell she didn't appreciate my answer, but she forced her mouth shut.

I went through the slides showing the financial and social benefits, and they really were dramatic. It costs eighty thousand dollars a year in Massachusetts to house an inmate in a maximum security prison, and my proposed system would reduce that to less than ten thousand dollars. The social benefits were equally dramatic. Every year violent criminals were either released early or given reduced sentences because of lack of prison space. With my system, there would never be any space problems. My audience, though, sat stone-faced through my presentation.

As I wrapped up the slides, a bony man in his early fifties with pale fish eyes started to question the moral integrity of what I was proposing. I stopped him and asked if I could answer him after the demo. He looked insulted, but agreed to wait.

I led them from the conference room to the lab. In the middle of the lab, a purebred boxer lay in a container with about a dozen electrodes attached to its body. A catheter was also attached, as were intravenous feeding tubes. Several optical wires, each the width of a single human hair, ran out of the dog's skull. The animal appeared to be asleep. One of my audience members let out a gasp. I ignored her and inserted a tape into the VCR.

"This specimen was chosen," I said, "because of his antisocial and aggressive behavior. This video was taken hours before attaching the dog to the MP100—or Mind Prison system."

The video showed the dog being taken into a room with several other dogs. Almost immediately, the boxer forced itself on one of the smaller dogs and tried to mount it. And just as quickly, it lunged at one of the other dogs. Fortunately, I had a firm grip of his leash and was able to keep him from doing any damage. The video ended with me throwing a Frisbee to the animal, which he watched with indifference.

I turned off the video and walked over to the dog.

"He's been connected to the system for a week now," I said, as I scratched him behind one of his ears. "Technology has existed for several years which converts digital images to rudimentary signals that the brain can process. This has proven helpful to the blind. My technology is a revolutionary improvement over that. What I'm doing is converting complex computer images to impulses that are fed directly into the prefrontal cortex, right angular gyrus, amygdala, and hippocampus areas of the brain. This in effect allows me to simulate consciousness."

I turned on a flat-panel monitor that sat above the dog. The images on it showed a Black Labrador being thrown a Frisbee. The Labrador chased after it and caught it in mid-flight. He then brought it back to his owner and dropped it at his feet and barked. Simultaneously, the boxer made a slight noise.

"The test subject is right now experiencing what is being shown on the monitor. Although it's nothing but a computer simulation, as far as he's concerned, he's chasing and catching Frisbees. We call these simulations scripts. The Labrador script has been running for two days. A two-day script, though, might actually simulate a month or more of activity. The script we ran before this was of a Basset Hound. In that one, the dog spent his time socializing with other dogs and their owners."

I looked at my watch and saw it was almost twelve. I had to hurry things up. I started removing the electrodes, catheter, and feeding tubes from the boxer. I then used a special instrument to remove the optical wires from his skull. The dog opened his eyes and then pushed himself up and jumped off the table. He was wagging his tail, greeting the stunned members of my audience. He was quite a bit different from the vicious beast they had seen in the video. I took a Frisbee from a shelf, called the dog over, and then gave the Frisbee a short toss. The dog took off and caught it in mid-air. He then brought it back to me and dropped it at my feet and let loose with a bark, his tail wagging a mile a minute.

The bony guy with the fish eyes seemed impressed. "Can this rehabilitate prisoners?" he asked.

"They're going to be spending their days living productive and enriching lives. Yes, it should be a positive influence on them."

He thought about that, and then asked, "If the prisoners are going to be lying for years at a time, how do you, uh, keep their muscles from atrophying?"

"We electrically stimulate the muscles," I said. "Muscle stimulation, feeding, cleaning, and health monitoring are all automated." I showed a thin smile. "The average prisoner will be healthier when they leave than when they entered."

I had won most of them over, but not the heavyset woman. Her eyes were shining brightly with moral superiority.

"What type of existence could they possibly have," she demanded, "if they're simply plugged into a computer with all free will and thought taken away from them?"

"What type of life do they have now?" I asked. "Right now, prisoners' lives are filled with boredom, drugs, brutality, and worse. We're developing scripts to let them live as Albert Einstein, Thomas Edison, Mark Twain, and countless other great thinkers and artists. We'll allow them to spend their days discovering the theory of relativity, inventing the light bulb, or writing *Tom Sawyer*. And every few days a new script will be selected and a new adventure will begin. What we're offering is paradise."

The woman started to argue with me but I held up my hand. "I have someplace I have to be right now," I said. "My assistant, Dr. Allison Hanson, will answer any further questions you may have."

I called Hanson on the phone and less than a minute later, as arranged, she entered the lab with several small dogs on leashes. The dogs backed up at the sight of the boxer, but the boxer ambled over to them civilly and wagged his tail.

I introduced Dr. Hanson to my audience and then left.

I was fifteen minutes late and I could see Svetlana through the restaurant window, her dark beautiful face smoldering with anger. She had gotten up from her table and was buttoning her suede jacket. Of course, any restaurant manager would seat her by the window. She was so damn beautiful. Long black hair, dazzling green eyes, a thin athletic body that only a twenty-five year old could have, and legs that could stop a man's heart. I felt light-headed just looking at her. I knocked on the plate glass window and her eyes seethed as she glanced at me. Then she looked away and left the table.

I caught her as she rushed from the restaurant. "You told me twelve-thirty," she said coolly, her voice thick with a Russian accent. She pulled her arm free from my hand and started to walk quickly away. Along with her suede jacket, she was wearing a short black skirt and suede boots that went half-way up to her knees. I watched her for a moment and felt dizzy. I don't think I ever wanted anyone as badly as I wanted her right then.

I ran up to her about the time she was opening the door to her BMW convertible, a car I had bought her after our first month together. "Please, Svetlana," I said. "I couldn't help it. I had a meeting that ran late."

"I don't know why I agreed to see you," she said. "There's nothing left to say."

"Please."

She stood quietly for a moment. Her eyes seemed to soften. "Okay," she said. "You can get in, but I don't know what good it will do."

She got into the driver's seat and I joined her on the passenger side. As she drove I looked at her profile and felt a lump form in my throat. "You're all I can think about," I said.

I reached over to kiss her, but she pushed me away. "Nothing has changed," she said dispassionately. "I'm not going to be just your mistress."

"You love me too, don't you?" I asked.

She sat quietly for a long moment, her eyes focused on the road. "It doesn't matter," she said at last. "You're married."

"I can't divorce Cheryl. I've told you that. She's funding my research. But if you could just wait three years, four at the tops—"

"I'm not waiting three years. I want to enjoy life now while I'm young, with or without you."

"If your wife would disappear everything would be fine," she said at last.

I didn't say anything.

"You don't love her," she said. "I remember all the times you told me she'd be miserable without you. That you didn't even think she could live without you. You'd be doing her a kindness."

I didn't say anything. Of course I had been thinking the same thing for months. About how much better everything would be if Cheryl didn't exist.

"If it wasn't for your wife, I'd be all yours. Body and soul," she said.

"It wouldn't work," I said quietly. "The police would know it was me."

Svetlana kept staring straight ahead, her face hard and beautiful. I noticed the whites of her knuckles as she gripped the wheel with her small hands.

"Let me think about that," she said after a long while.

I didn't get home that night until past eight. As I made myself a drink in the kitchen I could hear the droning and thumping noise from the basement of Cheryl running on her treadmill. She must have heard me because the noise stopped. A minute later I could hear her clumping up the stairs. Another minute and she joined me in the kitchen.

"Hi, honey," she said as she reached over to give me an overly wet kiss on my cheek. "I just finished three miles on the treadmill."

Cheryl was wearing her workout leotards. It kind of firmed her up some, but even still her body over the last few years had lost most of its definition and was becoming shapeless. To be fair, she was forty-six, a good seven years older than me and twenty-one years older than Svetlana. Still, all the countless hours running on her treadmill and performing aerobics didn't seem to stop her body from spreading and growing small unsightly bulges. As I looked at her, I noticed how puffy her face had become. Maybe the sheen of her sweat exaggerated the puffiness, I don't know, but it almost seemed as if a layer of stucco had been applied. I took a sip of my martini, wished I had put in a little less vermouth, and muttered something about how great she looked.

Cheryl put a sweaty hand on my drink hand—she was really sweating all over, dripping in it really—and twisted her body around to give me a slobbering kiss on my lips. All I could think of during it was how she smelled like sweat socks and how much that contrasted with Svetlana's sweet jasmine scent. Even when Svetlana was sweaty after making love, she still smelled of jasmine.

"How'd the meeting with the Corrections Board go?" she asked.

She had a sweaty hand resting on my arm. I took a sip of my martini, using that as an excuse to disengage myself from her, and then took a few steps away from her.

"I think I sold four of the five members. But even if I hadn't, it wouldn't matter. I've got the Governor and the State Senate behind me. The clinical trials are a go. Sometime in the next few weeks, the first human test subject will be connected."

I could tell Cheryl was both happy and a bit disappointed by the news. She knew once the clinical trials started she'd see even less of me. For a moment I felt sorry for her. And for a moment, I even felt a pang of regret about how I now felt about her. But the regret was fleeting.

Cheryl warmed up some dinner that she had prepared for me earlier. Later, when we were in bed she was all over me. I tried to pretend I was sleeping but she wouldn't give up and after a while I couldn't ignore her. I tried my hardest to think of Svetlana and somehow got through it.

The next morning, I received a call from Svetlana and we arranged to meet. When I saw her, her eyes and skin were flushed with excitement and it drove me crazy. It just made me feel weak in my knees. She gave me a long hard kiss, letting me taste her, letting me feel her warmth. Then she told me how we were going to get rid of my wife.

Her plan was for me to arrange a trip to Paris for me and my wife. I would explain to Cheryl that I wanted to squeeze the trip in before things got too crazy at work. We would first spend a long weekend at our summer home in the White Mountains and then fly to Paris. I knew Cheryl would be thrilled with the idea and I knew she'd tell her friends about it. At the last minute, while in the White Mountains, I would have to postpone my flight for a few days due to an emergency at work. I would insist that Cheryl still leave on her original flight and that I would catch up with her later. Of course I'd have to make sure she told her friends about the change in plans. Then I'd kill her and bury her. Svetlana would find a Russian look-alike for Cheryl. She wouldn't have to look exactly like my wife, just enough to match Cheryl's passport and for people on the flight to remember her. Later, she would disappear back to Russia. Svetlana would also arrange with her Russian contacts for a corpse to be found in a car crash along with Cheryl's passport and suitcase.

As Svetlana told me her plan, her voice came out in a breathless whisper. I touched her cheek and felt a hotness from her skin. She was burning. Before I knew it I had her in my arms and could feel her body tremble and push into mine. I told her we would do it. It seemed like an eternity before we separated. She told me she'd need a photo of Cheryl, and I told her there was one on my company's web site.

That night, I told Cheryl about our trip to Paris and she burst out crying. She gave me a flurry of wet kisses and then told me how happy she was. Later that night, I overheard her calling her friends, telling them about how we were going to spend the weekend at our home in the White Mountains and then fly to Paris.

The next day I got a call from Svetlana letting me know that the look-alike was en route from Moscow. We arranged the final details of where and when she would be waiting for me with Cheryl's look-alike. Then I hung up.

The rest of the week felt rather normal. I was surprised at how indifferent I was about what was going to happen. I was able to focus on work and really felt no nerves or anxiety. Thursday before leaving I modified a software module so that our weekend test would fail. I knew that sometime around Sunday morning I would get a panicked call from my assistant, Hanson.

Friday morning, Cheryl and I headed off to the White Mountains. It was a beautiful fall day and Cheryl could barely contain her happiness. I felt oddly at peace. The whole ride up Cheryl rested against me.

The weekend went according to plan. Sunday morning I got a frantic phone call from Hanson that the weekend test had failed. I told Cheryl that I would have to book myself a later flight. I could tell she was disappointed, and she started to argue that she would postpone her flight so she could be with me, but I insisted that she fly out Sunday night as planned. I'd rather have her enjoying herself in Paris than sitting around waiting for me to fix a critical software bug. In the end she relented.

I had a few mildly anxious hours waiting for her to relay the bad news to her friends, but by four o'clock I heard her on the phone. After she put the phone back down, I walked over to her and gave her a kiss. My hands were resting on her shoulders and slid slowly up to her neck. Before she realized what was happening, I was choking the life out of her. I just stared at her indifferently and kept squeezing, putting all my muscle into it. There was something about the look in her eyes that got to me, though. And there was something about how blood-red her lips became, and her tongue, the way it just sort of thickened as it pushed through those lips. Something oddly familiar about it all....

She fought feebly for a few moments and then her arms went limp. After it was done, a wave of nausea rolled over me. My knees buckled and I collapsed to the ground. It was a long while before I could push myself back to my feet and dig her grave. Afterwards, I went back to the house and had a few drinks to steady myself. Then I took a shower, put on some clean clothes, and got in the car to meet Svetlana.

I couldn't stop thinking about Cheryl—about the way she looked when I had choked the life out of her. I just kept seeing her the way she was during those last few moments: her eyes wide open, bulging, her tongue thickening as it pushed its way through blood-red lips. And those wide-open eyes, Jesus, staring at me with nothing but sadness. There was no fear or hatred in those eyes, only sadness. Then the sadness just sort of dried up and there was nothing left in them. After a while it was like looking into empty glass.

I pulled over to the side of the road and stopped the car. I had to get that image out of my head. I squeezed my eyes shut and tried to concentrate, tried to stop that image from playing through my mind. But I couldn't. It was like a movie that was wrapped around in a loop, playing over and over again. With a start, I realized I had seen it before, maybe hundreds of times, maybe thousands.

The air became still. It was so damn quiet. I couldn't hear anything, not even my own heartbeat. I realized why the scene of Cheryl being choked to death seemed so damn familiar. It all finally hit me. I wasn't Graham Winston.

As I sat there, I could remember every detail about my life with Cheryl. I could remember us meeting when I was twenty-two and she was twenty-nine. I remembered how beautiful she was then. I remembered how much she loved me almost from the start. I could see the years of us together and all the things she did to care for me and support me. I felt ashamed thinking about the last few years, and about all the little things I had said to her, all the snide comments, the innuendos. There was no wonder Cheryl was always running on her treadmill and doing aerobics. Anything to try to keep her body trim for me—to try to keep me from growing bored with her. I remembered other things. Really horrible things, things that I just wouldn't want to admit to. The one thing I couldn't remember, though, was her supporting me through medical school. Because I never went to medical school. And I sure as hell never went to engineering school. I had no memories growing up as Graham Winston.

I remembered that my real name was Bob Coggins. That I had bought a chain of supermarkets in the Denver area with Cheryl's money. I remembered killing Cheryl at our summer home near Estes Park, not the White Mountains.

As I sat there other memories came rushing forward. They were memories of events that hadn't happened yet but were going to happen. I remembered the phone call I received from France notifying me about Cheryl's death. And I remembered how Svetlana and I waited a year after that before getting married. And then how she betrayed me only a few days later. She had called the police, claiming that I had bragged to her about murdering Cheryl. With Svetlana's help they were able to dig up Cheryl's body. There wasn't much I could say or do after that. There was really no evidence to implicate Svetlana. She had been careful to make sure that there was no evidence.

They charged me with first degree murder. The trial was quick and the jury took less than an hour to convict me. Svetlana ended up with the millions that Cheryl had left me, and I was sentenced to life without the possibility of parole.

I remember being taken to prison, or at least what had become prison. It was really nothing but a large warehouse filled with coffin-sized containers. They had me drugged at this point, so I couldn't really do much of anything but look around. But I remember those containers, one stacked on top of the next. There must have been tens of thousands of them in that room. They placed me in one of them and attached electrodes all over my body. Then they stuck intravenous tubes in my arm and attached a catheter. And then they drilled those holes in my skull.

I sat in the car with my eyes shut, trying to concentrate, fishing for more memories, but that was all there was. And I realized I was now living a simulation. I guess either because of ego, or because Graham Winston had a hell of a sense of humor, he had developed a simulated script of his own life. So all I was doing now was living his script. Except there was a flaw in the system. Instead of simply re-enacting the script, my old memories were bubbling through and changing it. The script had been perverted and merged with my own past.

The image of Cheryl dying was so damn vivid. Probably every simulated life I lived got corrupted with memories of Cheryl and Svetlana. Probably every single one ended with me choking the life out of my wife. And I knew every future one was also going to end that way. I knew there was no escape from it.

I looked down at my hands and watched as I clenched and unclenched my fingers. I didn't know how much time was left before I'd be switched into a new simulated life, but I hoped I had at least enough time to meet up with Svetlana. I knew it wouldn't do any good, I knew what I was living now wasn't real, but I wanted Svetlana to go through once what Cheryl had gone through all those countless number of times.

I started the car up and pulled it back onto the road. Svetlana was waiting down the road for me. With a little bit of luck I'd meet up with her. With just a little bit of luck.

THE RAVINE
Steve Weddle

When I came around the corner into his back yard, he had his glasses in his hands, rubbing the lenses with a blue bandana.

I cleared my throat, and he looked up. We were about twenty feet apart.

"The fuck you want, boy?" he said, standing up and grabbing his shotgun from the table. He was more than twice my age, in his mid-60s, I'd guess. Thin, rough at the edges. And there were plenty of edges to the guy. Old snakeskin boots. Jeans. Brown flannel shirt hanging out of his pants.

The sun was coming up over the treeline, past the acre-long field behind his house. Midmorning. About this time of year.

"Mr. Greer, my name's Roy Alison." I pulled some papers out of my back pocket.

"I know who you are, shitface." He raised the barrels of the shotgun to my face. "Everybody knows who you are. You're the piece of shit who killed his parents."

That stopped me. I guess I'll never get used to that. Never get away from it. Which is fine. I did kill my parents. But it wasn't my fault. And it was ten years ago.

I was sixteen. Sitting in my room. Not bothering anyone. Put on some Blue Oyster Cult. Dropped a couple tabs of pumpkinhead. An hour later my mom busted into my room. My dad had been having kidney trouble a while and had passed out. She didn't want to wait for an ambulance because we were out in the country. And she hated ambulances. Said they were a rip-off. So she loaded my dad into the backseat of the Impala and I was supposed to drive them to the ER. Yeah. Funny story. I thought the oncoming headlights were calling to me. Calling me home. So we all made it to the ER in ambulances. Of course, my mom and dad didn't need ambulances by the time they got there.

I was locked up for a while. Full of the empty darkness, if that makes sense to you. The sort of nothing that fills up everything. Spent the whole time running down the "what if" crap to fill up my soul. What if I hadn't dropped then? What if they'd buckled up? What if this and that? You can go crazy with that. And maybe I did. And maybe when I got out and was all of a sudden an adult and alone, yeah, maybe I did some things I shouldn't have. And maybe those were my fault. But that's the old me. That's not who I am now.

Yeah, I'd had problems. But that was then. All I wanted in my new life was no trouble.

Now I'm working for Caldwell Parish, driving around handing out paperwork, trying to live whatever a normal life is when you're someone with my record, my past. As if anyone is normal.

"I'm here for the parish, Mr. Greer." I held the paperwork out for him. "I need to talk to you about your outbuildings. They're not up to code."

He set the gun down on the table and sat back down in his chair, pulled a Buck knife from his shirt pocket and starting cutting chunks out of an apple.

He had the same kind of metal lawn chairs we'd had at our house. Light green. Kind of a clam shell. Iron bars folded underneath so you could rock back and forth, humming a little something to make the pain go away.

"How long you been working for the government?" he asked me.

"Started at the building office last week," I said, still a little nervous looking at the gun, the violence within reach. I had three more visits to make before lunch, so I couldn't waste the whole day here. And I had to get back for a birthday party at the office. I hadn't been a free man for long and this job was the biggest piece of normal I had. My big hope for getting back on track, for keeping the darkness away. "I just need to give you a copy of this report and schedule a time for you to come by the office, Mr. Greer."

"Sit down, son."

"Thank you for the invite, sir, but I need to get moving."

He reached for the gun, then turned it on me, again. "Maybe my polite tone confused you, asshole. Sit the fuck down. I wasn't asking."

I sat down.

Mr. Greer set the shotgun in his lap, then ate an apple piece from his blade.

"Wanna tell me how you ended up here?" he asked.

I looked down at the paper, made like I was reading something. "We got a call. Tip. Said you were breaking the zoning ordinance."

He shook his head, spit out part of the apple. "Not that, you dipshit. I know that. I made the call. I mean how you got here." He emphasized the last word, looked around the property.

He made the call? Why would he make the call? "I'm sorry, Mr. Greer. I don't understand."

"Here. How did you end up here. Where you are now?"

Ten seconds or so went by. Felt like longer. I wasn't sure what he was talking about, but figured I had to say something. "Google Maps. Took 577 to a CCC road. Down that a ways until I hit what I guess was a logging road. You're all alone back here."

"Yeah. I'm all alone." He folded his knife back into his shirt pocket and stood up. He looked up to his outbuildings at the back of his property. "'We live as we dream—alone.' That's from a book, son." He grabbed the shotgun and walked over to me. When I started to stand he put the barrels of the gun against my chest. "I was asking how you got here. Walking around like a free man. After you killed your parents that night. After you killed my daughter."

My arms were at my side and I wasn't even close to ready when the butt of gun hit my jaw and knocked me cold.

I'd given up drinking a few years ago. Drugs a year before that when I was back behind bars. And I tried not to cuss. Tried not to speed. Tried to live a good life now. Make up for what I'd done.

"No reason you should know me," Mr. Greer was saying. Mid-conversation. Like he'd been talking for a while. But I was just coming back around. I rubbed my jaw where he'd hit me. Scratched through my beard. Something was flaking there. Blood. Dirt. I blinked. Rubbed my eyes with my hands, which were tied together. "She kept saying how it was so sad, such darkness." He was running a sharpening wheel, sparks flying off the knife blade. I looked out through the windows but only saw sky. I was pretty sure we were in one of the outbuildings I'd come to complain about. Yeah. Another funny story. "You know anything about darkness, shithead?"

Yeah. I had some ideas. Some ideas I tried to stay away from.

"I didn't kill your daughter."

"The hell you didn't," he said. "You kill everything, don't you? People like you? You're a curse. A blight. A bringer of darkness."

For what must have been the twentieth time in the past however long I'd been at his place, I had no idea what he was talking about. "I didn't kill your daughter."

Looking through the windows, I could see the sun at the top of the sky. Guess I'd been out a little while, but not too long.

He stopped sharpening the knife and turned around to face me. "Maybe you should stop talking about my daughter right about now."

I'd wanted this job. I'd wanted to work outside. Drive around, listening to Drive-By Truckers, Heads of State, Little Feat, all windows-down and fields full of sunshine. Sounds like a great day, backroads in the Louisiana country, grabbing a sandwich at the gas station, being your own boss in a sense. Staying away from trouble. Living a normal life.

Yeah, I'd done things I wasn't proud of. The accident with my parents. A few other things that ended up with people dying. Put a man down in self-defense. Finished a fight I hadn't started. The neck is a fragile twig. But I'd served my time for some of that and that was behind me. Someone else's life. Not who I'd wanted to be, who I'd become. I knew that if I lived clean from here on out, woke up every morning in the light, things would be fine. I was starting from scratch. Only this point on counts. A good job. Co-workers. Friends. The sunlight. The glare from the road. The summer brightness of things not yet destroyed.

He had me up, blade at the back of my neck, pushing me out the door to the edge of ravine behind his field. He hit me in the shoulder with the hilt of the knife, and I dropped to my knees.

"My girl was impressionable," he said. "Young. Innocent." He sounded like he was going to cry, sniffling a little. But he didn't. Just stood there looking out at the ravine. "What you did to your parents sent her over the edge. She was young. Troubled. Artistic. Like her mother." He pointed the knife at one of the other sheds. Another cinderblock box that brought me out here in the first place. I was sluggish from the head shots, but focused where he pointed.

"That one there," he said, "with the lock on the door. Full of her paintings." I wasn't talking, so he kept on. "She did thirty-seven paintings of you and your mommy and daddy. The car crash. Dark. Locked herself in her room and painted. And screamed and cried. And painted. All 'cause of you and your goddamned fool life. Broke her soul."

"I didn't kill your daughter."

"Damn sure did." He walked to the edge of the ravine and looked down. "She couldn't take it. The emptiness. The darkness. Whatever it is these kids feel. I just tried to get her through it after her mother died. Just hoping she'd be OK. Hope." He spit. "Damn hope."

"I'm sorry about your daughter, but I didn't kill her. I've done a lot of bad things, but I didn't kill her." Back here was dark, muddy, seeping through the knees of my pants.

"I been watching you. Waiting for you. Thought I was gonna have to come after you. Then I hear you're working for the parish now that you're a free man. Made a call. And here you are. Come to deliver paperwork. Just like the social services people when they took Lily away. They take your daughter and give you forms. Then they come back and tell you she ate a bottle of pills. And then there's all that other paperwork to bury her." He walked up to me, put the point of the knife to my neck. "You killed her. Sent her over the edge."

I tried to hold my head still as I talked. "Not my fault."

I could carry the blame for a lot of stuff. But not this. All I wanted was a new start. Fresh on the job. A blank slate. Not knowing someone was waiting for me. Waiting for me to start my new life. Holding on to something I'd let go. Something not my fault. Waiting to bring trouble back into it. He put the heel of his boot into my chest, my breath falling in sputters on the ground. "You took my daughter from me, you piece of shit. After all those years. The past is the past. But you never get out of it. You can let it go all you want, boy, but it ain't up to you. It don't let go of you."

I thought he was talking about me. What I'd done. My parents. The time I'd spent in juvie. The week I was free before I'd been pushed around enough and went out looking for a fight and found it. The year and a half I went inside for the stabbing. Trouble inside. More trouble outside.

I was face-down on the ground, trying to push myself up. "Trouble's a dog, son. A goddamned fucking dog. It gets your scent and hunts you down." I thought he was talking about me.

He wasn't.

"Yeah, I did some shit I ain't proud of. Some 'fucked-up, repugnant shit.' That's from a movie, son." I was still struggling to get up, and he kicked my arms out from under me. I fell back into the dirt, hit the side of my head on a rock, something hidden just below the dark ground. "I thought I was clear. That I'd left it behind. Then Claudia, that's my wife, she gets sick and leaves. Then Lily gets depressed because of your stupid shit. Says there ain't no point anymore." He looked at the buildings that held her paintings. "She got artistic. Woman at her school said that was good. An outlet." He spit. "Outlet, my ass."

He walked over to me. He was close enough that I could snap his neck, but I was passed that. I was good now. I could get through this without violence. Let him talk. Let him free himself. Let him come through the pain, the broken glass in the belly like I had. Just let him talk.

"You understand what I'm saying to you?" He leaned into my ear. "Can you hear me?"

He turned his back on me, but I didn't have the strength to get up. My eye was covered in dirt and blood. My head was liquid, moving around, looking for balance.

Five years ago, I could have taken out his knee in a couple of seconds, sent an elbow into his Adam's apple. Five years ago, that is what I did. What sent me back inside. I didn't want to go back inside. And I didn't want that, that darkness he was talking about, back inside of me. If you've never felt it, then you don't know what I'm talking about. The emptiness. The darkness that fills in from the edges. You think you can hold it back, but it seeps through like mud through door cracks.

He turned around to look at me. Take the knife, then I could settle him down. Talk to him. I didn't want to have to break him. I didn't want that life back.

"Claudia gone. Lily gone. All payback, son. For the shit I'd done when I was a young man." He shook his head. "It comes after you. Takes a while, but it finds you." He kneeled down near my face. "Like I found you. And that's what I'm gonna do. You see, some people get bit by a dog and they get scared of dogs. They run and hide. Wet their pants when a dog barks." He spat. "And some people, well, son, some people get mad at the fucking dog. Some people get real fuckin' pissed at the dog. And some people find that dog and carve a fuckin' hole in that piece of shit's head to clean out the darkness."

He aimed the knife at me, reached back into his belt for a pistol in the other hand. "You're not the first piece of shit I've had to settle a score with." He looked at me, then down to bottom of the ravine. "You know how many bodies they've found down there?"

I didn't say anything, kept my eyes on his. Tried to fight the desire to send my head into his jaw.

He said it again. "You know how many bodies they've found down there?" He leaned down into my face. "Not a goddamned one."

I stood up, heart beating, filling my ears with thumps and blood. I was good now. The pressure coming back, again. I'd given up drugs. Pressing against the inside of my skull. I didn't even cuss anymore. Pushing and pulling. Filling me. I could feel the blood moving out from my chest into my arms, my thighs. "I didn't kill your daughter."

My hands were still tied, which was fine. I didn't need much freedom anymore.

I got back to the office in time for lunch. A birthday cake was there for Shirley. Her fortieth, so it was all black with balloons here and there in the office.

When I walked in through the side door, everyone stopped and looked up at me. The mud on my pants, dark stains on my arms. The painting I was holding. A ravine filled with darkness.

My boss, Jerry, stood up, walked towards me, and asked me if I'd had any problems that morning.

"Problems?" I asked. I shook my head, wiped my palms on my shirt. "Not a goddamned one."

THROUGH THE VALLEY OF THE SHADOW OF ROOSEVELT'S NOSE
Craig McDonald

This one was as bad as that other he'd put down.

That pious old bitty in Georgia who'd yapped her family right into an early grave.

She was a talker, okay. She said more than plenty, but didn't really say *anythin'* in the end. Mostly, she seemed in love with the sound of her own shrill voice.

This one, the tall, handsome man with the graying brown hair and pale blue eyes, seemed even more chatty. It was almost like the man was enjoying their dialogue. Like the fool didn't sense how this was bound to end.

Bobby was losing patience with the man, too, he could see. Bobby's finger softly rubbed the trigger of his automatic.

Just now, they learned the man was something more than a talker.

Other than a talker...maybe that was how to put it. *Cussed words*.

Either way. Hell, they was probably all the same thing in the end.

Anyway, the man was a writer...an author. A writer known,

or so Bobby said, as "the man who writes what he lives and lives what he writes." A man named Hector Lassiter.

This Lassiter wasn't alone. He had a woman with him. Pretty woman. More than pretty, most would likely say. But tarted up fetchin'. Perfumed and painted like some Whore of Babyl'n. And they had a kid with 'em, too: a tow-headed boy-child of no more than seven. The boy, Tommy Lee, had this thick cowlick up front that would not be tamed. Wide, scared eyes on the boy. So they'd take care of that tyke first, as was custom. Bobby would see to that, of course. Get it over fast-like for the child. They always put down the youngest ones first. The so-called "innocent."

Then it would be the woman's turn.

The man would be the last to go.

Let him see it all, first. Take the challenge out of those eyes.

Though I walk through the valley of the shadow of death... I will fear...

Shaking his head, snorting softly, the killer looked down the barrel of his gun at the man in his sights. He said to the writer, "An author, eh? And I thought *I* was a misfit. Y'all just an artsy coward. A fool rewritin' the world 'cause he's got no stomach for this one. Mister, I don't see need during these mean times for any more writers. Not no need since the prophets. And ain't them prophets proven themselves to be sorry liars anyhow? It's a mean old world. A good man is hard to find, and anyway, what would you do with one if you did find him?"

The killer cocked the hammer back on his revolver. "And I can tell you just this much for certain, sir. This is one part of your life you will *not* be writin' about. Not never. Reckon you just had the bad luck to wander into my story." He looked at the writer's natty sports jacket and said, "Could use me a new coat."

With two fingers, the killer pushed his silver-rimmed glasses back up his nose. "Ain't no pleasure in this, mister, not for me, despite what you might be thinkin'. But you will all be at peace."

Glancing up at the granite heads of the presidents staring sightlessly forward into the void, he said, "Like the Lord, they are. Right there and yet not there 't'all."

He spat into the dust, said, "Look at them, lookin' and not

seein'. Starin' off to where it don't none matter." He shook his head and said, "Ain't no carin' in this world."

It had started as a simple film gig: Hector was to come up with some suspense stuff for a thriller that Alfred Hitchcock was just beginning to fiddle with.

Hitch had this notion of setting a climactic chase scene across the faces of Mount Rushmore. He'd paid Hector, novelist and sometimes screenwriter, to fly out to South Dakota and wander around the national monument. See what that soaring scenery might stir in the crime novelist.

Hector had taken up with this local woman from the F. O'Connor ("The *F* is for *Friendly*!") car rental agency. She was a comely divorcée named Emmylou Thorp; all legs and pouty lips. At first the woman had resisted: "You have a reputation, Mr. Lassiter. A kind of high-tone liver, I hear tell. An adventurer and a ladies' man. A scrapper. A hard man."

Hector had smiled and said, "Don't believe all that loose and low talk, darlin'. That's just to sell books and movie tickets. I'm gentle as a kitten."

He'd taken Emmylou and her son, Tommy Lee, out for a picnic around the monument, aimed to squeeze in a little film scouting expedition.

Down here in the basin—the scrublands of the Black Hills—in the shadow of all the massive heads, they had run afoul of this bespectacled killer and his bloodthirsty friend, Bobby.

The writer's rental car's radiator had taken a stone along the unpaved road snaking below the monument. As Hector was standing there, staring at the smoke roiling from under the hood, an old black heap that looked like a hearse had rolled up and two men had climbed out. One, somber and bespectacled, said, "Lend a hand, mister?"

Hector had heard radio reports about the men. He'd heard they were believed to be in the area. He'd seen some newsreel footage and read the newspaper reports of their cross-country killings.

Sure: Hector knew this man and his partner's fearsome reputations well enough and he'd made them *like that*.

But Hector had also known enough not to show any signs of having recognized them. He'd played it casual. Or so he thought.

Somehow, the man with the glasses and gray hair had in some way correctly intuited that Hector knew *exactly* who he was.

As they stood there, considering one another with dawning realization of recognition, a meadowlark trilled. The shadow of a still-winged, high-gliding turkey vulture swept silently over them.

The stranger pulled his revolver, pointed it at Hector's face and said, "This *is* unfortunate."

They were faced off now in the shadows of those giant heads; standing in the dust, staring at one another.

Low and steady voiced, Hector said, "Get in your car and drive off *now*. Not as if I can chase you or go phone ahead to the police with my car broken down as it is. You'll have more than a fair head start. And you won't have any more murders stacked against you in court."

The killer shook his head and said, "Ain't no sense in any of that. You can't know the future any more than me, mister. We've gone this long without no police catchin' us. I reckon we can go on for as long as there is left us, and that might just be plenty." He shook his head and said, "And you're in no spot to be sendin' us along and leavin' you here. That's not our way. If you know anythin' about me, and I suspicion you do, then you know that."

Hector wet his lips, looked around, stared a moment up at Teddy Roosevelt. Well, looked up Teddy's nose, really. The writer didn't fear much for himself, not yet. But the woman and the boy—the boy, particularly—well, they shouldn't have to feel this flavor of fear. Shouldn't have to see what was likely to come.

"You boys really best be movin' on," Hector said. "This road's not lightly traveled by all accounts. Someone's apt to happen by and soon."

"We was on this path a long ways and didn't see more than y'all," the killer said. He pointed at the dusty road in the other direction and said, "Don't see any tracks headed out that way you all were goin', neither. I'd say we are plenty alone." He rubbed his jaw, said, "We're always alone, even in company."

Hector frowned: Tommy Lee was shaking now, his teeth chattering despite the heat. The boy's knees were knocking. This needed to be wrapped up, pronto.

Hector said, "Just shut your goddamn mouth, pal. You're nothin' more than a blood-simple jackal. Your buddy here more so, maybe. But you're just as low and mean and bad as that psycho you truck with."

A little flare there in the killer's eyes. Much more in Bobby's.

The one with glasses, the leader, said, "Can't much argue with you about Bobby here. He can be a handful, and he does like the work too much. Takes pleasure in it. But there ain't no real pleasure in life. That's what makes me different."

"That's what makes you more pathetic—more the monster," Hector said. "Your buddy here has at least found his sorry love. He's bloodthirsty. You are, too, but you pretend not to be. That's what makes you the lower creature on the totem pole."

Bobby convulsed into this donkey bray of a laugh and said, "Thet's perfect, mister! Thet's *ex*actly right! He kills like me but salves his conscience by saying it ain't no pleasure! Hell, way I see it, he's just trying to keep options open in case he's got it wrong and he *does* have to face the judgment."

Hector said, "Didn't there used to be three of you?"

The one called Bobby said, "There was a misunderstandin'." He flashed an accusing glare at the bespectacled, older man. "Guess it's true what they say. Never go jawin' 'bout politics or religion." A beat, then: "'Specially not religion, eh, Boss? One cross word and Boss here put down poor Hi like Hi was some rabid cur."

So, the man with glasses had a temper on him. Hector smiled: *Good*. And so much for honor among thieves...or killers. Hector said, "Best close your eyes, Tommy Lee...Emmylou, you too."

The gray-haired man swiveled his gun at Bobby's head. "You keep them eyes open," he said to Emmylou and her son. "And *you*, Bobby Lee, you commence to apologizin', and askin' *me* for forgiveness, *right now*. Soon as you do that, Bobby, then you can walk them two into the woods a ways and take care of business."

Bobby said, "You turn thet goddamn gun away from me! You've got no right in hell to—"

"Have me *every* right," the gray-haired killer said, "Got me every right 'xactly 'cause there is no rights in this world. In a world with no rules, falls to thems who can and thems who'd dare to make the new ones. To... restore the balance."

Hector said again, softly, "Close your eyes, Tommy and Emmy. Keep them tight-closed, 'til I say."

The killers were ignoring Hector, the woman and the child for the moment.

Bobby, clearly flustered now, said, "You cow-simple son of a bitch! You sorry-ass—"

There was a crack and Bobby's right eye and most of his forehead dissolved into pink and white spray. Even as Bobby swayed, already dead on his feet, the gray-haired killer was swiveling his gun back toward the writer, aiming to get Lassiter back in his sights.

There was another crack, and the killer's gun hand was enveloped in another spray of blood and bone chips. The killer's revolver tumbled to the dust.

Uncomprehending, the gray-haired killer stared at his ruined hand. All but the pinky finger were severed to bleeding stumps.

The man, Lassiter—this *writer*—had an old Peacemaker pointed at the killer's head. The wicked-long antique Colt looked like a museum piece.

The writer's pale blue eyes were mocking now. He said, "Figure this is the price you pay for not bein' a reader. That silly phrase, 'the man who lives what he writes and writes what he lives,' for instance. I don't have much patience for it. But I suppose there is a kernel of truth in there. Enough so that had you ever read a story or book of mine, you'd have known to frisk me."

Hector checked to see the woman and the child still had their eyes tightly shut. He said, "Keep those peepers closed, you two, but don't worry. I've got the gun, now. You're safe."

Emmylou said, softly, "Thank God!"

It came as a snarl: "Ain't no God!" The killer was trying to wrap his shirttails around his bleeding hand.

"Don't bother with that," Hector said. "You're not going to bleed to death. Not from the hand. Use that good paw to get a hold of old Bobby's belt. You're going to drag what's left of him into that glade, yonder, where you meant him to take mine."

Huffing, struggling to drag his dead partner into the trees, the killer said, "This is no ways right. My story, it weren't never meant to end. Not this way."

Following behind, his Colt trained at the killer's head, Hector said, "These things are a matter of perspective. Sometimes, I think the wrong point of view makes for much of this world's misery. Take you for instance."

They reached the copse of pine trees, out of sight of the woman and her child.

His teeth chattering, his knees threatening to fail him, the killer said, "I don't understan'."

Hector shrugged. "*Your story*. You said your story isn't meant to end this way. That's your whole problem—one of perspective. Point of view. Well, this isn't your story. It never was. Way I see it, you stumbled into *my story*," Hector said.

The killer fell to his knees, like he might beg or pray for mercy. He said, "Mister, you don't believe in anything any more than I do, I can tell. You're no different than me. Ain't no God, and you know it. You're—"

"I am different than you," Hector said. "Fella said, if you gaze into the abyss, the abyss also gazes into you. Well, you and me, we maybe looked into that same black hole. Difference between us is, you flinched."

Emmylou heard the single gunshot.

She grabbed Tommy Lee and hid among the trees on the other side of the road, terrified something had gone wrong.

The writer, this Hector Lassiter, wandered out from among the distant pines. He was carrying the Colt in his right hand.

Emmylou ran to meet him, hugged Hector hard. She said, "It's over?"

The writer smiled. "It's over."

She held him close, said softly in his ear, "A hard man is good to find."

LAUGHING AT DEAD MEN
Keith Rawson

When I was twelve, my brother Sam found a body. Despite the fact we grew up in Gary, Indiana, little kids finding a corpse wasn't a normal occurrence. Usually the goombahs who'd make ditch runs in from Chicago were pretty careful. Most guys who used our slum of a city as their personal graveyard took the time to dig a hole, spread lye, and push black earth back on top.

The sloppier guys would take their fly magnets to the county dump, douse it with gasoline, and throw it on top of a burning pile of tires. You knew you were dealing with amateurs when a citizen or the cops made the discovery.

The dead guy Sam found was an obvious local. Black kid, early twenties, double tap to his chest, one to his throat...the guys who did him were cruel motherfuckers who left him out in the cold to bleed out and freeze to the ground in a puddle of his own blood and body fluids. When Sam found him, he came bursting into my room, bundled from head to toe in his snow gear, shaking me awake from a mid-afternoon nap.

"Get up, fuckface, I've got something to show you." I hated Sam growing up (and I'm still not a fan, the guy's a born asshole) because he spent ninety percent of his day thinking up creative ways to beat the shit out of me. I'd gotten to the point of jumping to action anytime the big retard said boo to avoid taking a slap or punch (it didn't work, like I said: asshole) and seeing that he was in his snow gear, I immediately started crawling into my big brother cast-offs and tromped off out the front of my mom's old single-wide.

The body was a mile or two walk from our place, through the weeds and the garbage people were too lazy or poor to haul to the dump. The corpse was flat on its back just past a cluster of burnt-out refrigerators. The cold and rigor had twisted the kid's limbs; his hands like claws, his long fingers digging into the frozen ground; his legs bent at the knees, spread like a woman trying to push out a newborn. His neck was cocked to the right and his thick lips had pulled away from his teeth, locking them in a permanent sneer, like a blood-caked black Elvis. At first, I stared down at him, bug-eyed, my breath chugging out of my lungs in short, sharp gasps; my stomach churned, bile crawling up my throat, burning.

Then Sam threw a rock at the guy; it hit him square in the teeth.

His front teeth and left incisor shattered.

That one rock opened the flood gate and instead of puking, I started laughing.

Sam chucked another one, not so lucky with his second shot; the stone glanced off the dead boy's cheek bone and opened a bloodless gash.

We spent the next two hours pummeling the body with rocks, stomping his legs and arms trying to get them to lie flat, poking at the gassy muscles with sticks, and we laughed the entire time, like two freaks jacked on weed and tequila; we laughed so much my stomach hurt and hitched from the strain.

That day was my best memory of Sam when I was a kid. Hell, it was my best memory of childhood, period.

I never thought I'd be one of those dead guys dumped out in the middle of nowhere that little kids stumbled across. With my choice of profession, I knew it was a possibility that somebody would get pissed enough at me to put a bullet in my head, but you know how it is when you're 6'3" of gym-worked muscle and know how to throw it around, plus you carry enough hardware to take out a third world country. I walked through this world feeling pretty much invincible. Shit, some days I felt downright immortal.

But then you start talking shit about the wrong people, maybe you pocket a little kickback cash, a little dope...you get the picture. My mistake was that I got a little lippy with my boss—who at the time was on a two week bender consisting of methamphetamines, coke, and countless bottles of Johnnie Walker Black Label—which pissed him off enough to send me out into the desert for a product pick-up with one of his dumbass hillbilly cousins. I should have known what was going on; my pick-ups were typically within city limits and solo drives.

I guess I was lucky that I got teamed up with Pervus, or Jim Bob, or whatever the little cracker's name was. The guy was so cockeyed from too many generations of inbreeding that his shot glanced off the side of my skull and only managed to take off my right ear. It was a shitload of blood and the slug knocked me cold, but it was enough to convince him that he'd gotten the job done proper. Now, if it had been me doing the shooting, I would've double-tapped myself, especially with such a small caliber weapon as the guy had decided to use on my thick skull, which I guess was lucky for me?

I came to a few hours or days or whatever later. My body felt beat to shit, the ringing in my head like a version of the tone the emergency broadcast people use at three o'clock in the morning amplified by a thousand. The gaping red hole that was my ear burned, and my body felt like it had been pelted with a hundred rocks. What hurt the most was my left eye. I was originally thinking the little cracker had pulled some kind of crazy Oswald magic bullet bullshit and had somehow managed to take out my eye along with my ear. The only thing was even though my body was a constant throbbing ache, the pain in my eye kept getting worse, as if something was jabbing into the socket.

I finally worked up enough strength to open my eyes and discovered the reason why my eye felt like it was being poked with a sharp stick.

Because it *was* being poked with a stick.

I squinted through the pain and saw them. Three little kids, dirty faced and slack-jawed, staring down at me like I was a ghost, which, I suppose in their eyes, I was. Looking at the three of them, raw rage welled up in me and I made a grab at the one standing closest to me. The three of them jumped in unison, emitting panicked squeals. I clambered to my feet, my muscles rusty iron hinges. The three kids were like statues, their eyes growing bigger and more disbelieving with each pained movement. I was a zombie getting ready to eat their brains…which wasn't all that far from the truth. I made another grab for them and that got their asses in gear. The three of them bolted and I somehow willed my body after them.

The little fuckers were quick, but I kept a step behind them even though it felt like I was missing half my head. They poured on the speed, their feet kicking up clouds of yellow dust, and I made one final grab and managed to twist my fingers into the straps of the slowest kid's backpack. I pulled and the kid started speaking in tongues and slipped his arms out from under the straps. I stumbled, clutching the backpack to my chest as I did a header into the dirt.

I passed out again after my little impromptu jog, waking up some time near dusk, and shambled towards the flitting headlights of the distant freeway. It was slow going, I remember passing out a couple of times before finally hitting the blacktop and waving down a trucker. When I swung up into the cab, the trucker nearly vomited in his lap either from the sight or smell of me and he wouldn't shut up about getting me to a hospital. It took a swift, hard slap to his fat face to convince him I didn't need a hospital and that he would need one if he didn't drop me off at the closest motel.

I holed up, I licked my wounds.

The motel the trucker dropped me off at was a dilapidated Bates-style squat just outside Buckeye, AZ, run by a tweeker named Jed. When I walked into the office at 1 a.m. missing half my head, good old Jed didn't blink twice when I forked over a hundred dollar bill. Thank God the boss's half-wit cousin didn't rob me after blowing off my ear. Once I was in my room, I stripped, boiled myself in the shower, and slept for 16 hours.

When I came to, my body was a sweat-soaked mass of fever, infection and stiff muscles. I dragged myself down to the office and bribed Jed with another Benjamin to head down to Wal-mart and grab me up some non-blood-drenched threads and an extra-large bottle of Advil. Once I made it back into my room, I hit the phone and started making calls to Phoenix. Despite its shitty, end-of-the-stick conclusion, my career had been a prosperous one. I had enough scratch laid away that I could disappear without my former employer finding out that I was still sucking down oxygen. First order of business was lick my wounds and track down some medical attention. I dialed a spaced-out quack who was in deep to me.

Despite being a degenerate dope fiend, the doc was a top-notch healer. He stitched up what was left of my ear, the same with my empty socket. By the time he left me, I was conked and half-crazed with fever, but I had enough dope to make me not care. I blanked in and out, sleeping uncomfortably, my awake hours bombed out of my gourd, watching bad daytime talk shows and stroking the backpack.

I focused more and more on the boys who'd found me out in the middle of the desert. Trying to recall their faces, attempting to burn their features into memory. Close to the end of my recovery, I finally decided to open the backpack and I found a name and address:

William Wilke
1256 Dowser St.,
Lot 23
Buckeye, AZ

Surprise, surprise, little Willie lived in a trailer park.

But then again, it seemed that the entire population of Buckeye, AZ, lived in some type of metal shack or other. Willie's trailer was a luxurious piece of engineering and if it hadn't been surrounded by a bevy of rusted-out, piece-of-shit single-wides, I would have never guessed the trailer was a trailer.

I rapped on the front door, stuffed my hands in my pockets and rocked on my heels. It was a Saturday, so I knew somebody would be home. A squat, plug ugly fatty with fire engine red hair answered the knock.

"Can I help you?" she drawled in some overdone, pseudo-Southern accent.

"Yes, ma'am. I was wondering if Willie was home?"

"Well—" She turned her head and I spotted the boy standing a few feet behind her. His eyes went wide, his mouth dropped open. Yeah, he remembered me, he remembered the boogie man.

I squared myself and planted a solid right to Willie's mom's teeth. The shot dropped her flat on her back and I charged in, leaping over her prone body. Willie tried making a run for it, but a healthy me is pro linebacker fast. I tackled him around the waist and we shattered the glass coffee table.

I turned him over onto his back, mounted his chest and gave little Willie a couple of sharp jabs. Not enough force to knock him out, but enough to break skin with my knuckles. His eyes were still big and disbelieving. I wrapped the fingers of my right hand around Willie's throat, squeezed just enough to make sure he knew I meant business and asked:

"Which of you little shitheels found the body?"

It's surprising what will keep you breathing. What will get you out bed each morning instead of begging for the big black to come swooping down. For me, vengeance is the shit. It wasn't revenge against my former employer that kept me rolling. My boss plugging me was business, it was dollars and cents, I got that, I understood *that*. What I didn't get was three little kids defiling a dead man, making even more of a joke out of him than death already has. As I healed and plotted finding the boys, I cursed myself, shamed myself because I'd done the same thing to the kid Sam had found all those years ago.

I guess we can call what the boys did to me *Karma* with a capital K.

Difference being I lived and could teach the boys a lesson before they grew big and strong and their transgressions would be revisited like they were visited upon me.

Good old Willie was quick to give up names. Michael Stuart and Chad Durante. Durante was the one who found me and went running for his buddies. I decided to save him for last and went after Michael.

Little Mikey was big time white trash. He lived with his dad a couple of miles down the road from Willie. Mikey's place was a sagging single-wide. I found Mikey and his dad out front of their place, playing plinko with pellet guns and empty Miller High Life bottles. Mikey glimpsed me and tried siccing his dad on me. Dad came at me with drunken bravado and I broke his arm in three places for the effort. I snarled at Mikey and said, "This is what you get, kid, your dad's gonna take your licks for you." I took a cinder block to Dad's left leg and watched him glaze over with pain.

I decided to stalk Chad. Chad was a rung above Mikey. Still lived in a single-wide, but well maintained, flower beds out front, a fairly new Toyota four-door parked under the carport, and a not all that bad looking forty-something bottled redhead of a mom paying the bills. My head sparked big ideas and slow revenge.

I rented a nondescript Chevy to play super spy on Chad's mommy. She was easy to track, suburbanites are all about routine. Chad's mommy was up at six, out the door with junior by 6:45, dumped him at before-school care at 7:00 and at her job at the nuclear power plant by 7:30. I didn't know how her work day went because you needed a pass to make it through the front gate. She was done at 4 and stopped at a local bar, called Duke's, a couple miles down the road from the plant. She drank with a group of five male co-workers. All of them thought she was hot shit. Radioactive hot, which she was. Roomy around the hips, nice pair of tits, perky ass. Straight up Mother I'd Like To Fuck. After drinks, she'd pick up Chad from after-school care, home for dinner, homework, bedtime for the boy at 8:00 and then 45 minutes on the treadmill for herself, then bed.

Friday nights were her big night out. Instead of heading home from afterschool care, she dumped Chad at the grandparents, drove home, whored herself up in too-tight western gear and headed back out to Duke's to drink with the same cronies. You could tell she wasn't boning any of her buddies. Clearly, they all wished they were putting it to her, but she had her eye on any piece of strange that *wasn't* one of her co-workers.

I fit the bill perfectly.

True, my features were a little bit on the fucked up side, but I've always kept myself in shape and chicks like Chad's mom dig scars and dangerous-looking strangers with scars and an eye patch. I didn't even have to make the approach. She accidently/on purpose bumped into me, spilling my piss yellow tap beer. She bought me another one, introduced herself as Tami.

When closing time hit, she was all over me, and I drove her over to my flop.

It's been two weeks now. By day three of week one, Tami had me spending the night. Chad went bug-eyed when he saw me. He didn't say a word and he trembled when we shook hands. Afterward, I rubbed my eye patch, gave him a wink and grin, letting him know:

I *know* you were the one holding the stick.

Tami's got a sweet set-up, she keeps her shack tidy, but the walls are paper thin and Chad's bedroom is right next door to Tami's. I can hear him whimper every time I'm stovepiping Tami's brown eye. Tami's a howler and she likes screaming out whatever I'm doing to her until I blow my load.

I figure I'll keep this up for a couple of years, let Chad get comfortable, let him think that he's out of the woods. And I figure, I'll stick around until Tami starts letting herself go or I can't stand her bitching anymore and I'll take Chad out to the desert for a stepfather and son outing with a couple of pellet guns, and then I'll do a quick turn right as I'm targeting a lizard and leave him screaming out in the middle of nowhere.

SHAFTED
Leigh Redhead

Barry Milton was dead for eight hours before anyone even realized.

He sat, wedged into the cracked red vinyl cinema chair, leaking fluids while his muscles stiffened and his body steadily emitted the fruity stench of decay. His milky eyes remained fixed on the screen where men with outsized penises pumped pneumatically at pigtailed blondes, and he remained deaf to the groans, slaps and sprightly synthesizer tunes emanating from the speakers. Between films, strippers pranced across the stage, strutting into the audience naked but for platform stilettos, perching on the backs of chairs and spreading their legs for customers holding two dollar "chair dance" cards. They avoided Barry, and not just because he hadn't paid for a dance.

"That guy in row eleven fucken stinks," Chantelle told Kylie when she emerged from the cinema, holding a latex nurse's uniform to her sweaty torso.

"No worries, love." Kylie was a big, lumbering woman who had previously worked as a cook at a sheep station. She grabbed something from behind the counter, hoisted herself out of the booth, and marched straight into the cinema through the swinging, saloon-style doors. When she got to row eleven, she didn't say anything, just looked pointedly at Barry and gave him a blast of Woolworth's air freshener, in Forest Spa.

"Problem solved," she told Chantelle as she crammed herself back into the cubicle and lit a Horizon from a pack of fifty.

It was my second day at the Shaft Adult Cinema and I'd just finished an hour in the peepshow. Back in the girls' room, I fixed my long dark hair and re-did my makeup in the age-speckled mirror. A short blonde in a cutoff mini, Perspex heels and nothing else fronted up. I tried not to stare at her tits.

"You new?"

"Yep."

"Worked before?"

"Crazy Horse. Elizabeth Street."

"Why'd ya leave?"

"Kept giving me Sunday nights. Money was shit."

"Got another job?"

"Not at the moment, but I should be out of here soon. I've applied for the police force, actually."

"Why?"

"Long story. One saved my mum once. And I'm not much good at anything else."

The blonde sung a few verses of "Women in Uniform."

"How'd you go in the peeps?" she asked.

"About eighty bucks."

"It's Friday night," she scoffed. "You should be making at least one-fifty an hour. Show me your vibe."

"You serious?"

She was, so I produced the vibrator from my wash bag. Nothing fancy: slim line, pink, fifteen bucks from the sex shop after a staff discount.

"No wonder you're not making any money. You need to upgrade," she said, and showed me hers: black, veined, and so large I inadvertently staggered back on my high-heeled boots.

"I'm scheduled for a dance downstairs," I said, and got out quick.

After flinging off my hot pants and bikini top to "Fastlove," I slipped from the lip of the stage, sashayed into the audience and immediately knew something was wrong. I'd lived in the country and recognized the smell: a mouse trapped in the wall insulation; a rotting roo by the side of the road. I strode straight out, wearing nothing but my thigh-high boots, and leaned on the front desk.

"Hey."

"How are you, sweetheart?" Kylie was sucking the guts out of her ciggie. "Bit of a short dance."

"Yeah," I admitted. "But the guy in row eleven is dead."

Not long after, the cops and the paramedics fronted up and even a couple of firemen whose only function was to perv at the girls, far as I could tell. The dancers had all clomped downstairs, shitty 'cause the punters had cleared out, but the sight of the boys in uniform cheered them considerably.

The ambos dragged the body into the foyer and zipped up the bag while Kylie emptied another can of alpine freshness into the air. What with the blokes flirting with the strippers, everyone making cracks of the "talk about a stiff" variety, and my George Michael CD still playing, the place had taken on an almost carnival-like atmosphere.

The short blonde who'd brandished the terrifying vibe sidled up. "I'll flip you for the young copper in uniform."

"You can have him."

"Go for firies, hey?"

I was about to tell her that discovering a dead body didn't inspire me to immediately jump a member of the emergency services, when a detective in a long black coat came up, carrying a clipboard. He gave us a quick up and down and I reflexively crossed my arms over my bikini top, while the blonde thrust her boobs out, flipped her hair and lit a Winfield.

"Which one of you bright sparks discovered the body?" The detective smirked. He was in his early thirties, tall, with crew-cut dark brown hair, and the arrogant look of a man who knew he was not only handsome, but had a Smith and Wesson strapped to his person.

"Not me," said the blonde.

"And you are?"

"Paris."

"Real name?" He clicked a pen.

"Chloe Wozniak."

"I realized he was dead," I said.

"Nice one. Only took you a day. Name?"

"Simone Kirsch." I was beginning to hate him. "So, who's the guy?"

"No wallet. Who pinched it?"

I narrowed my eyes.

"Someone going to search our lockers?" Chloe asked him.

"Maybe."

"Should I get rid of my bong?"

"Be a good idea."

Chloe and the rest of the girls quickly clattered up the stairs.

"You're not going?" he asked me.

"Nothing to hide."

The detective raised an eyebrow, but it was true. I hadn't taken any drugs for nearly a year. Police recruitment tested all applicants.

"How'd he die?" I asked.

"Ambos reckon heart attack, happens all the time. Just last week a dude carked it in a Carlton brothel."

"Embarrassing for the family."

"We always tell them he keeled over on the street outside."

"Nice. So, no suspicious circumstances?"

"You've been watching too many cop shows, honey. However…" He sidled closer and handed me his card. "If you do recall information which may be of assistance…"

"Detective Constable Adam Fitzgerald," I read.

"You have beautiful eyes," he replied, but he wasn't exactly looking into them at the time.

"I found the wallet!" the blonde, Chloe, announced at the end of the night. The toilet door was open and she had her hand down the "feminine hygiene" unit. I nearly gagged.

"What the fuck are you doing?"

"Collecting my stash. No jack was gonna go through there." She triumphantly held up a small bag of weed and chucked the wallet in my direction, where it skittered across the dusty floor. While she scrubbed her hands, I gave it a good going-over with one of the antibacterial baby wipes we all used. You didn't want to touch door handles, or anything really, at the Shaft.

There was no cash, but I did find a driver's license in the name of Barry Milton. Fat, bald and sixty-two, he had an address in St. Kilda, not far from my Elwood flat. I also found a medical card which advised he'd had a pacemaker fitted, all the usual bank cards, and a couple of small photographs of what must have been his grandkids. I felt bad for the dead stranger, and guilty for the jokes, even though I hadn't been making them. What a sad, sleazy, way to go.

I immediately rang Detective Fitzgerald and told him what I'd discovered. He wasn't impressed.

"We already know who he is. Informed the wife."

"How?"

"Medical bracelet. The excitement engendered by your fine establishment must have caused his heart to give out."

"Doesn't a pacemaker regulate heartbeat?"

"Not in his case, obviously. What you doing now?"

"Finishing work."

"Me too. Wanna grab a drink?"

I might have accepted, if he wasn't such an egomaniac.

"Too tired, sorry." I hung up.

Chloe came over and looked at the license. "I know that guy. Monique's regular."

"Monique?"

"She was working day shift. That dude used to come in and get a dance in the private booth with her all the fucking time. She'll lose a lot of money now. Not that I care."

"Why?"

"She's a thieving, junkie moll. Found my Chanel foundation in her makeup bag, fought the bitch, nearly got fired; now they don't roster us on together."

"Physical fight?"

"Uh-huh."

"Who won?"

Chloe smiled and I made a note never to fuck with her.

"Wanna go for champagne and a souvlaki?" she asked.

"It's two in the morning."

"Stalactites on Lonsdale Street's open all night."

I hesitated.

"They have fried haloumi."

"Let's go."

Next day, I decided to jog round to Barry Milton's, give the wife his wallet and my condolences, and back up the bullshit story that he'd had a heart attack strolling down Swanston.

The house was one of those red-brick, corner-block numbers built in the thirties: ornate tiles, sweeping verandas, rose garden. Not exactly a mansion, but it would have sold for more than a million.

I rang the doorbell and a crisp, middle-aged woman with an expensively highlighted blonde bob answered. She wore beige trousers and a light gray cashmere sweater and her blue eyes were clear. She took in my jogging gear, ripped tights, old Mickey Mouse tee, Nikes that had seen better days.

"Can I help you?"

I held out the wallet. "I just wanted to say I was there on Swanston Street when your husband, uh... I'm really sorry. I actually found this in the gutter and wanted to return it."

"How kind. Thank you so much." She gave me an arctic look that I recognized and I was shocked, even though I'd seen it plenty of times before.

"I have to go," I said quickly, and jogged towards the beach.

I was supposed to have the next day off, but Kylie rang in the morning, sounding stricken.

"Simone, thank God. Monique's quit and I need a girl to do the privates. No one else is answering. Can you cover?"

I hadn't done a private dance shift yet and wasn't sure I wanted to. Although management assured me it was just a lap dance, it didn't take a genius to realize other shit went on for tips in the closet-sized booth beneath the stairs.

Shafted

"Please?" Kylie begged.

"Okay."

The day was a disaster. Monique had been booked solid and none of her regulars were happy with me.

"So, love, you do any extras?"

When I sweetly informed them that sexual services were illegal outside of a licensed brothel, most walked, and I spent the day leaning against the counter, talking to Kylie.

"Why'd Monique leave?" I asked.

"No idea. She used to make a shitload of money here. At least three hundred a day. I'm busting for a pee. Mind the desk?"

"Sure." I sat behind the counter, thinking that if you combined Monique leaving with the way Mrs. Milton had looked at me, things were very suss indeed. On my first day at the Shaft, I'd filled out an application and they'd photocopied my ID. A gray filing cabinet sat under the desk and I hooked the tip of my boot under the handle and slid it open. Keeping a look out for Kylie, I flicked through to the M's. Melissa, Misty, Monique. I pulled out the piece of paper, shoved it down my boot and kicked the cabinet shut just as Kylie thundered down the stairs.

"I'm going up the girls' room for a bit," I told her. "Buzz me if anyone wants a dance."

Monique was a pinched-faced thirty-three-year-old with too-black hair: real name Tracey Gordon. According to her driver's license, she lived in the north of Melbourne, up at Preston.

I'd gotten Chloe's number after what had turned into a big night out, and I called her first.

"What's up?"

"I think Barry Milton was murdered."

"Why?"

"Monique quit and his missus looked at me funny when I gave back the wallet."

"Funny how?"

"It's hard to explain, but when I first started stripping, I told some chicks I'd gone to uni with about my new job. Even the right-on, do-what-you-want-with-your-body feminists gave me the same look. Condescending. That woman knew I was a stripper. And how could she if the cops said her husband died on the street?"

"You could've been mistaken. Maybe she was just a bitch."

"She didn't look too upset about him dying, either."

"Why do you care?"

"This is what I want to do, one day. And if I'm right, and I can help the coppers, maybe they'll want to take me on."

"You'll get in easy."

I wasn't too sure about that.

"You going to call Fitzgerald?" she asked. I told her I was, and she started laughing. "You don't need to make up a conspiracy theory to have sex with a D. Jesus."

"I don't—"

"Oh come on. You wouldn't stop bitching him out the other night. You hate him so much, I'd swear you wanna root him."

"Do not," I said, feeling the blood rush to my face.

Detective Fitzgerald suggested we grab a drink at a place called the Gin Palace after I'd finished work at the Shaft. He gave me directions to a laneway off Bourke Street and told me he'd see me there at five-thirty.

The joint was below street level, decorated with velvet curtains and upholstery and dark to the point that I staggered over a leopard skin pouf. I found Fitzgerald hiding in a cushioned booth, two martinis at the ready. He was wearing a suit with a sky blue shirt and I was in jeans and a striped top.

"You don't look so bad in clothes," he said, as Dean Martin crooned "Sway" from hidden speakers.

Fitzgerald didn't look so bad himself. His eyes matched his shirt and were framed by straight black brows and long dark lashes. Pity he was such a prick.

I sat opposite and took a sip, not expecting much. The last martini I'd drunk had been at an undergraduate cocktail party and was so vile I'd had to pour it down the sink. This one was sublime, like licking a glacier. Glacier? The booze must have hit already.

"So, how long you been in Melbourne?" he asked.

"I didn't tell you I wasn't from around here."

"You didn't know where the Gin Palace was."

"Always detecting, huh?"

"I ran your name through the database. You've applied for the service. I'll tell you now that the stripper thing is not going to work in your favor."

"I had to put it on the form; it's an offense to lie. Anyway, I thought the department didn't discriminate."

He laughed.

"What do you reckon my chances are?" I asked.

"Fifty-fifty. I could put in a good word...." He sipped, chewed an olive. "What was Sydney like?"

"It's nice of you to take an interest, but I want to talk about Barry Milton."

"Why?"

"I think he was murdered."

He sputtered so much a bit of olive flew out of his mouth and landed on a silk cushion. I took a big swig of my drink and told him what I'd told Chloe. Fitzgerald's perfectly formed lips were twisted with amusement and I wasn't sure whether I wanted to slap or kiss them. Another martini suddenly appeared and I went at it, hard.

"Let me get this straight. Some old cunt gave you the evil eye, so you think she killed her husband?"

"Plus the Monique thing." I pulled her employment form out of my bag and put it on the table. He gave it a once over.

"And how was this tart supposed to have knocked him? Bumped and ground him to death?"

"I don't know. He had a weak heart. Look, if you don't want to listen." I made to walk off, but he grabbed my hand. He'd taken off his jacket and rolled up his sleeves and his forearms were muscular, covered in dark hair. My mouth went a little dry.

"Simone, look, sorry. It sounds crazy, but you may be onto something. Have one more drink and I promise I'll look into it."

"Serious?"

"Yeah, it's pretty flimsy stuff, I'll admit, but you're showing initiative, thinking outside the box. Working tomorrow?"

"Off."

"We'll go and check out this Monique, together. She seen you before?"

"No."

"I'll pass you off as my partner."

"That's not legal." I drank. Was this the third martini? I wasn't sure.

"I won't tell if you won't."

"Okay." I was really trying to keep my shit together. "Guess I'll see you tomorrow."

"Lift home?"

It was inevitable, looking back. The drive to Elwood was a blur, then we were upstairs, in my flat, and I was ripping off his tie and dragging him onto the carpet in the foyer. He had soft lips, scratchy stubble and although I was naked, he'd only unzipped his fly. I could feel a strong chest and biceps beneath his shirt, and a hot, hard cock that was quickly inside me, and I was grabbing at his back, talking dirty, telling him to fuck me hard. Detective Fitzgerald obliged. I vaguely remembered him telling me he had to go, then nothing until I woke with the dry horrors at eight in the morning in a patch of sunlight, still on the carpet, hissing like a vampire. I popped four codeine, sculled a liter of water, had a pee and checked myself out in the mirror. Two hickeys, a bite mark on my boob, gravel rash and lips swollen like starlet on a collagen binge.

Martinis. Jesus. I showered, slammed down a plunger full of coffee and called the Constable's mobile. Switched off. I tried the Melbourne CIU landline, got the runaround. Detective Adam Fitzgerald was unavailable. Detective Adam Fitzgerald was not in today.

Detective Adam Fitzgerald was an asshole and I'd been an idiot. He'd had no intention of checking out my hunch, let alone having me ride along.

Still, the sex had been pretty damned good and I didn't need him anyway. I could look for evidence and hand it over to homicide myself.

I unwrapped a cheese single, about the only foodstuff I knew

I'd be able to keep down, shakily sipped a glass of cask wine to take the edge off, and got in my crappy '67 Ford.

Monique's was an unkempt weatherboard with seeding grass and an old Corolla parked outside. I was far too hung over to have a plan, so I just crept around to the back of the house. Blankets tacked to the windows stopped me from peering in, but I found something interesting in the concrete back yard. A whole bunch of boxes secured with packing tape and labeled with black marker: kitchen; bedroom; lounge. Monique was moving.

A green wheelie bin was wedged beside a rusting shed in the concrete back yard, and I flipped open the lid. Pizza boxes, garbage rotting in supermarket bags, yellow biohazard boxes for used syringes. And an expensive looking bejeweled and sequined bra. Why would she throw that out? Maybe she was giving up stripping. But she'd have chucked all her outfits. I picked it up and the thing was heavy—felt like something metal inside one of the pads. Weird, but what I really needed was something to connect Monique to Mrs. Milton.

Fuck it, I was going in.

On the other side of the house, a window gave and I climbed into an empty bedroom and crept through the house. When I reached the lounge room, I froze. Detective Adam Fitzgerald was slumped on the floor on the far side of the room. Packing tape covered his mouth, bound his ankles, and secured his wrists to a wall mounted radiator. Dried blood covered his face and shirt—the same sky-blue one he'd been wearing when we'd fucked.

In the center of the room, Monique and a thin guy with long, scraggly hair had nodded off on an old brown couch. The coffee table in front of them was littered with bent spoons, lighters, cigarettes with the filters pulled out, old fits and overflowing ashtrays. A large ceramic bong shaped like a wizard sat in the middle.

Fitzgerald was conscious and his eyes bulged when he saw me. I quietly slid my mobile out of my bag and pointed at it. He nodded, and I tiptoed up the hallway, opened the front door, and called triple 0 from the front gate so no one inside would hear. I gave the police the address, told them what was going on, but refused to stay on the line. Those junkies could come to at any moment and I didn't know what they'd done with Fitzgerald's gun—I needed to untie him, pronto.

I left the front door ajar on the way back in, checked the kitchen for a knife—all packed up—and finally lucked out on a pair of nail scissors in the bathroom. Sneaking back to the lounge, I crouched by Fitzgerald and struggled to snip through the layers of wrist tape. I'd just finished when his eyes widened and he whimpered behind the gag. I turned my head. The junkie guy had woken up and was staring at me. "The fuck?" He nudged Monique then staggered toward us, pulling Fitzgerald's gun out of his waistband. I scuttled back. Fitzgerald pulled the tape off his mouth, started doing the cop thing.

"Mate, put down the gun. Everything's gonna be okay."

Monique rubbed her eyes and watched her boyfriend swing the gun at me, then Fitzgerald.

"Who the fuck are you?" she screeched.

"Another jack," suggested the junkie with the gun.

"A stripper from the Shaft," I said, but she was yelling over me.

"Shoot the fucken both of them!"

Gun guy looked panicked, but pulled the trigger. Fitzgerald still had his ankles taped but threw himself to the side and the bullet smacked into the wall where his head had just been. At the same time, I heard people stomping up the front porch—so did the others. The junkie lined up another shot at Fitzgerald, so I launched myself at him. He was skinny, and I'd put on a fair bit of muscle dancing around in high heels, so the both of us crashed to the floor. He still had hold of the gun and I clawed at his hands. Boots thundered down the hallway and I looked up, hoping to see a SWAT team. Instead I clocked Monique, snarling and swinging the wizard straight for my temple.

And that was the last thing I saw for quite some time.

Chloe came to visit me in hospital with flowers, cheap champagne in plastic cups, and a copy of the *Herald Sun*.

"I heard you got whacked on the head with a bong. Didn't

know you got punched in the mouth." She nodded at my grazed, puffed lips.

"Not punched, kissed, if you'd call it that. Detective Fitzgerald."

"I hope the root was worth it 'cause you're going to be dirty on him now."

"He cut me out of the case. I already am."

She showed me the headline.

Hero Cop Solves Murder and Saves Stripper.

"I saved *his* ass. Prick."

Chloe read the article to me.

Turned out Mrs. Milton had fallen apart under interrogation and admitted everything. She'd thought her hubby was having an affair, and had hired a private detective, who told her he was visiting the Shaft, day after day. Mrs. Milton had staked the place out herself and seen Monique lead Barry out the door and kiss him on the cheek. When Monique left work, Mrs. Milton was waiting with an offer she couldn't refuse: a hundred grand to sew a neodymium magnet in her bra and rub up against Barry's chest while wriggling around on his lap, or whatever else they were getting up to. A sidebar in the paper explained the magnets were so strong that constant exposure was as bad for a pacemaker as an MRI. Her motive had been to keep the house, get a hefty insurance payout and punish her cheating husband. It had almost been the perfect crime.

A superior officer praised Fitzgerald, saying he'd shown great initiative and had really "thought outside the box." There was talk of a promotion to the Homicide Squad and the front page displayed a very nice photo of the detective, one arm around his wife, the other holding his two-year-old son.

A couple of weeks later, I got the letter from Victoria Police. We regret to advise...thank you for your interest...I called Fitzgerald and told him cutting me out had been a dog act, and I was sure that he'd not only failed to put in a good word, but had actually sabotaged my application. Of course, he swore it had nothing to do with him, then asked me out for another martini. I hung up.

• • •

Three a.m. Chloe and I had long finished the fried cheese and were halfway through our second bottle of sparkling.

"I'm jack of working for other people. Want to start my own agency," she said.

"Need a twenty-seven-year-old stripper who can't dance for shit?"

"Can't keep doing this job forever. What's your plan?"

I drained my glass. "Don't have one. I'm no good at anything except flashing my gash."

A couple at the next table looked over.

"You're good at investigating." She refilled our glasses. "You solved a goddamned murder!"

"So? I'm never getting into the police."

Chloe got a funny look in her eye, darted from the restaurant to the takeaway counter and picked up a day old newspaper. She turned to the employment and training section, slid it over the table and pointed to an advertisement.

"The Australian Security Academy," I read. "Certificate Three in Investigative Services?"

"You'd make a great private dick." She smiled.

2,984,000 POUNDS OF PRESSURE
Anonymous-9

Plodding past Training Room 1, the gas man recognized a voiceover from a familiar video: *The explosion happened at approximately four-fifteen in the morning when a water heater turned into a device of destruction, leveling a vacant bungalow to the ground. As the clean-up crew hauled away debris, the importance of never obstructing a temperature pressure relief valve was very, very clear.*

The gas man wondered how many times he'd heard it during the last seven years of work.

Here at West Los Angeles Gas and Electric, you will learn our three most important rules—one: safety, two: safety, and three: safety.

Audio faded as the gas man shouldered open the door marked Men's Change Room. He fished for a key to one of the identical steel lockers, row on row, and finding his, changed into a clean uniform with a blue flame on the shirt and a motto embroidered in red: "Keeping the Flame for Our Customers." In every available pocket, he placed small tools of his trade: a crescent wrench, a combination wrench, safety glasses with UV protection, company ID, and a pair of needle-nose pliers. A full-size pipe-wrench holster hung on his hip.

He locked up, tugged on a hat, and signed out a Toughbook

laptop before trudging to a Silverado 2500 truck with lettering on the side that matched his shirt.

Inside the cab, he snapped the Toughbook onto its docking station beside the steering wheel and looked at the day's orders. First was a home in Culver West: a potential gas leak. A GPS device told him the best way to get there, in the nicest voice possible. As the automatic gate rumbled back to let him off the base, he noticed a new banner fixed on the chain link. "Focus on Safety" drifted past his peripheral vision as the big Silverado rolled out onto Santa Monica Boulevard.

It was a nice little house on a nice little street. He wouldn't exactly call the owner house-proud, but at least the lawn was mowed, no trash on the porch. He'd been in more than one dump with moldy linoleum and cockroaches skittering in all directions, so he always took a good look before getting out of the truck.

On the porch, he tapped and called, "GAS MAAAN," in a loud but friendly voice.

A female inside barked for somebody to answer the door and when it opened, his world glitched and wobbled, as if God had just clicked the "Start Game" icon on his life. He stared down into the hazel eyes of a twelve-year-old girl. Eyes identical to his own. Set in the face of a child. "Uh, here about the, uh, gas leak," he fumbled, and as the girl stepped back, a stench of cat shit from inside the house hit him in the face.

"Manuela, don't let the cats out!" the voice inside shrieked.

"No, Mom, I know," the girl called over her shoulder, motioning him in, and suddenly he knew that voice inside, too. He felt for the safety glasses in his pocket, and slipped them on. Three ginger cats by the door shrank to let him pass.

The girl was wearing a school backpack, and by the looks of it, just about to leave. Instead, she led him down the hall.

The house had been nice once. The paint wasn't too bad, but cat feces were everywhere along the baseboards of the house, as if a dozen animals urinated and defecated wherever the urge struck. The reek was like a left-right combination punch to the sinuses.

They entered the kitchen where cats perched on the counter,

tip-toed across the top of the fridge and weaved themselves around the kitchen table-legs.

"I can smell gas," she said quietly.

The sadness in her eyes stung him, as if a wasp had flown inside his chest.

"I think it's the stove," she added. "We don't use it."

"Need to take a look," he managed to say, knowing most likely the pilot lights were knocked out, and it was a simple fix.

"Mom, I'll be back at three-thirty," she called.

Another shriek, "Did you feed those cats?"

"Yes, ma'am." The girl left him with a sideways glance starved of hope. A half-dozen cats followed her into the hall.

No reply from the front room, just a crescendo of canned laughter and a cascade of tinny music.

Alone in the fetid kitchen, thoughts clattering and banging inside his skull. Outside the kitchen window, he caught the flash of her hair and backpack bouncing. Then she was gone.

Eight years ago, she was five years old. He was twenty-nine. It was classified as an international abduction. He'd hired an attorney and obtained a custody decree. But Christie had vanished with their child, deep inside Mexico. It was just like something Christie would do—she graded poorly in the impulse-control department. When they married, he thought age or motherhood might improve her. Never dreamed she'd bolt and take Madison. That was the girl's real name. His girl, Madison. Now she was Manuela. Did she even remember owning another name once?

Off the kitchen was a small walk-in closet. The door was open, and he could see a cat box jammed to the rim with shit, and piled like a pyramid in the middle. The cats had finally given up; he didn't blame them.

"Did you find it?" a voice rasped close behind. His stomach flopped as he turned around. Eight years hadn't been kind to Christie. The stained housedress, the bleary face, gave away serious drinking. She held an enormous Angora cat in her arms, like a baby, and when her mouth opened to speak, he saw the pre-molars were missing.

"My mom passed, so we moved in a while back. It's mine now," she added unnecessarily. "Kid says she smells gas. I don't smell a damn thing. You?" She stroked the armload of fluff reclining on her defeated breasts.

He touched his hat brim in a show of respect, really to shield his face. "Need some stuff from my truck."

Her pale lips pursed at him, and she tramped back into the living room where the TV screamed for attention. The mother of his only child seemed hypnotized by it, as if the rest of life had disappeared.

Outside, he drew fresh air in deep and tried to exhale the stink. He opened a bin on the back of the truck and pretended to sort through valves and elbows. *She's back. Madison and Christie are back.* He could call an attorney, child welfare, the police, even. He could press charges, file for custody. The memory of Madison's photo sprang to mind, posted on the website for Missing and Exploited Children. *Have you seen this child? Ha visto usted a estos menores?* Eight hundred thousand like her missing, every year.

Flashback to red-tape hell. His attorney's voice, "Crime moves swiftly, justice grinds slowly. We're doing all we can within the law." He hired an investigator to go to Mexico and track them. He paid insanely high *mordida* bribes to grease jurisdictional wheels. All for nothing.

He used to wonder if there was any pain more intense than losing a child. On the worst nights, wracked with loss and rage, he bargained with the dark. "Tear out my eyes," he would beg. "Break my neck, grind my bones, just let me rescue my little girl." The dark never answered.

After three years non-stop, something told him to quit. Let them think he forgot. He knew Christie. She would try to come back.

This time, he knew how it would go: court-ordered visitation, lengthy evaluations, a court battle—courts favored mothers, even crazy ones. Most likely, Christie would disappear and take Madison, again.

Not this time. No.

In slow motion, he gathered a gas detector, a bag of tools and fittings. Inside, his eyes watered as the ammonia-cloud of cat urine hit. Christie lay slack-jawed in a living-room recliner, with the Angora still attached to her chest. A TV tray held a mickey of Southern Comfort with the twist-cap off.

He passed deeper into the house. Three bedrooms, one empty except for trash. The next had to be Christie's with empties beside the bed. The third was a sad little room with an air mattress on the floor and an overturned grocery carton for a nightstand. A little lamp sat on top, with a blue unicorn on the cracked shade. The house made him sick, this made him sicker.

In the kitchen, he relit the stove pilots and adjusted the flames. The walk-in closet gave up what was really on his mind—the water heater—a veteran, only slightly dinged. *The importance of never obstructing a temperature pressure relief valve was very, very clear.*

Lots of people saw water dripping from a TPR valve and their first instinct was to plug it. Fortunately, most people checked before acting and learned that a plug would turn an ordinary water heater into a grenade. Some people didn't check though, accounting for a number of explosions every year, some of them fatal.

It was just a matter of fitting a plug. Cutting the safety link. Turning the thermostat to max. A good couple of hours and 2,984,000 pounds of boiling steam pressure would detonate the tank and blast the house down. He crossed to a kitchen window, cats scurrying out of the way. They were about fifteen feet from the house next door. Every window would blow out from the shockwave, but the force wouldn't penetrate the next home. Neighbors would be safe.

Still, he didn't touch anything.

Eyes stinging from cat-box fumes, he set his tool bag on top of the heater and returned once more to the truck. Madison had said she would be home at three-thirty. Right now it was just past nine in the morning. The house and everyone in it could be gone before noon. Movement on the porch caught his eye as a calico cat poked its head out the front door and ventured into the sunlight. It dawned suddenly why the yard was kept clean—devious Christie avoided drawing attention with a dirty yard, but let the inside go to hell with impunity.

He checked the Toughbook for time on the order. Amazingly,

only thirteen minutes had passed. He was still within the normal estimated time for a gas leak.

His mind drifted down a timeline of possibilities. The heater explosion would leave a pile of steam-cleaned rubble. His work record was spotless, and Christie would go down as another unfortunate do-it-yourself homeowner, deceased. State budget cuts would help keep the investigation superficial—he'd be clear if nobody dug too deep. A few months on, he could slide into another job and put distance between himself and anything to do with heaters. He tapped the steering wheel and thought about this, as three more cats left the house, and strolled over the lawn.

If he went through with this thing, Madison would go to foster care today. No matter where she was sent, it would be healthier than this. He could safely collect her in about a year and get the best therapy that union medical benefits could buy, for both of them. On the other hand, she might recognize him as the gas man. At thirteen, she'd be old enough to connect a few dots and figure he had a motive for murder.

He looked out at the sunny little street in Culver West, and contemplated the misery beyond the front door of the pleasant little house. The Toughbook screen flashed: *seventeen minutes*.

He decided it came down to what was more important: his own skin or his daughter's. Should he do it? Or should he play it safe? Would Madison tell? Or would she keep the secret?

The gas man got out of his truck. He walked back to the house. He let a few more cats out the door.

HEARING VOICES
Jonathan Woods

"She loves me...she loves me not..." Like a game remembered from childhood, the words circled around and around and around in Bill's head.

He lay cadaver-like, arms at his sides, eyes staring across his saggy bed in the ratshit room he rented month to month in Mrs. Hughes' low-down apartment. Second-hand moonlight oozed like toothpaste through a dirty window with an airshaft view.

He had not bothered to remove his work clothes. A cheap mint-green dress shirt, worn gray pinstripe pants, black brogues.

An apparition hovered just out of reach above his head, a buxom wench wrapped in a silvery robe, her hair a twisted bramble of gold, the lure of lust writ large on her piquant lips. One hell of a woman.

His eyes untied the robe. The robe fell away, revealing plum-colored lace, soft curvaceous flesh, raucous breasts. A blowsy well-endowed wet dream.

Bill moaned. Forehead beaded in sweat, he reached down and uncinched his belt. The sound of his zipper descending was a metallic scream; but of pain or pleasure?

Four days ago, everything had taken a dangerous turn. *Like scoring big time in the Lotto. Or being run over by a fucking bus.*

It had been just another Monday. The first day of Bill's new job at the Thin Agency. Assistant mail clerk. Thirty-third floor of the Winstar Tower.

Still half asleep, Bill zombied across the lobby and into the elevator, minding his own business. One hand held a vinyl SpongeBob lunchbox he'd liberated one day from the trash left on the street for pick-up. Inside were a tuna on whole wheat, a Ziploc of sliced carrots and a grape-apple juice box.

A woman in a power business suit stepped into the elevator. Her colorless eyes appraised him from knees to nose. Deciding he was some kind of deviant, she turned her back. Then leaned forward and pressed the button for a lower floor.

As the elevator doors closed with a soft pneumatic sigh, a woman spoke. No, not the woman who had just entered the car. It was the elevator talking, a recorded voice emanating from a speaker hidden in the murky ceiling of the car: "The door is closing. Please step back from the door."

The voice was deep, lush, oozing with sexual suggestion, with an ever so slight mechanical undertow. It reached into Bill's head, calling up images of Loren Bacall in *The Big Sleep*.

Bill's eyes blinked.

The car shimmied then began a rapid ascent.

With ear-popping suddenness, the elevator slowed. A tiny bell dinged. The voice again: "This is the twelfth floor. Be careful when exiting the car."

Careful of what? Bill wondered.

As the doors closed behind the exiting woman's symmetrically diverting ass, the voice said: "The door is closing. Please step back from the door."

Bill fell into a standing doze.

"What's your name, sailor?"

Bill's eyes shot open. "What did you say?"

The sweet scent of some nameless *eau de cologne* mixed with heavy machine oil hung in the enclosed air. The voice repeated itself: "What's your name, sailor?"

Bill's eyes swiveled left, then right. But there was no one else in the car.

His gaze traveled upward searching for the hidden speaker.

"Are you talking to me?" he said.
"I just asked your name."
"It's Bill."
"Nice meeting you. I'm Angie."

His mouth grew instantly bone dry. When he tried to speak, his voice sounded like the wind susurrating across the West Texas high desert where he'd grown into manhood.

"Is this some kind of trick?" he whispered.

"God's truth? A girl gets lonely going up and down all day long with nobody to talk to."

This is somebody's idea of a joke, he thought. *A lousy fuckin' joke.*

What he said was: "Sure you do."

The elevator slowed.

"This is the thirty-third floor. Be careful when exiting the car."

Just before he stepped out of the elevator, the voice spoke again: "See you later, Bill."

"Yeah, sure."

It was a long friggin' day. At five o'clock, exhausted and hungry, Bill found himself in the HR Department watching a video about sexual harassment in the workplace and filling out a variety of redundant forms. It was after seven p.m. when he finally pressed the elevator call button. Alone in the Thin Agency reception area, he waited, brain in neutral.

The elevator doors opened. Bill entered the empty car and slumped against the back wall, closing his eyes. A headache ricocheted inside his head, like a skinhead lout out for blood.

The husky female voice spoke her preset words: "The door is closing. Please step back from the door." The elevator started to descend.

Next moment a breath of fingertips brushed his cheek. "Hard day?"

Holy shit! Bill cringed as if a red hot wire had grazed his skin. Fear licked his gonads like an ice-cold tongue. He pressed his eyes more tightly shut.

"Don't touch me!"

Her cloying cherry blossom fragrance wafted up his nose. Terror swirled like a jinn in Bill's brain. A riptide of nausea tore across his stomach. He retched, his hand holding back the bile.

"You're cute," she said. He imagined her standing naked next to him, biting the tip of her thumb, a lunatic smile curling the corners of her mouth and eyes.

Her hand rested on his shoulder. He twisted away. *If I open my eyes, I'll go stark raving mad.* He saw his own hand draw the blade of a straight razor sharply and deeply across his throat, blood spurting helter-skelter.

Her hands began to massage his shoulders. Slowly the fear began to ease away.

"A girl gets lonely in here," she said.

Awake before sunrise from a tormented sleep, Bill arrived at the Winstar Tower at 7 a.m. on Tuesday. Except for a somnolent security guard, the lobby was empty. The elevator doors slid open and drew Bill inside. He stood against the back wall, shoulders thrown back, eyes tightly closed.

When she spoke, it was as if she were standing right next to him: "Bill, you're so sweet to come early. I thought about you all night."

"Aren't you going to tell me to step back from the door?"

"I thought we were beyond that."

"I had an uncle who went nuts," said Bill. "Died in a loony bin down in Texas. After he killed and ate a bunch of people."

"Oh, Bill, that's such a sad story."

"Maybe I inherited the same genes."

He could smell her wild cherry perfume mixed with 3-in-1 oil. He sensed her closeness, her tropical breath on his earlobe. She kissed his cheek.

This is absofuckinglutely nuts, he thought. But it didn't matter. He was along for the ride wherever it was going.

Eyes still tightly shut, he reached out, encircling her softness in his arms. In a rush, he drew her electric flesh to him. His mouth mashed into hers. She twisted and slithered against him, her hand clutching at his tumescent cock through the thin polyester of his Goodwill pants. For a time, time ceased to exist. Then with a gasp her mouth broke free: "This is the thirty-third floor. Be careful when exiting the car."

He staggered from the elevator.

The day seemed as though it would never end. He kept putting mail in the wrong boxes, dazedly sitting in his cubicle trying to piece together an explanation for the inexplicable. At 7:30 p.m. Bill left the mailroom and walked to the elevator, his mind as twisted as the Gordian Knot.

It was a wild ride down. A wild fuckin' ride.

At the bottom, he reeled drunkenly across the lobby. His shirt unbuttoned, one shirttail hanging loose, the other peeking through his open fly.

At the hiss of the doors opening, the security guard nodding off behind his marble reception counter jerked awake. Observing Bill's dishabille, he frowned and started up.

Bill, winking and waving wildly, lurched for the revolving door and the emptiness of the night streets.

On Thursday, Bill entered the elevator at 6:05 a.m. Angie cooed: "Good morning, peaches." Not accidentally her hand grazed his privates. Bill's cock crowed.

Outside, a shaft of sunlight exploded above a line clouds.

"We've got to amscray out of Dodge," she said wiping the sweat from his brow. "I can't go on living this elevator life. A girl needs to get out more, see the world."

"What do you mean?"

"I mean we should head down to Mexico where the living is el cheapo. Where nobody knows your name or gives a fuck about your past."

"But there's all that the drug violence down there? Kidnappings, beheadings, revenge killings."

"The world's a dog-eat-dog place. You could end up dead as easily here as there. Besides, we'll be traveling under the radar."

"Okay, so just suppose we go to Mexico like you say. We'll still need money to live on."

"Hmmmmm. I'll think of something."

Twelve hours later as evening draped the city, within the dim interior of the elevator, the twin white orbs of Bill's buttocks rose and fell to the rhythms of love. Twin moons orbiting a planetary twat.

Afterwards while they shared a cigarette, she told him about the Benevolent Loan Co. located on the first floor of the Winstar Tower. About how every Friday afternoon, two canvas bags of cash, the week's receipts, lay slumped behind the counter, awaiting the arrival of an armored car. Twin canvas bags that never held less than $20,000 in used tens, twenties and fifties.

"How do you know all this?"

"A girl hears lots of stuff riding up and down in an elevator all day long."

"I don't think I'm ready for the Benevolent Loan Co. Last bad thing I did was jerk off on a photograph of Ursula Andress naked."

"Who's Ursula Andress?"

"That's not the point."

"The point is you'll make a great badass. No security guard. Manager on his break at the Dubliner across the street. Only two clerks, both dumb as dirt. You point the gun at them. Grab the money bags. I'm waiting at the curb in the stolen car with the motor running."

"What gun? What stolen car?" Bill's voice was icily sober, but she prattled on:

"We dump the car in Waco and catch a bus to San Antonio. From there it's an easy drive to the border."

"I hate to intrude on your Bonnie and Clyde fantasy, but we're almost to the lobby. We'll have to talk about this later."

"Oh, baby, I know we can do this. We can take a taxi instead of stealing a car."

There was a long silence.

"You're joking, right?"

At that moment, the doors opened to the lobby. Across the way, a lime-green neon sign read: Benevolent Loan Co. The offices beyond were as dark as the gates of Hell.

Bill scrambled into his clothes, grabbed his lunchbox and a week old *Time* he'd found in the break room. "I'm out of here."

"Call me. We need to reach closure."

• • •

Hearing Voices

When the sex dream faded, Bill sat up and tossed the used Kleenex in the wastebasket. One foot nudged a pile of paperback crime novels on the floor next to his bed. The stack listed, then tumbled sideways in a scree of lurid covers.

It was getting late. He had to make his lunch for Friday. When he stood up and started tucking in his shirttails, he realized he'd gotten sperm on the front of his shirt.

Shit!

On the way to the kitchen, he stopped in the bathroom and rubbed water on the stain. In the sink mirror, his eyes looked distinctly crazed.

At the kitchen door, Bill flipped on the overhead fluorescent light. Stove and refrigerator, both in basic white, Formica table-and-chairs set and an unreliable wall clock. He shared the kitchen with his landlady Mrs. Hughes and the other boarder Karim.

Or was it Kiram. Or Chiiram. Swarthy, odorous and unreliable, regardless. Studying bomb-making 101 on a student visa.

On his shelf in the fridge, there were still four slices of whole wheat bread twisted up in a Pepperidge Farm wrapper. And half a jar of peanut butter. In the staccato glow of the flickering florescent light, he made two sandwiches.

When he unzipped the SpongeBob lunch box, a gun stared up at him. *Holy quim hairs! How had she managed to slip the pistol into his lunch box? And where had she gotten ahold of it in the first place?*

It looked antique. A snub nosed .38 like the one Peter Gunn carried. He hefted the weapon in his hand. Opened the magazine. Counted five bullets. The spun cylinder made a ratcheting noise that sounded huge in the empty kitchen.

She'd probably had the gun for a long time. Just waiting for the right fool to come along.

Bill laid the gun back in the lunch box and set the sandwiches and a chocolate chip granola bar on top. Then closed the zipper and put the lunch box in the fridge.

Entering the next available Winstar Tower elevator at 11:05 a.m. on Friday morning, Bill was as wired as a pit bull scenting blood from the warm-up fight.

"I thought you weren't coming!" Angie snapped as the doors closed.

"I'm here, aren't I?"

"Okay. Okay. Everything's set for four o'clock this afternoon." She rubbed herself against him like a molting snake. Her tongue slimed deep into his ear. "You know you're the only one for me, peaches," she said.

Without warning, she bit down hard on his earlobe.

"Jesus!"

His hand flew up and he slapped her with enough meanness to make her stagger.

Her fingers touched her bruised cheek. Her big, glassy eyes stared at him.

"Why'd you bite me?" Bill asked.

"Just a taste of the fun we're going to have down Mexico way."

At 4:07 p.m. Bill pulled open the glass door of the Benevolent Loan Co. and strode inside. A chest-high counter with a wooden gate at one end divided the room in half. Behind the counter on one side were a couple of desks. On the other side, a glass windowed office, its blinds drawn, its door closed. At one of the desks, a young man in a white shirt and purple tie worked a calculator, shuffling through a stack of documents.

A young Hispanic-looking woman, her silky black hair swept sideways across her forehead, stood behind the counter. She looked up and smiled. "May I help you?"

Next moment, she cringed in fear as the short barrel of the .38 touched her forehead. "Oh my God," she gasped. "Please don't kill me."

"Hey, you!" Bill shouted at the guy hunched over the desk. He looked up anxiously, then froze. Bill pointed the gun at him. "Get the fuck over here!"

The young man obliged. When he was close enough, Bill belted him in the face with the barrel of the .38. With a sigh, the young man crumpled to the floor.

Like a snake with its prey, Bill's eyes held those of the woman. "I want you to hand me the two bags of money," he said. "Do it now!"

Her eyes knew the score.

Three seconds later, two fat but otherwise nondescript canvas satchels rested side by side on the counter.

Bill reached for the bags. "I'm going to leave now. I want you to stand right where you are and count to a hundred. Don't even blink your eyes. If you move, I'll come back and kill you."

Then the impossible happened. The door to the glass-fronted office opened and a man's head appeared. Heavy angular face, weasel eyes, graying razor-cut hair.

"Marge, get me..."

The voice trailed off as the manager cataloged Bill's startled visage, the revolver pointed at Marge, the twin bags of money in Bill's grasp.

It's the fucking manager who's supposed to be having a quick one in the bar across the street.

The man's head abruptly disappeared. The door to the office slammed.

He's getting a gun. Or calling 911.

Still gripping the two canvas bags, Bill turned and fled.

The security guard in the Winstar Tower lobby watched Bill burst from the entrance of the Benevolent Loan Co. and knew instantly that the shit had hit the fan.

As Bill skidded to a halt on the slick terrazzo floor, their eyes met and there was murder in both pairs. Bill squeezed off a shot. The guard dove for cover.

Bill hesitated, scanning the street through the thick plate glass of the lobby walls.

A scream of sirens was already approaching. Red and blue police lights flashed in the distance, drawing nigh with alacrity. At the curb, there was no sign of Angie with the stolen car.

In desperation, Bill turned and ran pell-mell toward the elevators.

The doors opened. A woman emerged. Bill grabbed her arm, jerking her out of his way. She sprawled across the floor. Her scream resonated in the tiny space as the elevator doors clanked shut behind him.

• • •

Two hours later, the police found Bill crouching in a maintenance closet on the thirteenth floor. He was stark naked and ranting about some stone cold bitch named Angie. The two bags of cash from the Benevolent Loan Co. were never recovered despite repeated searches of every nook and cranny of every floor of the Winstar Tower.

The next day, it was discovered that the voice announcement system in the building's elevators had shorted out and fused into an unrecognizable lump of plastic and metal.

The elevator maintenance company was called. In due course, they installed a new voice synthesizer system, this time with a man's voice.

JUAN HUNDRED OUNCES
Liam José

At the front of the Wilmington porno theater sits an electric wheelchair. Its chrome finish reflects the flashing neon dicks from the doorway.

The chair has to be left there because FIST AND SHOUT doesn't have disability access.

Instead, its driver, Juan Hundred, has to get carried down the staircase into the room marked PRIVATE. This isn't the easiest job, as Juan Hundred has put on a lot of weight since he lost the ability to walk. Luckily, the two men who carried him down tonight are more than strong enough.

See, modern pornography demands a huge level of fitness in its performers.

These performers:
1. Ozzie "The Aussie"
Star of:
The Crocodile Humper
I Cum From the Land Down Under
2. Malcumm X
Star of:
Do the Right Hole
The Gay Team
Black Shaft

Ozzie tears his hand away, causing Juan to tip on his side and almost drop.

"Jesus, Hundred, did you have to wear the sharpest fucken belt you could find?"

Juan steadies his large Stetson and winces, pinching the skin around his eye patch. He fights back vomit—when much of your CNS doesn't function, the slightest tilt can cause an upset.

"Fucking *cabrón*, can't withstand a little pain, no? How did you ever make it in this business?"

Malcumm stares at them, his lids drooping over his eyes. Disinterested.

"You muthafuckas gonna fuck and make up? I ain't gonna put up with any of this servitude shit much longer."

Ozzie swears again. Stretched vowels, clipped consonants. And the three make it into the room. Inside, Anderson Strong greets them. His day job: CEO of "Strong Arm Films," minor gay porn production and distribution house. Also: Owner of FIST AND SHOUT, gay porn theater.

Strong's balding head is cut into a restless mullet. Three gold hoop earrings adorn his right ear. He wears a gold locket around his neck that carries his own photo.

Strong dabs at his sweaty brow with a Kleenex and stands.

"Mr. Hundred, always such a pleasure to be in the company of a living legend."

Juan spits on the floor of the pokey office.

"Your men almost kill me on the way down those steps. It's incompetence. Incompetence. Do they not know who I am?"

Ozzie looks to the wall. His eyes say: Not this shit again.

"Well," Strong, every bit the diplomat, "their talents are limited." He thinks, *To fucking.*

Malcumm and Ozzie stare at him. Strong finds composure, clears his throat.

"Please have a seat, Mr. Hundred."

Juan stares death at Strong while his legs dangle free between the two studs.

Malcumm and Ozzie struggle to get Juan neatly into a chair while Strong unrolls a plastic mat onto his cleared desk.

"How's life been treating you, Mr. Hundred?"

Juan spits again. Speckles hit Malcumm, who adjusts Juan in the chair more aggressively than is needed.

"Bah. My trips across the border take all my time. I should be living the good life. Surrounded by friends, lovers, family. Instead, I'm being pulled around by you. These...boys exemplify the problem exactly. No respect anymore. I'm Juan Hundred, no? Juan fucking Hundred."

"Well, it's an honor, Mr. Hundred. If we're inconveniencing you, we could always renegotiate our—"

"Juan Hundred. I'm a pioneer. The first Latino porn star. The biggest porn star. The best. There is none better.

"And now my dick is useless. People say to me—'oh, the brain is the most erotic part of the body. You don't need your dick for everything. You can have a satisfying sex life or erotic life as you are.' Well, when I was at my peak, I could come once every ten minutes, each more powerful than the last.

"I could pull the train. Five other men at once couldn't keep up with me. I was up to my balls, spinning modern Spartans like tops. And people try to tell me anything could compare? This is why more people should do porn. They think their lives are fulfilling. Idiots."

Strong nods. Solemn. A tragedy.

Ozzie removes Juan's Stetson and, with Malcumm, carefully takes him to the desk, trying to not move him too quickly. They place him on his stomach, flat over the plastic.

"Are you comfortable, Mr. Hundred?"

"That suggests comfort. Do you think I've had a shred of it since I've been in this chair?"

"Ha ha. Well. I suppose not. Malcumm?"

Malcumm sighs. Pulls down Juan's pants. A fading MADE IN MEXICO tattoo that has stretched considerably adorns his right cheek.

"Are you ready, Mr. Hundred?"

"I did not come here for conversation with you pigs. Begin."

Malcumm wrenches his huge fingers into the rim of Juan's ass. He pauses.

"This okay, fool?"

"It's the most attention my ass is to receive, don't you hold back."

"Can you even feel it?"

"It's numb. I can feel the stretching though. Like someone pulling your T-shirt. You enjoy what you get."

Malcumm—timid—then—fuck it—he digs his hands right in. A gasping noise escapes Juan's asshole as it is stretched beyond believable dimensions.

"Fucken hell," Ozzie's eyes bug. "It's like you're a lizard with an arsehole the size of a volcano, mate."

"I was the king of the double, triple—whatever they could fit—penetrations. I wear my added girth with pride."

Malcumm's biceps bulge as he holds Juan open, his calm face not belying his surprise that Juan hasn't torn.

"Hey, you koala-rapin' muthafucka, you gonna get in there, or I gotta whup yo ass? Cuz my hands may be busy, but this whole body is built for ass-whuppin'."

Ozzie manages to get over the sight of the largest ass he's ever entered and fishes with his hands. They fit easily. He could give a round of applause. Ozzie starts digging.

Strong makes a filmic rectangle with his thumbs and pointer fingers.

"You boys. Cross-generational. Interracial. It's beautiful. If only I could record this. I can hear the fapping already."

Juan bares his teeth and grimaces.

"Wider. Wider. Never have I put up with such terrible workings in my ass."

Ozzie keeps digging. Through the greasy swirls of shit. Through the pockets of gas. The coffee grounds that are meant to fool the sniffer dogs. And finally he has it.

Ozzie's eyes speak again: I probably shoulda worn gloves.

"Fuck a duck! How much've you got in there?"

Strong, arms still outstretched framing the scene, rushes forward. Crash-zoom.

"Mr. Hundred. You are an artiste. Right there is our money shot."

Strong drops his hands and mimes ejaculate.

"It's nothing. It's only a little over six pounds. All that our connections could proffer. Juan Hundred can fit more, though. That is why Juan Hundred is best. I can't feel it, and even if I could, it would be no problem." He scorns Ozzie and Malcumm with his eyes. "It is what separates the amateurs from the professionals."

Ozzie places the six pounds of plastic-wrapped crack onto the desk. Malcumm lets go of Juan's ass and watches it retreat to an approximation of its regular size.

"Aww yeah, baby."

With a box of moist towels they clean up Juan. Ozzie looks at his hands and goes to leave for the bathroom. Strong stares at him: If you touch anything with those hands, you'll be on jizz mop duties the rest of your life. Ozzie frowns. Gropes at the doors with his elbows and knees, tries not to swear too much when he bumps a hand on his shirt.

Strong reveals an envelope fat with bills.

"Wow, Mr. Hundred. It is such a pleasure doing business with you. I look forward to next time."

"Eh. Save it. Don't bother me again until it is important. Juan Hundred has better things to do with his time."

Juan's wheelchair moves slowly through the dark L.A. streets. He rides toward a home where his cat waits for him. Where he, Juan Hundred, will sit, quiet, waiting for phone calls.

He looks at the ground and sees himself reflected in an oily puddle, and for a moment the face that looks back is flush with youth. The handsome Juan Hundred. The man who starred in *Juan Hundred Percent. El Burro.* The beautiful. The great. The proud.

His wheel crashes through the puddle, spilling the image.

He purses his lips. He scowls at the world he owns. He rides into the receding storm.

"I am the great lover. I am the king. I am all the things that have come before, and all that will come.

"I am Juan Hundred."

BUDGET CUTS
Dave White

When Paul Brown walked through the door, the first thing he felt was someone pressing the blade of a knife to his throat.

Paul dropped his briefcase and felt his knees give. Whoever was behind him wrapped the free hand around his waist and held him up. Paul gurgled and tried to catch his breath, but the air seemed to stop at the back of his mouth. Tears stung his eyes.

"Mr. Brown, you thought I wouldn't find you?" It was a male voice, full of phlegm, like he had a cold.

Paul reached his right arm over his head, trying to swat at the guy's head. The blade pressed deeper into his skin. A warm liquid rolled down his neck, pooling in his shirt collar.

"Stop struggling, this will be over soon."

Paul found his voice. Moving his jaw caused the blade to cut a bit deeper, but he had to say something.

"Wait," he said. "I'm just a teacher."

"I know," the man said.

The first letter came two weeks ago.

The envelope was white and bare, except for a stamp and a press-on label addressed to Paul R. Brown. Paul didn't read it at first, instead settling in with a beer, a sandwich and a stack of essays on *Rosalita's Hands*.

Paul wasn't a fan of teaching that book, the story of a rich

Mexican girl who is forced to move to America and become a migrant worker. While it was supposed to be inspiring to middle school kids, it was instead slow, tedious and filled with twenty-page chapters of Rosalita learning how to change diapers and sweep.

After finishing six papers and his beer, Paul got up and stretched, then went to the kitchen. He thought about another beer, but decided against it and washed the glass. Too many Kentucky Breakfast Stouts would knock a guy out before he accomplished anything.

When he got back to the couch, he picked up the envelope. He guessed it was his former church sending him something, hoping he'd return to the Parish. He opened it.

Instead, he found a letter from a concerned taxpayer. It berated him for daring to write a letter to the paper about voting YES on the town's school budget. Paul balled the letter up and threw it in the trash.

He opened his computer and typed another letter. People needed to understand.

The knife burned. Or at least the wound underneath it did.

Paul gritted his teeth and tried to focus on something in the room. Don't think about the blade, think about the lamp. The lamp was usually the first thing he turned on in the house. He'd drop his briefcase and flick the switch, before going for the TV remote or the fridge.

He didn't even get a chance to do that. The ambient light that filtered through his Venetian blinds was the only reason he could see the lamp at all.

Forget the lamp.

"Talk to me," Paul said. "Why are you doing this?"

"You know why."

The knife pulled a little tighter against him, and Paul's stomach finally gave in. He gagged and felt whatever was left of his lunch climb up. He tried not to spasm, and the vomit only dribbled from his mouth.

It dripped onto the knife and the guy's hand.

"What the hell?" the guy asked, and then stepped back. The knife clattered on the floor.

Paul fell to his knees. He got up and headed toward the door, but his assailant beat him there and leaned against it. He was older and mostly bald, only some flecks of gray hair at his ears. Laugh lines and crow's feet detailed his face. He wore a tight black t-shirt, and his biceps bulged underneath.

Paul had no idea who this man was.

And he didn't want to find out.

He turned and headed toward the kitchen, trying to get to the back window of his apartment. If he could get there and get the window open, he was pretty sure he'd survive a jump to the street. It was only the second floor. Maybe a fifteen foot drop.

The attacker had other ideas.

There was a sharp pain in his leg, and suddenly Paul was on the floor again. Fire shot up the back of his leg into his butt. He grabbed at the wound, but was pressed harder into the floor. He felt his jaw throb with the first punch. The second smashed his nose. Paul could smell his own blood.

He blinked to clear his vision, and saw the man, arm cocked back, smile.

"Don't you know who I am?" he said.

Jill Keenan came into Paul's room while his students were independently reading. Smiling, she held up a paper and approached his desk. Two of the kids oooh-ed, as if they couldn't believe men and women talked without being in a romantic relationship.

"What's up?" he whispered, ignoring the catcalls.

"You were the only one who didn't get one of these. I just put them in everybody's mailbox."

When he took the paper from her, he got a whiff of her strawberry perfume. Jill leaned on his desk as he unfolded the paper and read.

Faculty of Magellan Middle School,

You are no doubt aware that one of your colleagues wrote two letters to the local paper complaining about the residents of this fine town voting the school budget down. He reasoned voting the budget down was a sign we don't care about the students. He also said I didn't understand why a school budget is important.

Nothing is further from the truth.

I am tired of his logic. I do not wish to see our schools fail. I am tired of paying for them. I am tired of underachieving students and underachieving teachers complaining about money. I am tired of teachers speaking up about it. I am tired of them defying me.

To the teachers who have kept quiet, and gone about their business, I assure you, you have nothing to worry about. Your colleague, the letter writer, he should be ashamed.

He will be.

A concerned taxpayer.

Paul put the paper down on his desk and felt a lead ball form in his stomach. He folded the paper back up and looked at Jill.

"Everyone got one of these?" Paul thought about the anonymous letter he received two days earlier.

"Yeah. I don't look at mine until I put them all in the boxes, otherwise I never would have given them out."

"Don't worry about it."

"Are you okay?"

He looked at his class. They were staring at him.

"Get back to your books," he said. "Book talk is on Monday."

Jill crossed her arms and waited.

"I'm fine. You can't worry about these idiots."

"The letter you wrote was a good one," she said. "You said what we all were thinking."

Paul sat back. His chair rolled a few inches.

"We should show this to Andy," Jill said. "Or maybe the police."

"What could they do? It's an anonymous letter." Paul shrugged. "It's nothing. People who are too scared to sign their name are cowards."

Jill looked at the letter once more. "I guess you're right."

"Can you take all of these out of everyone's mailboxes?"

Jill nodded. "As long as no one picked theirs up. I have prep next."

"Duty, then prep? Your schedule sucks." He laughed.

She patted him on the shoulder, got up, and left the classroom.

Before the door could close, the bell rang. Students stormed into the hallway.

"I don't know."

"How can you not know?"

The man swung his arm down and connected with Paul's jaw. The shockwave traveled through his brain. Blood dribbled from his mouth.

Is that it? You're just going to lie here and get the crap beat out of you?

Paul balled his fist and punched the man in the stomach. The man doubled over, and Paul hit him again. Paul slid out from under the man. But as the attacker staggered in pain, he'd blocked the door to the kitchen. Paul ran back toward the front door.

And stopped right in front of the knife. He picked it up and turned back toward his assailant.

It would be self-defense, wouldn't it?

The man had gotten up and looked at Paul. In the eyes, not the knife.

"This is unexpected," the man said.

"What do you want?"

The man shrugged. "To kill you. To do away with shit like you."

Paul squeezed his hand tighter around the knife handle. It was a simple kitchen knife, stainless steel with a black handle. Paul had once cut himself cleaning one and needed six stitches.

The man coughed and spat on the carpet.

"Didn't you get my letter?" he said.

Paul didn't speak, but took a step forward. Jam the knife into this guy's neck. Show the cops the wounds on his neck and face.

"Answer me!" the man said.

"No. I have no idea what you're talking about."

Another cough. "That's the problem with you teachers. You don't listen. You think you're right and nothing else matters."

Paul resisted the urge to ask him to clarify. He couldn't believe how confident this guy was. Paul was holding the knife now, but the guy was confident and acting like he was still in charge of the situation.

Budget Cuts

And then the guy ran into the kitchen.

"You wrote that letter to the paper, and you thought no one would care. Or everyone would just roll over and vote the way you'd hope. But I wrote you a letter and I wanted you to reply. And when you didn't, I wrote to your school." The voice echoed off the tile floors.

As he advanced, Paul thought about Jill getting all the envelopes out of everyone's mailbox. How only two other people were able to read the letter, and they urged him to go to the police as well. He didn't listen. Argued against it.

"How could I respond to you? Your letters were anonymous."

There was movement. Paul thought about the other door to the kitchen. If the guy doubled back, he'd be able to sneak up from behind.

The man's voice seemed further away now. "You're a teacher. I thought you were supposed to be smart. Figure it out. I found your address, and you're not listed."

"You couldn't even sign your name. You're a coward."

More footsteps. He heard the thud of a kitchen cabinet swinging against the wall. A few dishes clanked.

Paul breathed out. He had the quintessential bachelor pad. No silverware sharper than a butter knife.

Now the voice seemed closer. "I'm the coward? Interesting. I'm standing here, unarmed. You've got the knife, and my heart rate's normal. How's yours?"

For the first time, Paul noticed his heart thudding in his chest. He could hear blood rushing through his ears.

"Here's what you don't understand. You never had to give anything up. All we do is pay you more each and every year. A four percent pay raise. And how do you get paid for it?" The man took another step forward. "How? We raise property taxes. And people who are barely hanging on to jobs have to pay you off. And you can't even get fired. Now they'll replace you with someone cheaper."

Paul blinked and almost responded. The argument had been rehashed in every newspaper in the state. And he did have a counterargument. How residents of this town hadn't passed a budget in nearly ten years. How the cost per pupil in his town was one of the lowest in the state.

But he didn't get a chance to say anything. Because as soon as Paul blinked, the man burst back through the open kitchen door.

They both toppled over and the knife skittered away again. The man pummeled Paul, hitting him in the head and stomach. Paul got his hands up, wrapped them around the guy's throat and squeezed. The guy kept swinging. Paul felt his eyes start to swell shut. His right hand got knocked free of the guy's throat.

The punches kept coming and Paul's vision blurred. He tried to keep squeezing with his left hand, but got nothing. He used his right to feel around.

And find the knife.

"Why won't you listen to me?" the man shouted.

Paul wrapped his fingers around the handle.

"Why won't anyone listen?"

Paul felt his triceps flex, and his wrist twist a little bit. It was as if he wasn't in control of his own body.

"I'm right! I've told them so many times, I'm right!" The man's voice was high pitched, as if he was crying at the same time.

Two more punches connected with Paul's face, and his grip on the knife almost loosened. He had no other choice.

Paul swung the knife up and jammed it into his attacker's side.

The man grunted and fell backwards. Paul got up and pulled the knife out. It was stained red. His attacker screamed. Without thinking, he brought the blade down again.

This time it dug into the man's chest.

His attacker's name was Mark Gardener. The police told Paul that after he'd been arrested. Gardener was considered a curmudgeon in town. A former locksmith, he now spent his time writing letters to the paper and showing up at Board of Education meetings with prepared speeches. None of the pieces were positive.

But no one considered him psychotic.

Paul was let go on bail, but knew he'd face trial. He had to hire a lawyer, and found one through the NJEA. The lawyer was optimistic.

The school board wasn't.

They couldn't have a killer working for them. He was suspended, without pay, and they were going to go through due process to fire him. The union rep told him he had no chance to keep his job.

Jill called him a month after the incident. He considered not answering, but he missed her voice.

"How are you holding up?" she asked.

"I'm okay," he said.

"You're lying."

She knew him too well. They'd worked together for ten years

"How's the new guy?" Paul asked.

"He's way behind. Barely a chapter ahead of the kids. Doesn't know how to deal with them. Always yelling. He sent Charlie Bellows down to the office for chewing gum the other day."

Paul closed his eyes. Administration's biggest pet peeve was sending children to them for discipline over something trivial.

"Did you give him any advice?"

"I told him what you told me when I started."

Paul remembered. Sometimes you want them to act their age. Then you realize they are.

Jill took a deep breath and when she spoke, her words were clipped. "I'm worried about you."

"I'm going to be fine," he said.

They talked for an hour that night. Once he hung up, he went to the computer and opened his email. He started typing.

The next budget vote was only a month away.

GREEN BY
Chris F. Holm

The bowl popped and crackled in Johnnie's hand as he set fire to the shake and seeds within. He took a long, slow pull, and his lungs filled with acrid heat. Then they filled with ash as the meager cherry fell apart and he sucked it down.

Johnnie coughed until he damn near puked. His face went red, then purple. Tears poured down his cheeks. After what felt like a goddamn hour, the offending ash came back up, and he spat gray onto the threadbare rug.

"Fuck," he said, voice hoarse. "Kicked."

"You shitting me?" said Quiggs. "It ain't even noon yet. How the hell could we be out?"

"Hey, fuck you—it ain't like you pitched in."

"I told you, dude—my mom snagged my stash. I'm lucky she let me come over at all. Probably wouldn'ta, if I hadn't told her we were watching Simon. The fuck is that kid, anyway?"

Johnnie shrugged. Like he gave a damn where Simon was. "Whadda you care? Little brat's probably off readin' or something. I told him not to come knocking—maybe he finally got smart enough to listen."

"That'd be a first. I swear, I don't know how you ended up with such a fucking nerd for a brother."

But Simon wasn't Johnnie's brother—not really. I mean, whatever, they shared a mom, but Duane sure as shit wasn't his dad.

Sure, Duane tried to play all buddy-buddy, with his whole *Hey champ! Wanna toss the ball around?* routine, but Johnnie wasn't buying it. He knew how Duane and Mom talked about him when he wasn't around; everything they said (and *did*—ugh) in their bedroom carried right down the heating duct to the basement where he slept. Johnnie, the fuckup. Johnnie, the high-school dropout.

Johnnie, who looks more like his father every day.

That last was the one that really pissed him off. It's one thing to try and bury anything that reminds you of your first failed marriage and start fresh with Family 2.0—Johnnie was pretty sure that's why Mom stuck him in the basement in the first place—but to compare him to some deadbeat asshat he'd never even met? That's fucking cold.

"Hey," Quiggs said, "you got any cash?"

"Got a fiver."

"I got four in change out in the truck. Another dollar makes a dime."

"Yeah? And how long's a dime bag gonna last us? 'Sides, that shitbag Howie won't sell to me no more since I hooked up with that chick he's banging."

"Sucks."

"Tell me about it—I lost my fucking dealer, and that bitch won't return my calls."

Across the room, a throat cleared, and Kevin's slow stoner baritone called out: "I know where we can score some weed."

Truth be told, the announcement scared the shit out of Johnnie —Kev had been camped out on a beanbag in the corner ever since he popped some of Duane's back pills a couple hours back, and somewhere around their second bowl, Johnnie'd forgotten he was even there.

"Whadda you know about scoring weed? You're a scrounge, dude—all you do is smoke other people's shit. You've never been carrying a day in your life."

Kev rubbed sleep out of his eyes and scowled. "That don't mean I don't know where to find some."

"Oh yeah? Where?"

"There's this dude out on 27 who's got a greenhouse fulla dank behind his house just begging to be broken into."

"Yeah? And how do you know about it?"

"I seen it. It's where my Grandma gets her shit. Says it helps her with her chemo."

"Dude," Quiggs said. "I wish I had cancer."

"I know, right?" Kev replied.

But Johnnie just frowned. "I don't know, dude—breaking into some drug dealer's private stash seems like a good way to end up dead."

"This guy ain't no drug dealer—he's just some fucking hippie with a grow license. 'Sides, he's like forty or some shit; dude probably passed a pipe at Woodstock, for Christ's sake. Guy that old gets in a tussle, he's liable to break a fucking hip—you really think he'd give us trouble?"

"Yeah, okay, maybe not. But a greenhouse fulla weed has *got* to have one hell of a lock on it."

"Yeah," Kevin conceded, "the front entrance has got one a them keypad locks on it, like from the movies. But the fucking place is made of glass—how hard could it be to bust a pane and make off with a little? In like thirty seconds, we could take enough to last a month. The dude probably wouldn't even miss it, and we'll be long gone before he ever knows we were even there."

Johnnie pretended to think about it a minute, just to remind the guys who was in charge. Really, though, he'd already made up his mind. It sounded like the perfect plan—and besides, what was the worst that could happen? They get caught, he spends a night or two in the county lockup instead of this lame-ass basement. Honestly, one dingy cinderblock room is as good as another.

But if they didn't get caught—if they pulled it off—they'd be fucking legends, like Clooney in that flick where he breaks into the casino vault to impress that *Pretty Woman* chick.

He cast a glance at Quiggs, imbuing it with as much Danny Ocean cool as he could muster. "Your truck gassed up?"

"Yeah."

"Then saddle up, boys—we got a job to do."

Kev and Quiggs broke into smiles, and Johnnie couldn't help but do the same.

This was gonna be fucking *epic.*

Quiggs' pickup truck barreled east on 27—that is, if a truck can barrel at twenty miles an hour. Quiggs hunched white-knuckled over the wheel like it was the last lap at Le Mans, his bloodshot eyes flitting to the rearview every ten seconds like he expected the five-oh would be descending on them at any moment. It was more grandma than getaway driver, and it was driving Johnnie fucking nuts.

"I thought you said you were good to drive?"

"We're getting there, ain't we?"

"Yeah, at a fucking walk."

Quiggs scrunched up his face as he worked on a rejoinder, and then started at a sudden noise. "Dude, you hear that?"

"Hear what?" asked Johnnie.

"Dunno. Kinda sounded like a cough."

"You're being paranoid. Nobody in here coughed."

Kev piped up from the bitch seat in the back of the cab: "I heard it, too, dude. I think it came from the back."

Johnnie glanced out the back window, but there was nothing in the truck bed but Quiggs' dad's landscaping shit, all covered with a ratty blue tarp. "No one's back there, man."

"You sure?" said Quiggs. "What if it's the cops?"

"Do you even hear yourself? The fuck would a cop be doing hiding in the back of your truck? We haven't done anything yet."

"Exactly," said Quiggs, pulling over into the gravel shoulder. "Which is why we oughta check *now*, before we do."

Kev, moron that he was, agreed with Quiggs. Johnnie thought they were both fucking nuts, and told them so, but they weren't hearing any of it. So over his objections, the three of them climbed out of the cab to confront Quiggs' imaginary copper.

They circled the truck, and stood in silence beside the tailgate for a moment, all looking expectantly at each other. Then Quiggs nominated Johnnie spokesperson with a nudging elbow to the ribs.

Johnnie sighed. "We know you're in there," he said, feeling

like a fool because in truth he knew no such thing. "You may as well come on out."

Nothing happened. Johnnie shook his head at the folly of his idiot friends.

Then something happened, and he damn near pissed his pants.

When that tarpaulin started moving, Quiggs, Kev, and Johnnie pulled their best Three Stooges act, all freaking out and running into each other in an attempt to get away. Johnnie bounced off somebody and wound up on his ass in the middle of the street. Kev and Quiggs clunked heads. Kev's head must've been the harder of the two, because he kept his feet, while Quiggs tumbled into the muddy, weed-strewn ditch.

Then Simon tossed off the tarpaulin, and Johnnie felt like a goddamn fool.

He was a beanpole of a kid in mousy clothes and tousled dishwater hair. His baby face belied his thirteen years, and a pair of wire-framed glasses sat perpetually crooked atop his nose. Johnnie couldn't believe to look at him he could be anybody's favorite, but the little apple-polisher was beloved by teacher and parent alike. Johnnie saw past all his math-club-and-soup-kitchen bullshit, though—saw him for the nosy little snot he really was. He was always all *What're you doing? Can I come? How come you never let me hang out?*

Fucking annoying is what it was—the kid had everything he could ever want, but still, he couldn't help but try and horn in on Johnnie's business. And now to stow away on his big heist? That was just too much.

"Jesus fucking Christ, Simon—what the hell are you doing here?"

Simon looked at his shoes. "Dunno."

"Not good enough, kid." This from Kev. "Spill, or I'm gonna hafta kick your ass."

Simon blanched. "I just... I heard you guys talking, and I thought... I don't know, that if I tagged along, proved that I was cool..."

Now it was Johnnie who went pale. "You were eavesdropping on us?"

"No! I mean, a little. There's this grate in Mom and Dad's room...."

"How much did you hear?"

"Enough to know that you'd be grounded for life if Mom and Dad found out what you were up to."

Quiggs dragged his muddy ass up out of the ditch. "You trying to blackmail us, kid?"

"Of course not! I—I just...I just wanted to be included is all. I'm not as innocent as you guys think, you know."

"Sure you're not," said Johnnie. "Only right now, all you are is going home."

"You bring me home, and I'll tell on you—I swear I will!"

"You do and I'll beat the hell out of you."

"Maybe—but you'll probably do that anyway. And either way, you'll still be grounded."

"Not if we don't go through with the heist."

"Sure you will. I tell them a story about knocking over some pot dealer and you think Mom and Dad are going to figure I made it up? It'll take them ten seconds to realize I must've heard it from you, and you'll be in trouble whether you go through with it or not. And if you're going to risk punishment, you may as well do the crime, right? Just let me come along, and no one will be the wiser."

"Kid's got a point," said Kev.

"Yeah," said Quiggs. "What's the harm of bringing him along?"

Fuck. Johnnie didn't like this. Didn't like it one bit. But what kind of choice did he have? Simon had him over a barrel.

"Fine," he said. "But you're staying in the goddamn truck, you hear me?"

Simon nodded, and tried his damndest not to smile. This was his ticket. His chance to show his brother what he was made of.

And once he did, things between them were gonna be different—he just knew it.

"Holy shit," breathed Johnnie, "that whole thing is fulla weed?"

"Yup," said Kev, who crouched beside him in the underbrush, a fragrant evergreen blanketing them in shadow. Quiggs and Simon were back at the truck, the former keeping it running while the latter no doubt peppered him with inane questions. "Thing of beauty, ain't it?"

"Damn right it is," he replied, and then, because it sounded like a movie thing to say: "Let's rock and roll."

They broke cover from the underbrush and trotted over to the wire fence—four parallel lines each a little under a foot apart, the lowest just above the brown-green blades of grass, and the highest at chest height.

"Fuck," said Johnnie. "That thing electric?"

Kev reached out a hand, tapped at one of the wires. "If it is, it ain't on."

"Cool." He snipped the wires with the hedge trimmers he'd snagged from the back of Quiggs' truck, and he and Kev strolled through the opening cool as Clooney. Then they trotted over to the greenhouse, its considerable bulk shielding them from view of the house beyond. It really was a thing of beauty—half a football field of glass and weed, glinting like an emerald in the midday sun, and just begging for a little smash-and-grab. Johnnie was amazed nobody else had ever thought of it. But then, not everybody had what it took to be a legend.

"All right, dude," he said to Kev, "go to it."

Kev stepped up to the side of the greenhouse and cocked back the tire iron in his hand. But as he reached his apex and tensed for the downswing, a voice from behind stopped him cold.

"I really wish you wouldn't do that," it said. "I'd hate to have to deal with cops *and* a broken window all in one day."

Kev and Johnnie spun around—Kev dropping the tire iron, and Johnnie the hedge clippers. Good thing, too, because keeping hold of them might've been perceived as threatening, and the guy behind them had a gun.

Not much of one, admittedly—just a little snub-nosed dealie-job that coulda fit in a lady's purse. But it was the only one that Kev and Johnnie had ever been on the business end of, and it looked big enough to both of them.

"Don't shoot!" squealed Kevin, not entirely manfully.

The dude—your basic hippie model, complete with Dead shirt, cargo pants, and ponytail—actually laughed. "Nobody's shooting anybody, dipshit. This is just to keep you here until the cops arrive, okay? Which ought to be any minute now, so just be cool."

"But how..." Johnnie began, and then it dawned on him. "Shit—it was the fence, wasn't it? Fucking thing's got an alarm."

"Wow, gold star, buddy! Shame you hadn't thought of that before you went and cut it, huh? Now do us all a favor and keep quiet, would you? I'm sure the nice policemen won't be long. And for God's sake, put your hands down."

Kev and Johnnie complied. Johnnie, for his part, didn't even know that he had raised his. He'd been too busy turning over in his mind what to do, but truth was, there wasn't anything *to* do. This guy had 'em dead to rights. If this were a movie, he'd be shouting at his character to run—telling him this dude wasn't gonna shoot him, so why not? But the fact was, this shit didn't feel like no goddamn movie, and he'd been wrong enough times already today he wasn't much up for gambling. Getting arrested sounded a whole lot better than getting shot.

So the three stood in silence for what seemed like forever, waiting for the cops to arrive and break up their little party. But it wasn't sirens that announced the end of their soirée. It was more of a wet, metallic *thunk*, followed by their hippie friend eatin' ground.

At first, Johnnie didn't understand what happened. Then he saw Simon, standing wide-eyed just behind the fallen hippie, and holding in his hands a spade smeared with blood and brain.

"The fuck?" said Kev.

"Si—" said Johnnie, dumbfounded by what had just occurred. "Si, what the hell did you just do?"

"I—that guy was going to kill you! I did what I had to do to save you!"

"Oh shit," said Kev, tears brimming in his eyes. "I think that fucker's dead."

"Shut up," Johnnie said. He approached the fallen man, felt for a pulse.

Nothing.

"He is, isn't he? That dude is fucking dead!" Kev was crying pretty good now. Simon, for his part, looked like he was gonna puke.

"Shut up," Johnnie repeated.

"What the fuck are we gonna do, Johnnie? Your brother fucking killed that dude!"

"I said shut up!" Johnnie didn't even realize he'd picked up the gun. But once he saw it in his hand, he knew what he had to do.

He wheeled on Kev, who just kept muttering that Simon had killed a dude, over and over to no one. Kev was so damn out of it, he never even saw the gun.

"Guys, I'm sorry!" came a call to Johnnie's left. It was Quiggs, breaking from the tree cover and sprinting toward them. "Kid said he had to take a leak, and by the time I realized he was gone..."

He stopped short when he saw the guy on the ground and Kev in Johnnie's sights. "Uh, guys? What the fuck is going on?"

For a tiny gun, that thing could make a lot of noise. Again and again it thundered, and soon Kev and Quiggs joined the hippie in the dirt.

For a moment once the shooting stopped, it was so silent, Johnnie thought he'd been struck deaf. Then Simon piped up with two quiet syllables that shattered the silence as surely as any gunshot, his voice thin and fragile like a child's.

"Johnnie?"

Johnnie dropped the gun and met Simon's terrified gaze. "Go," he said. "Run. Tell no one you were here."

"But I—"

"Simon, *now*!"

For the first time in his life, the kid listened to him. Johnnie watched him disappear into the woods, accompanied by the sound of sirens drawing closer.

Shit, he thought, eyeing the bodies at his feet—two of them his friends. This wasn't *Ocean's Eleven*, it was fucking *Reservoir Dogs*.

But what else could he have done? Simon was a good kid. Simon was his brother.

Besides, one dingy cinderblock room is as good as another.

LUZ VERDE
Frank Bill

Eyes burned with the inhale of rot. Hyena's Salvadorian pitch offered Crazy his ultimatum.

"Your time is zero."

Hyena ran a thumb across his throat. Laughed and turned back to disinfecting the pink meat. Crazy stood in the chicken factory, tired of waiting to become another statistic riddled across the land. Using a stainless-edge, he parted the dead and plucked chickens that hung from the steel shackle-line. Crazy wanted out.

With a latex covered hand, Crazy fingered out the bird's stringy opaque guts, splashed them into the metal trough. He'd been skimming cash from the dope he and his clique smuggled from the Illinois border to sell throughout Indiana and Kentucky. Drove the cellophane bricks in one van while another ran interference if needed for the state and county cops. Exchanged the product for a duffle of cash, taking a little off the top every other trip, planning to disappear. Start over. Then came the questions from Crazy's clique leader.

"The higher-ups wanna know why you comin' up short?"

Passing the pimpled fowl down the line, Hyena's words were a repetitive jolt. Crazy knew he'd been caught. The *luz verde*, the green light, had been sent.

The first break bell rang. Crazy slid the edge up his paper overall's sleeve, secured it between his braided leather wristband and forearm. He let Hyena and the other workers file out in front of him. Followed behind in shin-high rubber boots and white overalls stained with the heated insides that hid his inked flesh of Saint Death, gothic angels, clowns, roman numerals and knife scars.

Keeping his distance, Crazy thought about how everything started thirteen years ago in El Salvador. Where poverty and hunger had run cold. Callused his mother and father's gut in a driftwood shack with a tin roof nestled upon a mound of dirt and dreams of saving enough to immigrate to the States. Till Crazy found a new family.

Entering the chicken factory's tiled restroom with everyone else, Crazy pulled and tossed his rubber gloves into the metal trashcan. Took in the streaks of blood that outlined them as they lay piled with the other gloves. The memory of numbers ignited his mind. One, one thousand, knuckles vibrated his temple. Two, one thousand, a shin fractured his ribs. Three, one thousand, an elbow puttied his nose. Four, one thousand, a kick dented his thigh. To be accepted by his new family meant being *jumped-in*. He was central to the four surrounding young boys who mauled him. He wasn't allowed to fight back. It lasted thirteen seconds, felt like an hourglass filled with confetti falling instead of sand. When the beating was over, he lay like those gloves—wadded into a disregarded pile. Hands lifted him to his feet. He spit and coughed tears of ache while his new family embraced him.

In the restroom, Crazy stepped to the marble-circled washing station, grabbed a bar of soap and eyed two more clique members, Shank and Flame. With bristled heads and lean gnarled frames, they were the first two young men MS leader Angel and Crazy had recruited after crossing the Rio Grande. Paying the coyotes to bring Angel and him to the Midwest with ten other members six years ago with an objective: spread out to the small-cracker-ass redneck towns. Get a job with other immigrants. Blend in. Start recruiting members for the MS. Set up trafficking routes for drugs, humans and guns.

Mashing the metal bar to the floor beneath the rounded washing station, Crazy pushed a steady flow of water, lathered his hands. Then rinsed away the stink of his labor, stepped to one of the porcelain dryers that lined a brick wall, elbowed the chrome button that reflected his body and dried his hands. Caught Shank and Flame nodding to the handful of factory employees to get out. Footsteps and chatter exited. Hyena guarded the bathroom's doorway. Crazy took a deep breath, clenched his fists.

Shank and Flame stood in caramel-colored work uniforms, shirts buttoned to the top with their backs to a scuffed bathroom stall. Flame rattled his knuckles on the stall door. Beneath the door, boots dropped from toilet to floor. The door swung open. Crazy snake-eyed Angel. His clique leader, taking in the pitted and scarred facade that highlighted their past.

Angel tongued a question. "Why you do this, Crazy?"

Crazy didn't blink. His insides iced over. "Tired of this never knowing. Want a life of 'gevity without worry of when it end."

Angel chuckled. "You become worm-like. American bitch."

Crazy felt the others' eyes puncturing his frame from every direction with a zillion ice picks.

"No, I am El Salvadorian. Want to one day become elder Salvadorian."

In El Salvador, it was about belonging to survive. Here in the States, it was about separation by the language you didn't speak, clothes you didn't wear and cars you couldn't afford. Trafficking drugs gave you all of that till you realized you were a number waiting to be replaced by a new one.

Angel was granite-hard and said, "I am *primera palabra*. You were *segunda palabra*."

Meaning Angel was the first word, Mara, and Crazy had been the second word, Salvatrucha. The first and second in charge of their MS clique. Angel told Crazy, "But now you are *el ladron*, thief. Filch hand that accepted and nourished. You know how we deal with a Judas."

Crazy's heart redlined with alkaloid-rage and he said, "I'm done."

Angel's complexion was a rumpled hide as he gritted a wall of porcelain. "You been green-lit by big homies. You're dead."

Shank, Flame and Hyena swarmed Crazy like sharks to a raw

slab of loin. Flame feinted right and double-jabbed a point into Crazy's right shoulder. Pain ran red. Crazy grunted and ripped the butcher blade from his sleeve. Sliced across Flame's eyes, halved them into a permanent state of blindness. Flame screamed. Knees followed the blade that rattled onto the floor, with both hands patting the moisture that poured from his cleaved sight. Shank lunged and dug a serrated piece of steel into the meat of Crazy's left hip. Crazy winced. Swiped his butcher's edge across Shank's elbow flexer. Vein, tendon and ligaments ruptured. Shank jerked and broke the steel off. Dropped the handle, stepped back and palmed his wound.

From behind, Hyena roped a piece of braided cable over Crazy's head, noosed it tight across his throat. Lifted Crazy to the balls of his feet. Ripe-faced and gagging, Crazy staked his knife into Hyena's left thigh, over and over, tenderizing the muscle. Hyena released the cable, dropped backwards onto the tiled floor. The knife stuck in the flank of his leg. He chewed on the sting and burn, ripped the knife free.

Angel came with a jagged blade, divided Crazy's jaw just below the ink of a double teardrop and said, "In the hospital." Crazy staggered backwards, shoulder and hip burning, and fingered the wet from his face. Angel parted Crazy's chest and said, "In the jailhouse." Crazy pressed both hands to his chest. Eyed Angel whose eyes branded Crazy's as he rooted the jagged steel up into Crazy's stomach, twisted it from side to side and said, "Or in the grave." The three destinations of an MS member's life.

Angel backed away. Hyena rolled to his side and cut through Crazy's rubber boot with the butcher blade. Crazy's Achilles' heel was now just snapped elastic. His gauged outline oozed and splashed to the tiled floor as if a worn-out crankshaft.

Crazy lay floored by the moisture of his wounds, his heart slowed and he remembered in El Salvador, after the *jumping-in* he had to seal his initiation, spill someone else's blood. Crazy remembered watching a rival clique member steal a hen from a villager. Holding it upside down by its yellow-clawing hinds, he ran. Unseen, Crazy followed the rival to a yard knotted by cinder and soil where he heaved and smashed the chicken's head against the earth, stomped a foot down on its head, ripped it off like a rubber Halloween mask and tossed it into the dirt. Crazy pulled his knife free, came up behind the rival, slashed through the cartilage of his Adam's apple. Watched him wobble and stumble to the ground like the bird with its bloody knob of bone replacing its face, thrashing the earth till it bled out.

Now Crazy felt fingers dig into his head, felt the repetitive crack and give of his skull slamming into the bathroom ceramic, knowing to leave this life he had to offer the same thing he'd taken from the rival, his own life; blood in, blood out.

Flame lay on the floor moaning, the whites of his eyes divided and saucy. While Hyena, Angel and Shank stood over Crazy, smeared by his wounds, watching the rise and fall of his chest stop.

Each man traced the four points of an imaginary crucifix over their bodies, bowed their heads and asked forgiveness from *la Santa Muerte*, Saint Death. Then stepped to the washing station, shared a bar of soap, washed the red river from their arms and hands and down the drain.

The bell rang. The break was over. Angel, Hyena and Shank knew their working alongside the other immigrants would no longer camouflage who they were, the Mara Salvatrucha. That they would go to the second stage of their destination in this life. The jail. Inside they'd become initiated with new rituals and rules. On the outside more numbers would step up and take their place in this unending ecosystem of violence.

THE LADDER
Adrian McKinty

"Broke another squash racket! This is getting expensive."
"Quit slamming it down on the floor when you get mad, dude!"
"Are these the problems white people have?"

—Facebook Comment Thread, Failblog March 24, 2011

Donald sighed as the university loomed out of the rain and greyness. All morning he had hit nothing but red lights, and now although it was green, he had to stop because a huge gang of students was crossing the pedestrian walkway in front of him.

It was rag week and they were wearing costumes: animals, Cossacks, knights, milk maids. Predictable and drab, the outfits had a home-made look and they depressed him. The students were laughing and some were actually skipping. It was raining, it was cold, it was December in godforsaken Belfast, so what the hell had they to laugh about?

The traffic light went red and then amber and then green again and still they hadn't all got across. He was tempted to honk them off the road, but no doubt from hidden pockets they would produce flour and water bombs and throw them at him. He sat there patiently while the car behind began to toot. He looked in the rearview at a vulnerable, orange V-W microbus. Yeah, you keep doing that, mate, he said to himself and sure enough, a half a dozen eggs cut up the poor bastard's windscreen.

He chortled to himself, the mob cleared and he turned into the car park.

"Jesus Christ, is that a grin?" McCann asked him when he appeared in the office.

He nodded.

"What, have you got a job offer somewhere?" McCann asked.

"No, old chap, I am doomed to spend my declining years with your boorish self and my cretinous students in this bombed-out hell-hole of a city slowly sinking into the putrid mudflats from which it so inauspiciously began."

"Bugger, if I'd known I was going to get an essay..." McCann said, not all that good-naturedly.

Donald took off his jacket and set it down on the chair. "Is this coffee drinkable?" he asked staring dubiously at the tarry black liquid in the coffee pot.

"Drinkable, yes. Distinguishable as coffee, no."

Donald poured himself a cup anyway, added two sugars and picked up the morning paper.

"Before I lose interest entirely, why were you smiling when you came in? Some pretty undergraduate, no doubt?" McCann asked.

"No, no, nothing like that I'm afraid. The students went after some hippy driving a V-W Microbus, talk about devouring your own."

"Aye. I've seen that thing around. New guy. Been parking in my spot. Kicked his side panels a few times. Buckled like anything. It's an original. Those old ones are bloody death traps."

"A windscreen covered with eggs and flour won't make it any safer."

McCann took out his pipe and began filling it with tobacco. Donald went back to the paper. "So what's on the old agenda today anyway?" McCann asked.

"Nothing in the morning. Playing squash at lunch time and then we're doing 'The Miller's Tale' after lunch."

"'The Miller's Tale'? Which one's that?"

"Do you actually want to know?"

"Well, not really, I suppose," McCann replied, somewhat shamefaced.

The hours passed by in a haze of tobacco smoke, bad coffee, worse biscuits and dull news from the paper.

At twelve, Donald slipped off, only to be intercepted by a student outside the gym.

"Dr. Bryant," the student began in a lilting voice and Donald remembered that he was a Welshman called Jones or Evans or something.

"Mr. Jones, how can I help you today?"

"Uh, actually my name is—"

"Yes, Mr. Jones, how I can help you? Come on. Out with it, man. I'm in a hurry."

"Uhm, Dr. Bryant, I'm supposed to do a presentation next week on Johnson…"

"Ben or Sam or, God save us, Denis?"

"Uhhh, the playwright."

"They all wrote plays, Mr. Jones."

"They did? Uhm, well, it's Ben. Yeah. And, well, the library doesn't have the secondary sources, someone took them all and I don't know what to do really. I tried to borrow them from the University of Ulster library, but they're out too. I've read all the primary stuff, but I want the secondary sources to do a good job."

Donald felt a pin-prick of guilt. Mr. Jones seemed like a nice, sincere, young man. One of the few good students. He was studying engineering but was taking English as an elective. Perhaps that explained his curious dedication. The BA's in English were all perverts and pot-heads. "All right, Mr. Jones, come by my office at four today and I'll lend you my own books, they should be sufficient for a half decent presentation. You'll be careful with them, won't you?"

"Oh God, yeah, thank you, thank you very much," the student said.

Donald arrived at the gym feeling unnaturally buoyant—two quite pleasant incidents in one morning.

He showed his ID to Peter Finn, the ancient security guard at the reception desk.

"Afternoon, Dr. Bryant," Peter said in his rough country accent.

"Afternoon," he replied curtly.

"Going to give the wee shites another hiding, eh?"

"One tries, Peter, one tries."

"You still at the top?" Peter asked, knowing full well the answer. Donald swelled a little. "Still plugging away."

"Sixteen straight months, Professor Millin says. Yon's a record, ye know," Peter said very seriously.

"Is it indeed?" Donald said and this time it was his turn to pretend. "Well, all good things must come to an end sometime. This new crop of lecturers is giving me a run for my money," Donald said magnanimously.

Peter winked at him as if he didn't quite believe him.

Donald grinned, went to the basement, found locker 201 and changed quickly into his gear: a casual blue T-shirt, white shorts, white socks and an old pair of Adidas squash sneakers. He looked at himself in the mirror. He was in the prime of life. His eyes were clear, his cheeks clean shaved, his hair jet black with only a few strands of invading grey around the ears.

Fenton was late and Donald tried hard not to show his irritation. Fenton was a slightly younger man and he was nimble. He was number three on the squash ladder and by no means an unworthy opponent. Fenton playing above his game and Donald playing beneath his could pretty much even out the field. Fenton changed into his gear: pristine white shorts, Fred Perry top and a brand new racket.

They walked to the court, stretched, warmed up the ball.

Donald won the racket spin.

He served a high looping ball that died in the corner. Fenton made an attempt to return it but he had no chance. Donald served five more like that before Fenton managed to get one back and by that time, it was too late—his confidence was broken. Donald won the match three games to one, Fenton's sole game coming from Donald's largesse. When he was in control, it was Donald's policy always to let an opponent win at least one game so that no one would ever know the true picture of his ability.

They showered and had a quick gin and tonic in the bar before

Donald went off to his lecture. It was a nearly full house and a few of the students didn't ask stupid questions, and he was in good form when he set off for home at four o'clock. Halfway to the car, he remembered about young Jones and went back to his office. Amazingly the undergraduate was on time and he gave him the books without further ado.

"Quite the day," he said to himself as he walked to his Volvo estate under clearing sky. Susan noticed his good mood immediately as he picked her up outside the Ulster Bank on Botanic Avenue. "You're in a good mood," she said.

"Yes," he said. "Let's eat out at the new Italian."

"What about my eggplant lasagne?"

"We'll give it to the dog."

"What dog?"

"Any dog."

The drive to Carrickfergus was easy, the new Italian was acceptable, the sommelier complimented him on his choice of wine.

He parked the Volvo outside his neat, mock-Tudor detached house near the Marina. After another cheeky bottle of Tuscan red, he and Susan had sex only slightly less exciting than that he'd been lecturing about this afternoon in "The Miller's Tale."

As days go, it wasn't bad and when the University loomed out of the mist next morning, this time he didn't sigh.

Susan, getting a lift to Belfast for the shopping, smiled at him.

"It's growing on you," she said.

"Perhaps," he agreed.

"You're playing Fenton today in your silly squash thing, aren't you?"

"Oh no, that was yesterday. And it's not silly. He was the third seed. Psyched him out completely, poor chap. Went to pieces. Had to go easy on him."

"So you're still top of the ladder?"

Donald was a little surprised at the question. Of course he was still top. Did she seriously think he could take her out to the expensive new Italian restaurant, get the priciest plonk on the menu and be happy as a clam if he was off the top? My God, what kind of cipher did she think she'd married.

"Oh yes, still at the top," he said casually.

She started talking about something or other but he was replaying the game in his mind, wondering if his backhand was still quite as strong as his lob. He left her outside the bank.

"So you'll drive me to the soup kitchen on Saturday?" she asked getting out of the car.

"I'll drive you," he said and then after a pause added: "What soup kitchen, what are you talking about?"

"Haven't you been listening? Our reading group. That book really affected us and we're volunteering at the soup kitchen on Saturday. Christmas is coming you know."

He tried to think what the book could be. Something by Orwell perhaps, or Dickens, or some ghastly novel set among the poor of India.

"Of course I'll drive you. In fact, I think I'll even go. Help out."

"You?" she said incredulously.

"Me, yes. Why so shocked? I'm a Labor man through and through. Help the common people, each according to his needs and from, uh, you know... that's my motto," he said with only half sarcasm, for she had hurt him a little with her surprise.

The week went by like every other week, and on Saturday he did help out in the soup kitchen and it was by no means completely unpleasant. Some of the indigent were witty and grateful fellows fallen on hard times and he felt, if not happy, at least content.

The following Monday morning Mr. Jones gave his presentation and it wasn't bad, and that afternoon he played squash with Professor Millin in the gym. Millin was number six on the ladder, not a serious opponent. An older man, a physics lecturer, well into his forties, although last week he had taken a game off Dunleavy, who was currently in second place, and Dunleavy was the sort who never let anyone have a game, ever.

"Heard you gave old Fred Dunleavy a run for his money," Donald said conversationally as they walked down to the court.

"That Scots bastard, I showed him, he's slipping, he's really slipping, getting a paunch, I tell you, you'll cream him next time you play him, cream him," Millin said.

Donald was happy to hear this. Dunleavy was a young physical education lecturer and for some time it had been his fear that Dunleavy would one day pull a superb game out of the bag and beat him.

"He's been avoiding me for weeks, I suppose that's why," Donald said with satisfaction.

They paused outside the court to stretch. Donald looked at the squash ladder and was surprised to see a new name way down at the bottom, at number sixteen: V.M. Sinya.

"Who's that?" he said, pointing at the name. Millin was the Ladder Secretary for this term, so he should know.

"Oh yes, new chap, foreigner, bloody Pak... er, I mean, uh, an Indian fellow I think. Initials stand for Victor Mohammed, so I suppose he's a Muslim. He's from Computer Science. A lot of those boys do computers nowadays."

"Is he any good?" Donald asked with a hint of nervousness in his voice. Anyone new could be trouble and several world champions had come from Pakistan.

"How the hell should I know?" Millin replied with great indifference.

"All right, let's go in," Donald said, putting all ominous thoughts of the new-comer out of his mind.

He let Millin have a few points early before cruising to an easy victory in four games. He showered, picked up Susan and drove home.

On Thursday, the Dean told him that his student evaluations were up since last term and, after buttering him up, asked him if he'd ever considered standing for the University Council. He had no such intention whatever, but the thought that the Dean was interested in him pleased him immensely.

On Friday he had a game with McCann, who was number twelve on the ladder. McCann had been quite a useful little player until the drink had become the dominant force in his life. Now all he was left with was a powerful serve and a few trick shots. He had no stamina and he couldn't get about the court. Donald never usually bothered to play anyone this low down but McCann was a friend. When he got to the court, he was pleased to see that Mr. V.M. Sinya was still at number sixteen. He hadn't even been able to beat old Franklin at fifteen; clearly the man wasn't much of a threat. He found that he was tremendously relieved by this. Was the ladder so important to him that the thought of a mysterious stranger had given him the jitters? He laughed at himself. What a dunderhead you are, he said to himself, and to prove his good humor, he let McCann take a couple of games.

On Saturday he was still feeling sufficiently good to help out at the soup kitchen again. Also at the weekend he received a letter that one of his papers on Chaucer was going to be anthologized in the new collection by Dalrimple. Things, in fact, were going so well that he began to be suspicious that something terrible was going to happen. Perhaps he would be informed that he had some dreadful illness, or maybe he would crash the car.

Just in case, he took the train to work on Monday, sitting in a back carriage near the emergency exit and steeling himself for a sudden derailment.

Nothing happened except for fifty gum-chewing, messy, loud, obnoxious children getting on at Greenisland who tormented him all the way to Central Station with their music and pointless celebrity gossip.

His fears of impending disaster were somewhat realized when he showed up at the court to play Dunleavy and he saw that the mysterious Mr. Sinya was at number ten on the squash ladder. The man had demolished five opponents in a week! This meant, of course, he had displaced McCann, so at least he could interrogate his friend at lunch.

In an unusually brutal and hurried match, he thrashed Dunleavy, showered quickly and found McCann in the office eating toast and drinking tea mixed with whisky.

"What's Sinya like?" he blurted out before even saying hello.

"Sinya, I've no idea, mate."

"You played him."

"I gave him a bye; he wanted to play me on Friday lunch-time and I just couldn't be bothered."

"You gave him a bye?"

"Yes."

"So maybe that's why he's jumped up the ladder? People have been giving him byes."

"Aye, could be," McCann said, not at all interested.

Relief sunk over Donald like chloroform and again he chastised himself for the importance he had given to something so silly as the squash ladder.

The relief lasted until Wednesday when he bumped into Millin coming out of university bookshop. Millin informed him that Sinya had demolished him and that he, Sinya, was now number five on the ladder.

"What's he like?" Donald asked, trying not to sound frantic or panicked.

"Oh, he's good. Going to give you a pretty tough game."

"What's he like?" Donald insisted.

"Don't get your knickers in a twist. He's Pakistani. I suppose forty, perhaps older, it's hard to tell with them. He's fast and, my God, that serve, those returns. It's a nightmare, you give him any opportunity and he destroys you. Our match was over in half an hour."

Donald went home that night in a state of distress. He barely talked to Susan and he couldn't concentrate on his proofs for the Dalrimple book.

From his upstairs study, he stared at the boats in Carrickfergus Marina and the grey castle beyond. The boat halliards were muzzled by the wind, the granite castle walls kept their own counsel.

Could it be that the squash ladder was perhaps the one thing that gave him any satisfaction, any sense of accomplishment, in what was really a rather pathetic, little, nondescript life?

Not the teaching, not the writing, not even Susan.

And now, inevitably, he was going to face his Nemesis. It was a melodramatic thought but he couldn't shake it.

A few days later, the phone rang in his office. With a sense of dread, he picked up the receiver. Naturally it was Sinya. He had beaten Fenton and Dunleavy and he would like to play Donald whenever it was convenient.

His voice was pleasant enough, foreign but not very foreign and gentle. Aye, that's how they get you, Donald thought. Softly softly.

Lull you and then go for the jugular. Bastards. Well, he wouldn't let them. He wouldn't take this lying down. This was his league, his campus. Who did this guy think he was, for Christ's sake? He'd been going easy on these chumps, he could take them all with one hand behind his back. This guy was no different. Try to spook me? See about that. He realized that during this prolonged internal soliloquy, Sinya had been waiting for a reply on the other end of the phone.

"This afternoon's fine with me. 1 p.m.," he said quickly, hung up and attempted to bury himself in work until just before the match.

He arrived early, but Sinya was already there, changed, waiting for him. They shook hands. Sinya was tall, bearded, good looking. He had a very charming way about him. He smiled easily and was polite. He asked Donald how he was and inquired about Donald's new (bought yesterday) super-light, super-strong, carbon-fiber, state-of-the-art, Khan Slazenger Pro racket.

Sinya won the spin, served, and launched a tremendous dying serve that Donald barely returned, but of course Sinya was already at the front wall waiting to volley Donald's weak backhand. Donald, anticipating a crushing return, ran to the back right of the court, but Sinya placed a perfect drop shot in the left front corner, flat footing Donald and winning the point. Sinya won the next four points and then missed one. On Donald's serve, Sinya volleyed the ball back so fast, Donald didn't even see it until it was too late.

The whole match went that way, Donald's play got worse and worse, and forty-five minutes later, it was all over. Donald had managed to take a game but Sinya had well beaten him 9-5, 9-4, 7-9, 9-1. Shellshocked, he let Sinya prattle on about this and that and then watched with horror as Sinya stopped at the notice board outside the court and had the cheek to take out Donald's name from the top of the ladder and substitute his own. Couldn't the bastard even have the decency to wait until he was showering?

He drove home and after four hours of silence, Susan got it out of him and of course, he agreed that it was only a stupid game and it meant nothing. The next day he went to the court with his new racket and practiced serves and drop shots for an hour and called Sinya and asked him for a rematch.

The rematch was on a Friday, and this time Sinya took him in straight sets. He realized with horror that Sinya had given him the game he'd won last time as a courtesy, just as he had condescendingly done with the lesser players in his bouts.

They walked back to the car park and Sinya stopped at the repulsive Volkswagen Microbus Donald had seen egged by the rag week students.

"Do you want a lift?" Sinya asked. "You're in Carrick, aren't you? I drive all the way to Larne, so it would be easy to drop you."

The fact that Sinya lived in Larne, one of the grimmest towns in Ulster, gave Donald no comfort in the silent ride home.

Sinya's reign at the top began and seemed unbreakable. He was miles ahead of all the players. In fact, if he'd been younger, he could well have been an international. Weeks went by and Donald played him on and off with little effect. On a weekend game with Fenton, Donald unexpectedly lost, and after another few weeks he was only at number four on the ladder.

Despite the repeated assurances of his wife, his friends and even on one humiliating occasion, the university's psychological counselor, that it was only a senseless cardboard list of names, he felt that his work, his health, his libido and his mental outlook all were suffering terribly as he slipped down the ladder.

Christmas came and went, term ended and began again.

McCann was no comfort, but he found himself spending a lot of time with him in Lavery's or the Bot, enjoying increasingly frequent liquid lunches.

At the gym he noticed now that Peter Finn was cool to him at the door.

On a damp Tuesday morning, he played a man called Jennings, lost in straight games and found that he was now last on the ladder. He almost relished this final embarrassment. Now there was no place lower to go.

He slipped upstairs to the cafeteria, called Susan and asked if she could get a lift back to Carrick with one of her friends. He sat, nursing a coffee, watching the sky darken and the lights come on street by street, Sandy Row, the Shankill, the Falls, the illumination moving north to the old shipyards and then down around the university and the City Hospital. In Belfast tonight there would be violence and love and passion and death. People in the hospital would be passing away from cancer, accidents, heart disease, and in other wards, dozens of babies were being born. New lives for old.

"It really isn't that important you know, old man," he said to himself.

"What isn't important?"

He turned. It was Mr. Jones, his student from last term's course on the Elizabethans. He was holding a book called Automotive Engineering Mistakes.

"Oh, I was just talking to myself. Join me. Have a seat. What on Earth are you reading?"

Jones sat. "It's about design faults in cars. Not just the Ford Pinto. Some pretty famous cars. Even brilliant designers make mistakes."

He got Jones a coffee.

Something McCann had once said came floating back into Donald's mind.

"I heard those Volkswagen Microbuses are a death trap," he said.

Jones grinned. "Oh yeah! No crumple zone at the front to absorb a crash and the exhaust pipe runs the full length of the floor... oh boy, you get two holes in the rust and your vehicle's filled with carbon monoxide, death trap isn't the..."

But Donald was no longer listening.

It would be the easiest thing in the world.

Punch a hole through the floor and the exhaust.

Punch a hole. Let fate take over. If nothing happened, nothing happened. But if Sinya got into an unfortunate accident in the long drive from Belfast to Larne, well, it wouldn't really be his fault. It wouldn't be murder, or attempted murder. It was a design flaw in the vehicle; he was helping nature take its course.

He said goodnight to Jones, ran six flights to the first floor and out into the wet, cold January darkness.

He knew that it would have to be now. Tonight. If he thought about it he wouldn't do it at all. His conscience would kick in. His middle class sensibility. His morality. His cowardice.

It would have to be now or never.

He reached the car park. It was six o'clock. Most of the vehicles had gone, but the putrid yellow Volkswagen was still there. Sinya often worked late, trying to get ahead no doubt, Donald thought spitefully. He went to his Volvo, rummaged in the trunk and found a torch and his toolkit. He locked the trunk and walked to the Volkswagen.

"I'm not going to do this, it's not me. No. Definitely not," he said to himself.

He checked that the coast was clear. No one was within a hundred yards.

"I don't even know what to do. Should have asked Jones for details. Doesn't matter, I'm not going to do anything. I'm not a killer. What I will do is take a look under the car though, just to see if it's possible."

He scanned the car park again, turned on the torch, squatted on the wet tarmac and looked under the V-W. A great hulking exhaust pipe ran almost all the way from the front of the cabin to the back of the car. The pipe was rusted, the chassis was rusted. A few taps from a screwdriver might do the trick....

He stood, checked the car park one more time.

No one.

He was calm.

He lay back down again.

In five minutes, it was done.

He had punched a hole in the top of the exhaust pipe and another through to the cabin. He had connected the two holes with a paper coffee cup he had found lying around—squeezing the cup into a tube. If an accident did occur, the cup would burn in the fire, and if didn't, it was an innocent enough thing to find lying in the bottom of the cab.

He wiped himself down, got in his car, sped to the Crown Bar, had two pints of Guinness to calm his nerves and drove home.

In his study, he had a double vodka and a cognac, but he couldn't sleep.

Susan went to bed and he checked the radio for reports of road accidents, deaths.

He really didn't want Sinya to die. If the poor man was injured, that would be enough. Then Donald could resume his march back up the squash ladder and get his life back in order. Get to the top, stop drinking with McCann, start writing his book, think about kids....

Finally he drifted off to sleep on the living room sofa at about three. He woke before the dawn in the midst of a nightmare. Sinya's Volkswagen had plunged off the cliff at the Bla Hole just outside of Whitehead. Two hundred feet straight down into the rocks below. The car had smashed and it was assumed to be an accident, but the police had found a paper cup wedged in the exhaust. The murderer had left fingerprints all over it.

Five years earlier, Donald had been arrested for cannabis possession at Sussex University. His prints were in the database.

"Oh my God," he said.

He turned on the radio. A road accident in Omagh, another in County Down, nothing so far on the Belfast-Larne Road.

He paced the living room. What madness had overtaken him? To try to kill a man over something so preposterous as a squash ladder? He had obviously taken leave of his senses. That's would he'd do at trial. He'd plead temporary insanity.

Insane was the right world. Macbeth crazy. Lear crazy.

Susan woke and he was such a mess that she drove him to Belfast.

He thanked her and ran to the car park.

The Volkswagen wasn't there.

"Oh, Christ," he said to himself.

He cancelled his lecture, went to his office and waited for the telephone to ring.

"Is that Dr. Bryant?

"Yes."

"This is Detective McGuirk, we'd like to come over and ask you a few questions if that would be okay..."

He waited.

McCann came by to see if he wanted to go for lunch. He said he wasn't feeling well. It wasn't untrue. He felt sick to his stomach. McCann left. He closed the door and turned the light off. He sat there in the dark.

And waited.

Perhaps they wouldn't ring him.

The first he would know about it would be a knock at the door.

He wouldn't go with them. He wouldn't let them take him. His office was on the sixth floor. The window. The window. A brief fall through the misty air. A crash. It would all be over.

He waited.

Waited.

He sank beneath his desk.

The phone rang.

"Dr. Bryant?"

"Sinya?"

"Yes."

It was Sinya. He was alive!

"Yes?" Donald managed.

"Dr. Bryant, Professor Millin cancelled with me today and I was wondering if you could squeeze in a quick game?"

"A game? A squash game? Yes, yes, of course, I'll be right over."

He sprinted the stairs.

Sinya was already in the court warming the ball.

He waved to him through the glass, ran to the locker room, changed into his gear and ran back to the court without stretching or getting a drink of water.

He didn't care how suspicious or unsubtle he sounded. He had to know.

"I didn't see your car this morning. You're always in first," Donald said.

Sinya grimaced. "That thing tried to kill me. I was halfway home last night and I realized the whole car was stinking of exhaust fumes. I pulled over just before Whitehead. Would you believe it, the whole exhaust is rusted away to nothing and a paper cup had blown in there and gotten stuck between the exhaust and the car. I left it at the garage in Whitehead and got a taxi home. I suppose I'll have to get it fixed."

The Ladder

Donald grinned with relief.

Emotions were cascading through his mind: relief, happiness, gratitude.

He would inform Susan tonight that she should go off the pill. He would start going to that soup kitchen again. He would give to charity. He would really get started on the book.

This would be his last squash game ever.

"I have really screwed up my priorities, darling," he'd tell Susan. "That silly squash ladder! Something as banal as that. I'm going to be more Zen. Live in the present, live in reality. Real things. You, me, life, stuff like that. It's corny but, well, I've had a moment of clarity. It's about perspective. It all seems so bloody stupid now. Jesus. I mean, can you believe how obsessed I was?"

Sinya hit him a few practice shots which he returned with ease.

"Well, I'm sorry about your car, old chap, but I think you can afford a new vehicle with the money they're paying you in computers. And Larne isn't the priciest place in the world to live. You should be more like me. Enjoy life. Live for the moment. Get yourself a Merc or a Beemer. You deserve it," Donald said.

Sinya laughed. "Are you kidding? The University only gives me three hundred a week, you know. A BMW on my wages?"

"Three hundred a week? What are you talking about? A junior lecturer makes twenty grand a year. It's more in computers, I'm sure."

Sinya grinned. "I'm not a lecturer. I'm a technician in the computer department. I fix the machines, man. Hardware, software, you name it."

Donald gasped but said nothing.

The game began and Sinya took a mere thirty five minutes to beat him.

They showered, talked about the weather, shook hands, parted ways.

Donald walked to the English department building.

No one had to know, no one did know.

When he got to his office, he called Millin and told him. Millin was outraged.

"Doesn't the fellow know that the ladder is only open to faculty? My God, the effrontery."

"You'll do something about it?"

"Of course I will. Right away. I'll scrub the last two months results and put it back to the way it was at the beginning of December."

Donald hung up the phone. Leaned back in his chair.

Grey sky.

Black sky.

Night.

Stars.

In the car, Susan talked about the soup kitchen, birth control. He avoided giving direct answers. They ate separate microwave meals from Marks and Spencer.

When he got into work the next morning, he went straight to the gym. V.M. Sinya's name had disappeared and he, Dr. D. Bryant, was again in the number one spot, for the first time in nearly two months.

"The once and future king," Peter said at reception, startling him.

"Yes," he attempted to reply, but his throat was dry, and no sound came.

HUNDRED PROOF
Scott Wolven

I was off-paper, living in a rented cabin on a lake in the Adirondacks, when my old cellmate Jerry called. We had done two stints in county together, years ago. He was in for an assault charge. I ended up being in the state system for a couple years. He wrote me a letter while I was in. I wrote him back. He got my number from the boss at the shale pit where I used to drive a loader. It was April and raining. The call came way past midnight. I got up and answered. He sounded drunk.

"Hey," he said. "It's me."

"What's going on?" I said. I sat on the screened porch, looking out over the black lake and listening to the steady rain.

"I need you to do something for me," he said.

"What," I said. Thunder boomed in the distance. The line crackled.

He gave me an address about an hour south of where I was. A small town west of Albany, close to where he lived.

"Can you be there tomorrow?" he said.

"Yes," I said. "I don't work Sundays."

"What are you doing for work now?" he said.

"Running a Wood-mizer on a commercial site up here," I said.

"Least you got work," he said. "Be there tomorrow morning around nine."

"I will," I said.

"I'll be there too," he said. Drunk. Then he hung up.

I got up early, drank some coffee and got on the road. Drove through the forests to the highway. It was easy to find. A run-down neighborhood on the edge of town. Jerry was already there when I pulled into the driveway. Two cop cars were in the driveway. The house was one-level, red-brick. All the windows were busted out and stuff was strewn around the yard. I picked up a little muddy stuffed rabbit as I walked over to Jerry. There was yellow police tape around the house and the cops were inside. The front door was open and I heard their radios going off. I stood next to Jerry in the front yard.

"What happened?" I said.

"The landlady said when my daughter moved in, there was stuff—furniture and shit—left by the previous tenant. She told my daughter that my daughter could have it," he said.

"Yes," I said. I dropped the stuffed rabbit to the grass.

"Apparently they came back and wanted their shit," he said.

"Oh," I said. "Is your daughter okay?"

"No," he said.

"Jesus," I said. "How bad is she hurt?"

He turned and looked at me. "Dead," he said. "And we can't find her son."

"Oh, Christ," I said.

One of the uniformed cops came out of the house and looked over at Jerry. "You're not thinking of doing anything, are you?" the cop said.

"What do you mean?" Jerry said.

"You're not going after them, are you?" the cop said.

"No," Jerry said. "That's up to you."

"We'll catch 'em," the cop said. He walked to his cruiser.

Jerry shook his head. He knelt like a catcher in the grass, looking down, talking to someone who wasn't there about how much he missed and loved them. He picked the rabbit up and turned it over in his hands. Crying. Shaking.

We walked around the house, looking at the broken windows. There was a lamp in the side yard. Next to it sat an empty bottle of Southern Comfort. Jerry picked up the empty bottle. We walked around to the small backyard and there were a bunch of things in the grass—a hammer, a big kitchen knife, two rolls of duct tape and a plant in a broken ceramic vase. Jerry lit a cigarette as we slowly walked around. When we had made a full circle and were back on the driveway, he spoke to me.

"What do you think I should do?" he said. He took the empty bottle of Southern Comfort and put it on the front seat of his pick-up truck.

"I have no idea," I said. The cop radios were still going off. It looked like it might rain.

He nodded. "If you think of something," he said, "let me know." He held out his hand and I shook it.

"You want me to come to the funeral?" I said.

"Nah," he said. "My wife's family is coming from Binghamton and they'll just ask who you are and I'll have to hear about what an asshole I am for doing time, even though it was almost ten years ago."

"Okay," I said. "Keep me posted."

He opened the glovebox on his pick-up and we came up with a pen that wrote and a scrap of an insurance envelope and I gave him my mailing address. On the way back up to the Adirondacks, I stopped for gas and picked up a twelve pack of beer. I sat on the screened porch, sipping from those cans, staring at the lake. Thinking about that poor little boy's stuffed rabbit. I tried to remember what animals I had, when I was a kid, and for some reason, the combination of the beer and those memories made me cry. As the rain came down and filled the lake.

Two weeks later, I stopped at my mailbox on my way home from work. There was an envelope with messy handwriting on the outside. Inside was a note from Jerry. The cops used a sniffing dog and found his three-year-old grandson dead in the woods, a mile from the brick house where his daughter had lived.

The site I was working on got cleared. I milled the logs into boards for some rough-cut fencing, sent loads to the kiln for the finer work. The crew I was with put up the barns and houses. I went home every night and drank alone and stayed out of trouble.

At the end of August, the Adirondacks was as dry as a bone. The foreman shut the site down—a stray spark in the woods under those conditions was a risk he didn't want to take.

The phone rang, deep in the night. I answered. It was Jerry.

"Hey," he said. "You still working?"

"No," I said. "Too dry right now."

"I figured," he said. "Come down to my house and get drunk tomorrow."

I was sitting on the screened porch. I could hear the faint echo of my own voice off the pitch-black lake. "Okay," I said. "What time."

"Late afternoon," he said.

I could hear the liquor on his voice. "How's your wife holding up?"

"Sheila's gone to Binghamton to be with her mother," he said.

"Okay," I said. "Should I bring some beer?"

"Bring whatever you like," he said.

We sat in lawn chairs in the back of Jerry's house, drinking beer from a cooler full of ice and bottles and cans. He was smoking a cigarette. He had some brown liquor in a glass over ice going at the same time as his beer. The charcoal was heating up and we were getting ready to put some sausage on. Next to his little shed where he kept his motorcycle and mower and snow blower, there was a small beat-up wooden penguin lawn ornament. He pointed at it. Next to it was a glass liquor bottle.

"What's with the penguin?" I said.

"That's from my friend's brother," he said. "My old friend Brian." He pointed at the thin woods behind his house. "He used to live behind me, beyond those trees."

"What happened," I said. I sipped my beer.

"He used to hunt and fish with me. Talked about buying a motorcycle. He was a prison guard. I came home one day and there were cops over there." He pointed at the woods. "He'd blown his brains out in the backyard." He paused. He sipped his beer, then his liquor. "Sheila called me."

"You guys were married then?" I said.

"Yes," he said.

"Oh," I said. "I thought you and Sheila just got married recently."

He nodded. "We did. Sheila was married to him at the time and I was married to someone else."

"Okay," I said.

He hit the liquor, draining his glass and finished his beer. He got another and went inside the house and came back out with a fresh rocks glass full of booze. "She's been gone for a week," he said. He sat in the lawn chair next to me.

"You think she'll come back?" I said.

He shook his head. "I wouldn't," he said. "Given a choice, I'd get as far away from me as possible."

"What makes you say that?" I said.

He shook his head again. "It ain't worth talking about," he said. He turned his beer up so it caught the sun. "Did you ever fire a gun at a woman?"

"No," I lied. "I never did."

"I have," he said. "So there you go." He sipped his booze. "I haven't been right lately."

"Oh," I said.

He lowered his voice to a whisper. He pointed over toward the penguin. "See that bottle?"

"Yeah," I said.

"That's the bottle I took from outside my daughter's house in the spring," he said.

"Yes," I said. "I remember."

"She didn't drink Southern Comfort," he said.

"Okay," I said.

"So after it happened, I talked to Brian's brother about it. And yesterday, he came over here and talked to me."

"What did he say," I said.

Jerry held up one finger and went into the house. He came back out with a full bottle of Southern Comfort, and poured himself a fresh full rocks glass. He reached into his pocket and dropped a handful of bullets onto the picnic table. They were round-nose, flat-point bullets with a gray head and a copper-colored shell-casing. He picked out five of the bullets and put them in the rocks glass full of booze. Then he spoke.

"Brian's brother told me he heard three guys talking in lock-up, bragging about how they got away with something in the spring. About how all they drink is Southern Comfort."

"How do you know it's them?" I said.

"I don't," he said. "But I'm going to talk to them tomorrow morning."

I stood up. "Jerry," I said. "I know you're hurtin', but I'm not getting in that kind of trouble again."

He looked at me. He held out his hand and we shook. "That's all right," he said.

I started to walk to my truck.

He was sitting in a lawn chair by the picnic table, drinking a glass full of booze with bullets and ice in it.

AUTHOR BIOS

Dennis Tafoya lives in Bucks County, Pennsylvania, and is the author of two novels, *Dope Thief* and *The Wolves of Fairmount Park*, as well as numerous short stories appearing in collections such as *Philadelphia Noir* from Akashic Books. He is a member of the Mystery Writers of America, the International Thriller Writers, and the Liars Club, a Philadelphia-area writers group.

Andrew Nette is a writer based in Melbourne, Australia. He reviews for a number of on-line publications, including *Crime Factory* and *Back Alley Noir*, the official on-line forum of the U.S.-based Film Noir Foundation. The manuscript of his first novel, *Cambodia Darkness and Light,* was short-listed in the 2010 Victorian Premier's Literary Awards for Unpublished Manuscript by an Emerging Author. His blog, www.pulpcurry.com, explores crime film and literature, particularly from Asia and Australia.

Jedidiah Ayres lives in St. Louis.

Roger Smith was born in Johannesburg, South Africa, and now lives in Cape Town. His debut thriller, *Mixed Blood* (2009), was published in six countries and won the Deutscher Krimi Preis (German Crime Prize) and was nominated for a Spinetingler New Voice Award in the U.S.A. The movie version of *Mixed Blood* is in development starring Samuel L. Jackson, with Phillip Noyce directing. Roger's second book, *Wake Up Dead* (2010), was a 10 best pick of the *Philadelphia Enquirer, Times* (South Africa) and *Krimiwelt* (Germany). His third book, *Dust Devils*, will be published internationally in 2011. Visit Roger's website: www.rogersmithbooks.com.

Josh Converse is the author of "Glory B." His work has appeared in *Plots With Guns*, *Out of the Gutter*, and *Crime Factory*. Josh can name all past and present members of Guns N' Roses without any apparent embarrassment, and he once referred to the *Caldo De Siete Mares* at Cotixan as "the 'Chinese Democracy' of soups." In 2010, Josh was the recipient of Nick Tosches' final apology. He lives and works in Chicago.

Charlie Stella is the author of 7 crime novels dealing with organized crime. His last, *Johnny Porno*, is a look into the past (1973) when the mob ruled New York and the porno flick *Deep Throat* became the proverbial forbidden fruit. His next book, *Rough Riders*, will be published by Stark House Press in July 2012 and is a sequel to his first two books, *Eddie's World* and *Jimmy Bench-Press*.

Greg Bardsley has worked as a crime reporter, ghostwriter, speechwriter and video producer. His fiction has appeared in the anthologies *By Hook or Crook: The Best Crime and Mystery Stories of the Year* (Tyrus Books), *Uncage Me* (Bleak House Books) and *Sex, Thugs and Rock & Roll* (Kensington Books). Other stories have appeared in *Plots with Guns, Storyglossia, 3:AM Magazine, Out of the Gutter* and *Thuglit*. He lives with his family in the San Francisco Bay Area.

Hilary Davidson has published stories in *Beat to a Pulp, Crimespree, A Twist of Noir, Crime Factory, Spinetingler Magazine, Needle, The Rose & Thorn,* and *The Feral Pages*. In September 2009, she won first prize in the Watery Grave Invitational, a short-story contest for crime writers. She also won the 2010 Spinetingler Award for Best Short Story for "Insatiable," which is in *Beat to a Pulp: Round One*. Her story "Son of So Many Tears" appears in *Thuglit Presents: Blood Guts, & Whiskey* (Kensington, 2010). She's the author of the novels *The Damage Done* and the forthcoming *The Next One*.

Kieran Shea cooks better than you, rarely waffles from instinct, and takes great pride in curdling the status quo whenever he can. He considers himself lucky enough, but unfortunately he is also a glass-half-empty kind of guy. Kieran divides his time between 38°58'22.6"N - 76°30'4.17"W and 39°17'N -74°35'W.

Nate Flexer is the author of *The Disassembled Man* (New Pulp Press, 2009), which was named the second best crime fiction novel of 2009 by *Spinetingler Magazine's* Nerd of Noir. The book is set be translated and published in Italy in 2011. In addition to his work as a crime fiction writer, Flexer is also very interested in the behavior and evolutionary history of cockroaches. He currently lives in a ghost town somewhere in the mountains of Colorado.

Cameron Ashley writes and drinks in Brunswick, Melbourne. He is the editor-and-chief of *Crime Factory Magazine.*

Patricia Abbott is the author of more than seventy-five short stories published in crime and literary fiction outlets. She won a Derringer Award for her short story, "My Hero." She is the co-editor (with Steve Weddle) of *Discount Noir*, an ebook from Untreed Reads. Forthcoming stories will appear in *Needle, D*cked, Dark Valentine, All Due Respect, Mystericale E, Deadly Treats,* and several unnamed projects.

Chad Eagleton lives in the Midwest with his wife and dog. He is a two time WGI finalist and the Spinetingler Award nominated author of "A Ghostman on Third." His work has been published in DZ Allen's *Muzzleflash, Powder Burn Flash, A Twist of Noir, Bad Things Pulp Pages, The Pulp Pusher, Beat To A Pulp, Darkest Before The Dawn*, and *Crimefactory.*

Ken Bruen has been a finalist for the Edgar, Barry, and Dagger Awards. The Private Eye Writers of America presented him with the Shamus Award for the Best Novel of 2003 for *The Guards*, the book that introduced Jack Taylor. And in 2010, the Mystery Readers International bestowed the Macavity Award on Ken and Reed Farrel Coleman for their crime novel *Tower.* Ken lives in Galway, Ireland.

Jimmy Callaway lives in Sand Diego, CA and blogs at *Attention Children.* He is the fiction editor of *Crime Factory Magazine.*

Dave Zeltserman won the 2010 Shamus Award for "Julius Katz" and is the acclaimed author of the "man out of prison" crime trilogy: *Small Crimes, Pariah* and *Killer. Small Crimes* (2008) and *Pariah* (2009) were both picked by the *Washington Post* as best books of the year. His recent *The Caretaker of Lorne Field* received a starred review from *Publishers Weekly*, calling it a "superb mix of humor and horror" and has been shortlisted by ALA for best horror novel of 2010. *Outsourced* (2011) has already been called "a small gem of crime fiction" by *Booklist* and has been optioned by *Impact Pictures* and *Constantin Film*.

Steve Weddle is an editor and writer. A former English professor, he holds an MFA in creative writing from Louisiana State University and currently works for a newspaper group. His fiction has appeared in numerous literary and crime/noir journals. In 2009, Weddle and six crime fiction writers created *DoSomeDamage*, where he blogs on Mondays. In 2010, Weddle and John Hornor Jacobs created *Needle: A Magazine of Noir*. He lives with his family in Virginia.

Craig McDonald, author of the internationally acclaimed Hector Lassiter series, is an award-winning journalist, editor and fiction writer. His short fiction has appeared in literary magazines and anthologies. His fiction and nonfiction have earned him nominations for the Edgar, Anthony, Macavity and Gumshoe awards. He resides in Ohio. Craig can be found on the web at www.craigmcdonaldbooks.com.

Keith Rawson is a little-known pulp writer who lives in the alkaline desert waste of southern Arizona with his wife and very energetic daughter. His stories, poems, interviews, reviews, and essays have been widely published. He is the author of the short story collection, *The Chaos We Know*, and is a staff writer for

LitReator and *Spinetingler Magazine*. He is the publisher of *Crimefactory Magazine*.

Leigh Redhead is best known as the creator of the character Simone Kirsch, a stripper who leaves the sex industry to become a private investigator. Redhead drew upon her own experiences as a stripper in creating the character. She is the author of *Peepshow, Rubdown, Cherry Pie,* and *Thrill City*. She lives in Hanoi, Vietnam.

Anonymous-9 won the 2008 Spinetingler Award, Best Short Story on the Web, for "Hard Bite." She is currently writing it into a full-length novel. In 2010, a committee of the International Thriller Writers nominated her for a Thriller Award in the short story category. She has two Derringer nominations and another Spinetingler Award nomination for 2009. "2,984,000 Pounds of Pressure" is dedicated to Brownie, the beloved dog of a real-life gas man. A-9 lives in Los Angeles. Visit her on the web at www.anonymous-9.com.

Jonathan Woods divides his time between Dallas, Texas and Key West, Florida. His book of neo-pulpy noir crime stories, *Bad Juju & Other Tales of Madness and Mayhem*, was published in 2010 by New Pulp Press. New York Magazine called *Bad Juju* "Hallucinatory, hilarious, imaginative noir." Jonathan's stories have appeared *in 3:AM Magazine, Dogmatika, Plots with Guns, CrimeFactory, Pulp Pusher, Thuglit* and other webzines. He holds degrees from McGill University, New England School of Law and New York University School of Law. Jonathan's crime novel *A Death in Mexico* will be published in April 2012 by New Pulp Press. Visit his website at www.southernnoir.com.

Liam Jose co-edits and designs *Crime Factory*. He has been published online in various places, and occasionally in print for publications including *Pelican, Rough Cut, Farrago* and *Above Water*. In the scriptures it was foretold that he'd either be humanity's saviour or demise. Place your bets, folks.

Dave White is the two time Shamus Award nominated author of the novels *When One Man Dies, The Evil That Men Do, Witness To Death* and the short story collection *More Sinned Against*. He lives in New Jersey.

Chris F. Holm was born in Syracuse, New York, the grandson of a cop who passed along his passion for crime fiction. He wrote his first story at the age of six. It got him sent to the principal's office. Since then, his work has fared better, appearing in such publications as *Ellery Queen's Mystery Magazine, Alfred Hitchcock's Mystery Magazine, Needle Magazine, Beat to a Pulp*, and *Thuglit*. He's been a Derringer Award finalist and a Spinetingler Award winner, and he's also written a novel or two. Visit him on the web at www.chrisfholm.com.

Frank Bill is the author of the short story collection *Crimes In Southern Indiana* and the forthcoming novel *Donnybrook* (2012).

Adrian McKinty is the author of 11 novels, the most recent being the Spinetingler Award-winning *Fifty Grand* (2010) and *Falling Glass* (2011). He lives in Melbourne, Australia with his wife and two daughters.

Scott Wolven is the author of *Controlled Burn* (Scribner). Wolven's stories have appeared seven years in a row in The Best American Mystery Stories Series (Houghton Mifflin), the most consecutive appearances in the history of the series. The title story from *Controlled Burn* appeared in *The Best American Noir Of The Century* (Houghton Mifflin), edited by James Ellroy and Otto Penzler. Wolven's novels *False Hope* and *King Zero* are forthcoming in 2011. He is finishing another collection of short stories. Wolven is on the faculty of the Stonecoast MFA Program, University of Southern Maine.

ACKNOWLEDGEMENTS

Cameron wants to thank all contributors for their generosity, time and hard work. Also thanks Hadee, Claire, Jo, Annalise and Sharon at Roisin Dubh, Brunswick, for putting up with me every Saturday and serving me beer whilst this book was put together.

Jimmy wants to thank comic books and beer.

Keith wants to thank all the contributors for their time, generosity, and amazing stories. I'd also like to thank my wife Alicia and daughter Sadie for putting up with all my *Crime Factory* shenanigans.

MT. LEBANON PUBLIC LIBRARY

CPSIA information can be obtained at www.ICGtesting.com
Printed in the USA
LVOW041836200911

247103LV00006B/4/P